CW01210926

A Gargoyle's Delight

Monster's Duet, Book 1

Naomi Lucas and Mel Braxton

Copyright © 2023 by Naomi Lucas and Mel Braxton

All rights reserved. No part of this book may be reproduced or transmitted in any form without permission in writing from the authors.

Any references to names, places, locales, and events are either a product of the authors' imagination or are used fictitiously. Any resemblance to actual persons, places, or events is purely coincidental.

Painted Cover Art by Zakuga
Discrete Cover Art by Artscandare
Chapter Headers by Atra Luna
Edited by LY

CONTENTS

Dedication	VII
A Gargoyle's Delight	IX
1. The Statue	1
2. His Name	9
3. Cock-a-doodle Doo!	13
4. Curiosity Kills the Summer	17
5. The Awakening	23
6. A Plea for Normalcy	31
7. Peaches and Half-truths	39
8. An Unshakable Gargoyle	45
9. Adrial	51
10. Dazzled by Daylight	55
11. Jealousy and Desire	63
12. Branded	71
13. Breaking Bread	77
14. All Cats Recognize Demons	85
15. Waiting for Darkness to Come	91
16. Omissions	95

17.	The Taste of Desire	103
18.	Claiming a Gargoyle	107
19.	Sweet Delight	113
20.	When Day Becomes Night	119
21.	Blood Red Lace	125
22.	No Way Forward	133
23.	Ella, Carol, and John	139
24.	Murderer	145
25.	His Name	151
26.	Hard Truths	157
27.	The Last Straw	165
28.	An Unexpected Recovery	171
29.	The Long, Dark Nights	177
30.	Hopkins	181
31.	The Stranger at Dawn	189
Epilogue: The Vow		195
Authors' Note		209
The Scarecrow's Queen		211
Prologue		213

DEDICATION

To my dear friend, co-writer, and editor Mel. This book wouldn't exist without you.
-Naomi

To the lovely Naomi, writer and friend extraordinaire. Coauthoring was your brilliant idea.
-Mel

A GARGOYLE'S DELIGHT

For centuries I have suffered.

Petrified and silenced, all because I failed to destroy what I was created for.

Except now, after so long... There is a female.

One who always seems to be by my side.

Day after day.

Night after night.

She talks to me. Touches me. Tells me things. She shares stories of a world I no longer know. She is a reprieve from my punishment. A sweet delight. She liberates me from my solitude.

But when I rise, my adversary seizes his opportunity, and she's caught between us.

He only wants her to get to me.

She *isn't* his.

And I'll do anything to protect what's MINE.

Chapter One
THE STATUE

Summer

I push my glasses higher up my nose and glance over the small group of tourists in front of me. Like most of the people that find their way into the dusty depths of Hopkins' Museum of the Strange, their expressions are a mix of intrigue, curiosity, and... disgust.

The kid beside me, who couldn't be more than five years old, presses his hands against the glass display case. "That's a big tooth. Does it have a story too?"

I smile at him. "Everything here has a story."

"A dragon's tooth, eh?" the kid's dad says as he reads the label card out loud. He chuckles under his breath, making his skepticism obvious. "It looks like a cross between a megalodon and a sabretooth fossil... What creature is it really from?"

"A dragon," I state dryly. "Just like the card says." The dad holds back a laugh as I continue. "The Helmsdale Dragon was found off the coast of Scotland." Pulling out my keys, I unlock the cabinet and grab the faded polaroid pictures tucked behind the tooth, showing the excavation of the dragon's skull. I give them to the father and son. "No one knows where the rest of the head is. It vanished shortly after its discovery in 1983, though several of its teeth are still in circulation. There's a running conspiracy that the dragon's skull was seized by the Vatican."

The boy gawks at the pictures as he and his father flip through them. Several of the other tourists join us, looking over their shoulders.

"Dragons aren't real," the father says. He hands me back the polaroids, his eyes threatening to roll into the back of his head.

My smile turns saccharine. "Some would beg to differ."

They amble off to inspect the next curiosity that grabs their attention, and I return the polaroids to the display case. Every day is like this—the same people, just in different shapes and sizes, filtering in here hoping for magic, supernatural, and above all, the mystery of both. They're equally unwilling to believe any of it, despite the proof all around them. Hopkins' Museum of the Strange is full of things that don't belong in our reality.

It's the stories that actually draw the few visitors in, not so much the objects themselves. Anything could be strange… if there's a bizarre story attached to it. It took me several months of working here to figure this out because my boss wasn't going to connect the dots for me. Without a proper story, this dusty old museum would never stay in business. I'm sure of it.

Because like ninety-nine percent of our customers, I'm still skeptical. And I work *here*.

But it's my job to pretend I believe everything I say. It's how we make money, and with only a handful of tourists coming in each day, I fear each paycheck will be my last.

It doesn't help that the museum is in Elmstitch, a small rural town surrounded by farmland and far from big cities. It's a minor tourist trap. People only stop here when they need a break from the highway and someplace to stop for the night.

The wood floorboards creak as the visitors creep around, disappearing from my view as they weave through cluttered rooms of junk. After a few more minutes, I lead them into the windowless backroom, to a display of formaldehyde jars filled with animals and organs. Some have small fairy carcasses floating inside them.

I point at a large jar containing a rat with three heads and three tails.

"One of the Giant Cerberus Rats. The rat was discovered in NYC in the 1920s, along with dozens like it. To this day no one has figured out why these rats developed the way they did. The city had them hunted down and eradicated. There hasn't been another Cerberus Rat since."

We move deeper, toward a collection of dolls. Indicating one of the central displays, a doll of a little boy wearing faded blue overalls, I lower my voice and face them. "The Boy of Saint Krass. Handmade by famed dollmaker Royce Holl. The doll was commissioned by Saint for his son, Patrick, after the boy's twin brother, Brandon, died the year before. The very night the doll was delivered, the Krass's house burned while the family slept. Hours later, Patrick and the doll were found, completely unharmed, within the smoldering rubble. They say Brandon's spirit possessed the doll and saved his brother—"

"Really, a possessed doll?" the disgruntled father quips. "What's next, a vampire's coffin?"

I point to the heavy curtains behind him. "Viscount Hydes' famed coffin is through the room to your left, beyond the curtains."

He glances at them before turning back to me. "Seriously? You're serious? I pulled that out of my ass."

Yes, seriously.

Luckily, his son is several feet away, staring at the formaldehyde jars.

"Hydes and his wife, the Viscountess of Valin, traveled to America in the early nineteen hundreds where they patronized an orphanage in Boston. Several of the children died, completely exsanguinated, and the police visited the Viscount and Viscountess's estate with a warrant. In their initial search, they found crystal decanters of blood. Later, under the belief the Valins had skipped town, the police discovered them in the basement of their home, covered in blood, sleeping in a coffin."

The father looks behind the curtains. "What happened to them?"

I shrug. "They died. During their arrest, they were brought into the sunlight and their hearts gave out. Their bodies had completely crumbled by the time the officers took them to a hospital."

The boy, now at his dad's side, tugs at his father's arm, his face whiter than it was several moments prior. "I want to leave."

I almost feel bad for frightening the child, but who brings a young kid to a place like this? I warned the father upon admittance that some of the exhibits weren't suitable for children. My only hope is that the boy's nightmares don't last because I'm afraid the kid won't receive any comfort from his father.

By the time they and the other tourists leave, there's an ache behind my eyes and my mouth is dry. This work makes me thirsty. I flip the sign on the door to *Closed* and walk through the moldering, eclectic rooms of the museum, making certain I didn't miss any stragglers. When I'm certain I'm alone, I head to the front desk, grab my water bottle from behind the counter, and face the giant stone gargoyle behind me. Leaning back against the counter, I sip my water.

The gargoyle is one of Hopkins' most interesting exhibits, and he welcomes everyone when they enter the museum.

"Until this job," I tell him sarcastically, "I never knew how annoying dealing with skeptics was."

And I'm one of those skeptics, sort of, I think. I can never tell anymore. I've become too good at pretending. It was inevitable, after spending countless hours in this place.

Rain begins to fall, pinging the dusty front windows. A light flickers, and the gargoyle seems to grow bigger as a shadow dances across his hulking form.

There's a knock on the door, and I turn around. Through the glass top of the front door, I spot a shadowy figure on the other. "We're closed!" I shout.

"I think I left my phone inside!"

The father. Of course, it's the father. I put my water away, grab my keys, and head for the door.

"Thank you," he huffs, hunkering from the rain. "Do you mind if I take a quick look?"

I do mind. I don't like being alone with strange, *annoyingly skeptical* men. Every day, I'm burned by one of them. Regardless, I usher him inside. "Sure. I'm just closing up for the night."

"I'll be quick." He smiles and walks past me, his gaze streaking across the front room's displays before heading deeper inside. "I promise."

I follow behind him anyway, staying at the threshold of each room until he finds his phone near the dragon tooth display. He gives me another smile as he sighs with relief, and I lead him to the front.

"Thank you again," he says, but instead of dashing back outside, he nears the counter.

I glance at the gargoyle like he's a coworker who can hear my repressed sigh. Still, I head behind the counter, so at least the gargoyle has my back as I face the father. "Is there something else you need?"

Where's your son? is what I'm really asking.

His lips tilt upward. "Do you really believe this stuff?"

"I do," I lie easily. Too easily.

"It's nonsense, though." As he says it, the light flickers, and when his gaze streaks past me, landing on the gargoyle, his cocky smile slips.

"Is there anything else I can help you with?"

The father's gaze returns to me, his smile less certain. "Doesn't this place scare you?"

Sometimes. "Not at all," I lie again. "I enjoy the mystery of it all."

That last part wasn't a fib.

"I like a good mystery too... What do you say about joining me for dinner and telling me a few more of your favorites?"

The light shudders again as a heavy boom of thunder sounds. I swallow shallowly as another, far more annoyed sigh threatens to escape. Except as the shadows expand and retract, the father's eyes retreat to the gargoyle.

"That's kind of you, but I can't. I have plans already."

His gaze drops back to me, his brow furrowed. "That's too bad—"

"I'm sure your son doesn't need any more of this place."

"Don't worry about the kid. He'll be sleeping at the motel. What about a quick drink? Maybe you can show me the Watering Hole? It's right across the street."

Eww. I like this guy less and less the more he speaks. And that's the problem with small towns. The good partners are all taken, and the bad ones... well, they often remain that way—even if they're just a tourist passing through. "I am sorry, I do have plans," I say, heading to the front door to show him out.

My plans include finishing my book and sleeping.

Except when I glance back, he's not following me—he's not even looking at me. His focus is captured by the towering gargoyle statue. Pushing my glasses back up the bridge of my nose, I cough, waiting for him to join me. He continues to ignore my prompts.

"The Nameless Gargoyle," I say slowly, lowering my voice, and leaning into the creepiness of the story as the rain builds outside. It's impossible to hide my genuine admiration of this artifact. The exquisite carving greatly exceeds the time of his alleged creation, and the resulting figure is striking and formidable. His silent, nonjudgmental companionship is the best I've had since returning to my hometown. "No one knows who sculpted him nor where he originated from before he was in the ownership of Jean Motismo, a magician and supposed warlock."

The father shifts. "Warlock? Like a witch?"

"Similar. Jean Motismo found some fame in the early sixties, although he was never considered one of the greats. If you examine this gargoyle's mouth, you'll see one critical distinction: no drain. This stone was not shaped to be a water pipe, and the method used to carve the gargoyle, as well as the stone itself, predates the middle ages."

"Is that supposed to be the gargoyle's great mystery?" He squints at the statue.

I move past him, retreating behind the counter, drawn into the story. "Jean Motismo became obsessed with the gargoyle, featuring the statue in many of his shows. It was said that for the finale, he would bring the statue to life. One night, after performing for friends at their mansion, Motismo's wife found him backstage pouring a bucket of pig's blood over it, saying he had to free it... if he didn't he would be swallowed whole by Hell itself." I indicate the deeper crevasse of the gargoyle's wings. "Traces of that blood are still on the statue to this day."

The father peels his gaze off the statue and turns to me. "Free it for what?"

There's another boom, another flicker of light. He jerks his hand from the counter where it was inching my way.

"I swear it just moved," he gasps.

This time, I give *him* a cocky smile. "Everyone swears that. And it's not the only thing here that moves."

He shakes himself. "Right."

Backing up several steps, he takes in my smile, wincing with disgust at my enjoyment in all of this. Without giving me another glance, thanking me, or saying goodbye, he walks out the door, muttering under his breath.

I lock up for the second time this evening, hoping it's the last, and try to shake off the whole encounter. Pulling off my glasses, I wipe them on the cloth in my purse. I don't see much without them, and so my world narrows, time slowing as I reset.

The drum of rainfall sounds against the panes, and it's then I realize I didn't bring a jacket with me this morning. Groaning, I put my glasses back on, and hone my gaze on the gargoyle.

"Thank you for scaring him off," I say, studying his imposing form. Twice my size, even mid-lunge, he's nearly a foot and a half taller than me, and this close, I have to crane my neck to examine him.

His stony eyes stare partially upward. Those broad features, twisted with determination and rage, draw me in, past his bat-like wings, clawed hands, curved horns, and tail. Grotesquely appealing, the artist that sculpted him knew what he was doing.

Gargoyles were—are—said to ward off evil spirits and demons. Even going so far as to banish bad fathers who are looking for a quick hookup. Unlike any other gargoyle statue in existence, this one appears like it's actively vanquishing enemies. There is nothing static about the statue, poised mid-strike like he's about to deliver a death blow.

This is what makes The Nameless Gargoyle's story far more interesting than most of the oddities in this museum. Jean Motismo not only used the gargoyle in his shows. According to his wife, he had used the statue as a conduit for his spellcraft and dark sorcery, drawing power from demons.

"I know why Hopkins keeps you back there," I say.

He doesn't reply, of course. I know I'm talking to a stone. All the same, he's stood behind this desk for more years than I've been alive, watching the museum and its keeper.

"Thanks for all your help," I add, lifting my hand to stroke one of his wings. This isn't the first time he's saved me from customers who step out of line, and these small touches are my way of saying thank you.

The stone warms under my touch. Something stings, and I jerk my hand back. There's a cut on the side of my finger.

"Shit." With a wince, I blot the shallow wound with a tissue and turn to the gargoyle, wiping his wing where I bled. "Sorry about that. Don't tell my boss," I joke. "I need this job."

A yawn tears from my throat. It's been a long day, and tomorrow will be one too. Until Hopkins returns from his trip, I'm the only one here. That means I'm covering all shifts and tours, opening and closing, and cleaning up.

Turning back to the register, I count and collect the money, turn off the lights, and drive home.

As my hands land on the steering wheel, my finger tingles, turning icy cold where I'm cut. Mist rises from the staunched wound, but when I blink, it's gone.

Chapter Two
His Name

Summer

It's a struggle to fall asleep. The early autumn storm continues late into the night, and the rain pelts against the roof while the wind whistles against the thin walls. I bundle deeper into my quilt and try to drown out the noise.

These days, I'm sleeping in a converted attic, my childhood bedroom. Back then, it was a thrill to make this space mine. Dad works in carpentry, so it became a project we shared. The angled ceiling already gave the space a certain drama, and we installed a skylight window and added a balcony. I insisted on painting the ceiling a dark blue and dotting it with yellow so I could have my own night sky.

It's a great room except during storms like this, as summer becomes fall. Without proper insulation, the attic runs cold.

After a full day working at the museum, my imagination runs wild. I tell so many stories during the day that they often slip into my dreams.

I know there are no monsters under my bed, only books. Except when thunder booms and the rafters shake, I warily eye the door leading to the deck.

I'm thankful. I am. I have a roof over my head and a job. It's sheer luck that Hopkins needed help. In my tiny hometown, job prospects aren't exactly great for recent graduates with master's degrees in museum studies, or, well, for anyone. In all the years I've lived here, the town hasn't grown. It's antiquey and unique, even quaint, though depressed. There's little to no growth. People don't move here, and everyone who leaves never comes back.

Everyone except me.

I miss my friends and my life before, discovering what a real town, even a city, feels like. So whatever gratitude I do have comes easier some days more than others.

My limbs are heavy when the whole attic shakes. There's a heavy *thump*, and the skylight darkens more than it should—even in the rain, the outside house lights normally reach me. I grab my glasses, but by the time I can see there's nothing.

I lower my head back to my pillow, drifting somewhere between wakefulness and sleep.

"*My name is...*"

My eyes crack open, and I look around my room thinking I heard a voice. The cut on my hand tingles.

There's nobody. Yawning, I flip onto my side and snuggle back into my bedding.

Something cold brushes my lips. Softly swaying back and forth, it whispers like a kiss. I turn over and lift my hands to my mouth.

My lips are chilled like they'd been caressed by frost.

I run the back of my hand over them until they're warm. Squinting, I look around my room again. It can get drafty in here. Sighing with frustration, I drop back and throw my blanket over my head.

I'm drifting on the edge of sleep again when the sensation returns. Only this time it's more insistent. It doesn't simply whisper a kiss upon me—it crushes against my lips, cold as stone.

"*My name is...*"

It's that voice again.

Annoyed, I explore, running my lips against whatever it is, learning the shape of what's kissing me without bothering to search my room again. *It's just a dream. An interesting dream.* The rounded tip is rigid. I follow up its length and discover a thick, smooth stone.

I've dreamed up a stone phallus. I clench my thighs as I test it out. I've never given head or sucked a cock. It's surprising, how sensual this is.

The cock is so cold that my lips fail to warm it. And as the cold, tingling sensations become familiar, my lips part, determined to heat it, warm it to my touch. I invite it into my mouth, stroking it with my tongue, savoring the first bite of frost.

My hips buck. I gasp as the head is pushed into me, over my tongue. But when I open my eyes, there is nothing above me except the blanket.

I grasp at it, shifting the blanket off of me—finding the cock impossibly long and thick—only it's invisible, feeling like ice, and my fingers can barely brush its surface before they become numb. The cold is sensual, awakening my usually elusive desire. I lower my fingers under the blanket and toward my sex, twitching under the cold contact they bring to my sensitive flesh.

I work my fingers over my clit as my mouth strains. My hips sway against my hand, moving forward and back, my head swaying too. I gag as the invisible shape taps the back of my throat, forcing me to back off. It's so cold. The heat of my mouth changes nothing.

Like a popsicle that doesn't melt.

What am I doing? Confused, I pause.

"*My name is...*"

That voice... It's inside my head.

I chase my release with reckless abandonment, certain I'm alone.

I moan and shake, whimper and shiver as the cold rod thrusts in and out of me. I suck and suck, desperate to warm it, furious to do so. If I can... I can accomplish anything.

Frantic to reach my goal, I'm driven to completion, and when my body is overcome by an abrupt shudder, a climax follows. I twitch and pulse, pleasure streaming with the release of pressure. I settle back into my bedding, my legs tangling with my blankets.

Lifting my head from my pillow, the stone-cold phallus falls from my mouth.

"*My name is Zuriel.*"

I open my eyes again.

There's a large shadow beside me, leaning over my bed. I blink rapidly, and it doesn't go away. My mouth snaps closed as I right my glasses and sit up.

I haven't been dreaming of just any statue—I've been giving head to the museum's gargoyle.

He's rigid, his posture still that of a guardian mid-strike, except he's never had a cock before. His groin has always been smooth... My eyes widen in admiration. His cock is thick and erect, protruding severely from his form. It casts a formidable shadow over me.

I squint. Steam rises from it. Not steam, cold vapor. Mist. It fills the air between us slowly, soft gray and crystalline. When it touches my skin, it prickles.

I suck the vapor in, my mouth and nose flooded with it.

"Zuriel," I gasp.

His name.

The knowledge steadies, solid as a fact. It's unnerving how the information doesn't feel like something I dreamed up. I whisper his name again, watching the mist drift across my room.

"Zuriel."

Lightning strikes and his cock twitches.

My gaze trails up his muscled form, steadying on his bat-like wings and deeply snarled features. I look for the usual bloodlust in his expression, except now his eyes are wide, shocked, feverishly heated.

Staring at me.

I shift uneasily, unable to look away.

My nipples peak and my core clenches. Sitting up, kneeling with my legs under me, I remain trapped.

No matter how long we stare at each other, I can't decide if this is a dream or not.

Zuriel.

Chapter Three
COCK-A-DOODLE DOO!

Summer

I wake to sunlight trickling through the skylight. Groggy, I realize the bed is next to me, and I'm on the floor with my quilt wrapped around my naked body.

My glasses aren't on the nightstand, and I'm relieved to find them carelessly thrown aside. Achy and annoyed, my neck and back are wrenched from sleeping on the hardwood floor. Squeezing my eyes closed, I dig my fingers into stiff joints.

Great. The day is starting wonderfully. I groan, pressing my fingers harder into my trapezius.

Clear skies shine through my skylight as I knead my neck. The first wafts of Dad's coffee rise from the vent next to me, tingling my nose. I sigh happily. God, I love that man. No wonder Mom fell for him. A man who makes coffee in the morning is a man to keep. She's told me that countless times.

Coffee can fix a lot. Coffee does more than a diamond ring, tastes better than true love's first kiss. I didn't believe her at first. I do now.

Coffee is *love*.

My thighs slip against each other when I try to stand. I peer up at the ceiling, looking for a leak, but there isn't any.

This isn't water. This wetness… it's coming from *me*. My entrance is damp, and slick when I test it with my fingers. I'm wet. Like, really wet. A blush roars to my face.

I rub my fingers across my slit and twitch. Last night's dream was strangely lucid, thrillingly sensual, and recalling it makes me sad, realizing it was just a dream.

"Summer, are you up?"

It's Mom. I wrap my blanket tighter around my naked body. "Yeah?"

"The power went out last night. Your alarm probably didn't go off. If you don't hurry, you're going to be late for work!"

My alarm clock is blinking *12:00,* and there's far too much daylight streaking in from above.

When I'm slow to respond, Mom shouts, "Did you hear me? You okay?"

No, I'm not okay. I'm horny.

I choke out a reply. "Be down in a minute!"

Scurrying around the room, I grab the first clean clothes I find. Only as I'm about to rush downstairs to the bathroom, I freeze, looking around my room. I turn back and check the lock on my balcony doors. It's still in place. Everything in my room is the same as it was last night, minus the rumpled, throttled bedding.

It was just a dream. A hot dream.

And now it's over.

After a quick shower, I pull my hair into a messy ponytail and clean the smudges from my glasses. Rushing, I apply enough makeup to trick customers into thinking I'm put together. Jeans and a sweater are enough for this job, and I can wear Chelsea boots instead of heels. I would have to buy a whole new wardrobe if I landed a position at one of the fancy museums I keep applying to. It's a nice daydream, to be fancy. I've never been that way, and it sounds like fun.

A quick scroll through my email confirms that nobody is interested in interviewing me anyway. Not yet at least.

With no time to dwell on depressing job prospects, I dart downstairs for breakfast.

Mom reads at the table, drinking her coffee. Dad's already gone to work. There's a stack of pancakes left for me, which is far more generous than I deserve.

"Thanks," I say. Thanks for waking me, for pancakes, and for the roof over my head.

Ugh. I want them to be proud of me. I *need* them to be proud of me. I want it more than being fancy.

She puts down her magazine. "Your dad was running late too. I'm sure half the town is running behind after a night like that. Strange storm, wasn't it?"

I shovel pancakes into my mouth, grunting in agreement.

"You're too beautiful to still be single," she says. "Let me set you up on another date."

Oh, god. "No. And we've gone over this." She still speaks like being a single woman is unacceptable, that I should be married with children by now, and I suspect she would have suggested I accept the offer for drinks from the creepy father last night. "I'm only here until I can find another job. I'm not staying. I can't afford to get attached, and I'm not ready for a relationship." All my previous attempts at romance have fizzled into nothing, and I'm tired of trying.

"You've been here a year, Summer."

"Don't remind me," I mumble around a bite of food, trying not to hang my head.

"There are plenty of wonderful men in Elmstitch. You just need to try harder. I know the perfect man..." she continues, selling the attributes of today's eligible bachelor.

I'm pretty sure her definition of eligible isn't the same as mine, not with the way she keeps guilt-tripping me. It's only a matter of time before I give in and go on another blind date to appease her. I pretend to listen as I finish my food, clean up breakfast, and load the dishwasher. When Mom goes upstairs to retrieve the number of some guy she met, I check my purse, give the cat a hurried scratch, and bolt out the door before she returns.

My old station wagon is parked on the dirt driveway leading up to our farmhouse. The route to work wiggles through the country, leading me from the forested outskirts into town. It's a nice drive, a quiet one. Sometimes I'll see deer or hawks. Some claim to have seen Bigfoot, though that's clearly another hoax.

When my phone rings and Ella's name pops up on my screen, I put her on speaker.

"Guess what?" she shrills.

"What?"

"I'm engaged!"

"Oh my god!" I shriek. "Congratulations! I'm so happy for you!" And I am. Ella and Rebecca are ridiculously cute together.

Ella was my college roommate and now my closest friend. We've been through a lot together, wild frat parties, hard professors, and long exams. We went to the same graduate program, and unlike me, she got a job directly after receiving her degree, employed as a conservationist at a museum where she interned.

"Will you be my bridesma—"

There's a click. Then dial tone.

I try to ring her back, twice, but the line refuses to go through. Cellular service is spotty around here, especially in the forest.

I'm thrilled to be her bridesmaid. I'm already running numbers in my head, wondering where I'll squeeze some extra money for dresses and travel. I wouldn't miss her wedding for the world. Doing so would be a crime against our friendship.

My girl Ella is getting married!

Meanwhile, I'm... *stuck*. Everyone's getting married, starting jobs, buying houses, and having babies while I'm having sex dreams about a gargoyle—that's how far behind I've fallen, and I can't help the jealous lump that forms in my chest reminding me how many steps backward I've taken. Talking with Ella would help. It always does.

I don't have the chance to call her back, because when I leave the forest and turn on Main Street, there are three packed tour buses parked across the street from the museum.

My heart sinks into my stomach.

Three buses. On a *Monday*. Hopkins' Museum of the Strange was supposed to open thirty minutes ago.

I swallow down my panic, straighten my glasses, and quickly park my car nearby, giving the people loitering outside my most sincere apologies. I offer reassuring smiles and spooky antidotes, promising that the museum will be worth the wait. They're upset, and they should be. It's not like me to be late.

We need the business, and Hopkins has placed his trust in me. With how things are going, I can't afford to be fired.

I plaster on a reassuring smile. "Give me a moment to open up and you'll be free to examine Hopkins' mysteries for yourself."

There are angry whispers behind me, and they make my hands shake, my keys jangling while unlocking the front door. If I can just get through the next few hours, it'll all be okay.

The gargoyle is waiting for me as I flick on the front lights. He's right where he's supposed to be, behind the front desk, and not in my dreams.

Not in my mouth either.

"Good morning," I greet him, joining him behind the counter.

I stiffen, my gaze drifting down his body, because jutting out from his usually smooth groin, is a large, erect cock.

I dig the Tylenol out of my purse and take two.

Chapter Four
Curiosity Kills the Summer

Summer

d

He has a cock.

Taking off my glasses, I wipe them and put them back on. It's a smudge. It has to be.

The monster cock is still there.

My dream...

It wasn't *real*.

Right?

My whole body shudders as my mind reels and my cheeks heat furiously.

Oh, god. What the fuck is happening?

My gaze consumes his member, finding it exactly like I dreamed, the epitome of carved perfection.

As I lean forward, the tip glistens, slightly wet. My throat tightens as I jerk back, once again, checking the ceiling for a leak.

There's no leak.

Either someone is pranking me or I've finally cracked. Because it can't be real. It just can't. There has to be a reasonable explanation.

I'm about to reach out and grasp it, to make certain that his member is real—that it's not a trick—when the door rattles. I startle and jump, twisting in the direction of an impatient tourist. "I'm not ready!" It sounds too harsh. "Please wait. I'll be right there."

I don't have time for this. I can lose my mind after my shift ends.

Unfortunately for me, the gargoyle is placed *right behind the front desk*, and his cock... It's not something I want paying visitors to see. I don't want anyone to ask about it. If someone does, I don't know what I'll say.

He's mine.

The surge of possessiveness breaks my spell, and my lips flatten.

I find a white sheet tucked under the counter and throw it over him. It's not quite large enough to cover everything, but with a few tugs, it conceals his giant cock.

While the sheet protrudes in the middle, tenting over his phallus, the guests won't know what they're looking at.

I rub my face and make quick work of opening the shop, testing locks to exhibits that are never opened, chanting odd Latin rites that Hopkins made me practice over and over, and sprinkling "holy" water on some of the cases. Hopkins swears I must do these bizarre rituals.

Soon I'm throwing open the door taking my place behind the counter to start charging visitation fees and waiting for my Tylenol to kick in. "I'm sorry for the wait. I'll be available for questions soon. In the meantime, feel free to explore the unlocked rooms. Sorry again."

As one customer turns into forty, my back heats, practically feeling the gargoyle and his cock behind me whenever a tourist's gaze strays over my shoulder. The gargoyle's presence looms like he's staring at me through the sheet as intently as we held eye contact in my dream.

I'm not crazy. I'm not. I rub my temples.

Crazy or not, I keep my stomach flush against the counter for the remainder of the check-in process, putting whatever space I can between us.

When the last ticket is sold, I throw a sign on the counter that says I'm giving a tour and wander the rooms, fleeing from the statue, drawing crowds to exhibits with strange histories, sharing the creepy stories I know by rote. As the morning eases into normalcy, my panic ebbs.

By the time the tourists have seen it all, my voice is hoarse. They complain that there should be more people on staff. I agree, even if I can't remember anyone working here besides Hopkins. The faded *Help Wanted* sign plastered on the front window is the same one that was there fifteen years ago.

It's hard work, running the shop and museum on my own, but these days my boss is often away on his trips, presumably finding new artifacts though he hasn't returned with any, and I hardly have a choice in the matter.

When the tour buses leave, they're followed by a steady stream of visitors. Without taking a break, I quickly devour a protein bar for lunch. Finally, as my day nears its end, I shepherd the final visitors into the front room, urging them to buy their souvenirs because I'm about to close early.

I return to the front desk. Poised before the gargoyle, my mind returns to what's hidden beneath the sheet.

It has to be a prank.

It's nearly dusk when the final customer steps forward with his purchase, and my lips curl in a tired smile.

At last.

He slams a palm-sized reproduction of the gargoyle on the counter. Startled, I frown at the souvenir and the customer's vehemence.

"Why is he covered?" he demands. "I came here to see him."

Looking up at the customer, my mouth parts with awe. With windswept golden hair, a perfect five o'clock shadow, a cleft chin, and brown eyes so deep I could drown in them, the man is beautiful. His face is angelic, his muscular, broad body straining against his tight white shirt and faded jeans. He partially leans over the counter.

"We're in the process of restoring him," I say quickly, completely intimidated.

He looks past me at the gargoyle, clearly displeased. I don't like this. Everything about him rings warning bells.

Wanting him gone, I continue the sale, slipping my hand over the small replica of the gargoyle. A replica *without* a cock. "That'll be $15.99."

His eyes drop back to me. "What?"

"For the figurine." I motion to it, trying not to fixate on the carving's lack of genitalia. "Unless you don't want it?"

He honest-to-god *snarls* at me before turning away and storming out the front door.

I stare after him, my brow wrinkling. I don't remember selling him a ticket to the museum, and I certainly would have—it's not every day a man like him walks into the shop. He strides down the street, turns a corner, and I lose sight of him.

Shrugging it off, I lock the front door, flip the *Open* sign to *Closed,* and return to the counter.

My gaze lands on the figurine still lying there.

I pick it up and turn it over in my hand, rubbing my thumb down the replica's front, tracing over the gargoyle's face and along his chest. My thumb settles against his smooth groin before shifting down his legs.

I peer up at the real statue, increasingly uncomfortable with the white sheet draped over him. "Guess it's just you and me now." My soft chuckle sounds forced.

I rub my thumb over the figurine once more, eyeing the tent in the sheet.

When I take a step closer, my phone rings, and I shriek, dropping the figurine—porcelain clinks as it shatters at my feet. My heart pounds as I grasp the edge of the counter for support. My ringtone continues, and I curse under my breath as a cold sweat forms over my brow. I grab my phone with a curse, hoping it's Hopkins.

Ella's name appears on my screen. I shake out my nerves and answer her.

"So sorry about earlier," I say before Ella can speak. My voice sounds like a squeak, and I clear my throat.

"Girl, you need to get out of there. No one should have to live in a town with bad reception. It's cruel."

"I know." *I'm trying.* I change the subject to a happier one. "I'd love to be your bridesmaid!"

"Yay! Good! Because I need you. We're having the wedding at the Smithsonian American Art Museum. Neither of our families will appreciate it, and I'm hoping you can help with that."

"Art and history are my specialties," I reply with a laugh, glancing at the exhibits beyond the entry room. "I wouldn't miss your wedding for the world."

"Thank god. It's going to be tons of fun, lots of booze. Enough about me, how are you? It's been a few weeks. Any interviews?"

I cringe. "I'm... fine. Taking it day by day. And no interviews. Not yet."

"Don't stop applying."

"I won't." I can't, not even when the process wears me down. "Mom wants to set me up on another date."

The museum's lights flicker.

"Hopefully it'll go better than the guy who took you to his family reunion the day after your first date. What was his name again? Lionel?"

"Yeah. Don't remind me."

"Long day? You sound tired."

I sigh. "There was a bad storm last night. I ended up running late when there were three buses of tourists waiting." I can no longer resist the urge to look at the covered statue as I talk. My gaze drops to the protrusion in the fabric—is it damp or is that a trick of the light?

I look up for a leak and grimace. There is no leak!

"Is your boss out again? No new coworkers yet?"

"Unfortunately, yeah."

"That sucks. I'm so sorry. I hope no one gave you attitude."

"There was one guy at the end—the strangest part was he looked like he'd walked off a Hollywood set." I shake my head. "And really, the day wasn't too terrible. He was angry that an exhibit was... being restored. Do you mind if I call you when I get home?"

"No worries. Talk to you soon."

It's time.

I've come up with a dozen theories, and most of them are plausible. If the gargoyle now has a cock, there must be a hidden mechanism within the statue that released it. Maybe he wasn't built entirely of stone. The gargoyle *had* been the property of a magician.

Maybe the magician used him for more than magic tricks...

Slowly, I lift the cloth inch by inch, until the rounded, glistening tip of his phallus appears.

It's just a trick. I laugh. A trick that sucked me right in.

Soon I'll be free to unwind on the couch and mindlessly enjoy my true crime shows. A romance I'm dying to read was released today...

"What a day," I tell the statue, tugging at the sheet until he's completely revealed. I press my lips together, my gaze drifting from his scowling face to his jutting cock. "A big day for both of us. Sorry I covered you. You surprised me."

Except for his new appendage, he's completely unchanged. Hesitantly, I lift my hand and caress his bat wing. He feels the same as he always does, smooth and cold, hard as stone. My hand dips lower and traces his abdomen, searching for the magician's trick.

When my fingertips reach the base of his cock, heat surges to my cheeks and a buzzing begins behind my eyes. My legs cramp. Touching his genitals makes me feel like a pervert.

I glance behind me to double-check that I'm alone. This would be the perfect time for Hopkins to return. He'd look at me with those squinty eyes and bushy eyebrows. He'd click his tongue like he knew what I was all along. Checking the windows, I confirm there's no one outside.

I turn back to the gargoyle. "It's an impressive cock," I whisper, meeting his stone-carved eyes. "Anybody would be jealous of what you're packing. But it's time to figure out the magician's trick so I can put it away. We get kids in here sometimes," I trail off. "You know how it is. We can scare them, but traumatizing goes too far."

I put my fingers back on him, more forcefully this time, leaning in and eyeing his large testicles, his base, shaft, and pointed mushroom-capped tip. Wherever my gaze goes, my fingers follow, testing and pressing, rubbing and gripping.

He's larger than I remember. Along the underside of his shaft, there's a line of subtle ridges that vanish into his tip. His testicles, though appearing incredibly soft, are just as hard as the rest of him, just as smooth. I cup them and wince, rubbing them with my palm, my blush heating furiously.

He's as cold and hard and smooth as stone. The theory that there's some sort of mechanics involved in his design starts to seem farfetched.

I drop my hand and peer up at him, frowning. "There's got to be a release somewhere. You can't be hard everywhere. What are we going to do about this, *Zuriel?*"

I hear a crack, and he blinks in reply.

I freeze as my gaze narrows. I must have imagined it, simply another strange shadow. The creak of an old building.

Except the gargoyle does it again. Another blink. And this time, his entire face moves. The corners of his lips turn into a broad smile, revealing thick fangs. Groaning, shifting, crackling, and grunting noises fill my ears as I press my back against the counter.

"Summer." My name emanates from him, hollow and dry, dust drifting in the air.

I can't look away. My eyes widen as the gargoyle straightens, cracks his neck, and twists his spine like he's been sleeping in an awkward position for a very, very long time.

Finally, my body responds.

Screaming, I knock over a bookcase as I race for the front door. I scramble with the lock, sprint outside, and don't dare look back.

Chapter Five
The Awakening

Zuriel

d

"...Zuriel."

She uttered my name.

Heat rips through me, freeing my frozen limbs. It happens in a flash, streaking out from my center and spreading to the tips of my wings. I'm stunned by the rush of long-forgotten sensations.

She uttered my name, the female who's been my constant companion for the last bits of my fragmented memory, telling me odd stories, talking to me, and even sometimes... touching me.

I've never seen her, yet I know her. Her voice, her scent.

She has my name.

Time has passed since I last stirred, though I do not know how much. Scattered pieces of memories scurry into sequences, never sticking around for long. Sensation muddies my thoughts.

It's hard work, coming back to life.

Blinking my dry eyes, I suspect I've been stone for centuries. Looking around, I face the dim, cluttered room. Sticking out my tongue, I taste the air and feel it slip inside my lungs. It smells sweet, like... peaches, a comforting scent. They cultivated them at the monastery that once housed me.

Ruin came to that monastery, and I was removed from it.

Demons always find a way. Mine could not trespass on such holy ground, and since I had surrendered the privilege of movement, I do not doubt the monastery fell because of him.

For many years, I was in my demon's possession, mocked and taunted in countless voices as he shifted through them, testing each in the hope of breaking my resolve. His assault only ended when war came to his land and his host died. He lost everything, including me.

Since then, I've belonged to a few others. All were evil men who sought my name and were promised power if they could learn it. They were tricksters, all of them, and once I understood their self-serving natures I refused to extend my protection to them.

I could not allow them to share my power with my enemy.

Adrial.

I do know my demon's name. I always have.

He's bound to me, and I to him. He will hurt anyone and anything in his attempts to make me his servant and reclaim his strength. Since he cannot kill me without the angels sending my replacement, he longs to control me.

He's just waiting for his chance.

This female may be a trick. One for which I am falling.

"Summer," I utter as saliva rushes my mouth, bringing forth a smile. It has been so, so long... So long since I've stretched out my wings, so long since I could speak. I gulp down more air, pleased by the expansion of my lungs.

An excited delirium streaks through me, consuming me with a frenzied sensation. My wings loosen as my nerves reawaken. My hands clamp into fists. I test my limbs, spanning my wings and arching my back, and my body lightens from its shell. The movement thrills me.

I hear a crash, a scream, and then the racing footsteps of the woman who now owns me. She flees, afraid.

Waiting until details become clear, a groan pours out from my throat as I take in the swinging door and the sign on it. Dreary and dim, it's called *Hopkins' Museum of the Strange*. I've been here for some time, I believe. The smell of old books and dusty musk deliciously fills my nostrils, mingling with the peaches. There are no others nearby to witness me rise. I do not sense Adrial's presence.

Though there is no doubt that he has been nearby. Recently. I scent his rotting menace amongst the dust and musk. Faint as it may be, I cannot mistake it. It won't be long until he comes and finds me.

Rushing out of the building, a damp chill enshrouds me, eliciting another moan from my throat.

There are lights everywhere, and a vehicle drives by, scorching down the road, wheels screeching. I glimpse the female behind the wheel.

Technology has advanced since last I saw the world, despite having overheard much over the years, information slipping into my vague, detached awareness. It's a disconnection I'll no longer need to endure, now that someone knows my name. My very dangerous name.

Slipping into the shadows, I take to the sky.

Following her vehicle from a distance, I keep to the lower clouds.

I am not to be seen. I do not belong to the world of men—I strike fear into them regardless if I am trapped in stone or am in motion. The fewer humans know of my existence, the better. They will only get in the way.

Squealing, the vehicle leaves the town, slowing down as it reaches a winding street through a thick forest and past intermittent farms, homesteads, and buildings. After a while, it pulls off onto a dirt road, slowing down further and turning into the last driveway at the end. It approaches a house with a steeply pitched roof, ornate gables, and large windows. Light floods the first floor.

The house appears old, yet maintained, emanating a history that's entirely its own. There's a wraparound porch and a small balcony on the third floor. There's a large lawn, a garden, and a shed that smells of wood. Several large trees surround the home before giving way to a forest that separates it from the closest house.

The vehicle parks. The hum reverberating from it comes to a halt, but the woman, *my Summer,* does not come out. I drop from the clouds and land in the trees.

I wait.

I know Summer. Better than any human. She's the only employee of Hopkins, the eccentric male who bought me at auction and gave me a home, knowing my purpose. I know him too, though not well despite the many years I've been on display within his museum.

Hopkins once tried to learn my name, though he gave up rather quickly, laughing it off and patting my wing—as though it were a joke. He hasn't tried since, knowing better than to trifle with dangerous things, preferring to collect and preserve. To remain neutral. I have sensed many dangerous relics within the walls of his museum where he provides a home for those who would be used by others for their own perilous gains.

He keeps us like trophies. I was lucky to be picked up by him before Adrial amassed enough wealth to purchase me again.

Summer has been his only employee ever, as far as I know. Why a young woman would want to work in a dangerous place like Hopkins' Museum is beyond me, though I have ceased to care. I have no reason to interfere, despite wanting too, very much.

Even now, I can feel all the places she has touched and caressed. Her words and ideas, hopes and fears have fluttered through my thoughts, gifts she should not have given me. Her attentions have lulled me closer to the living than I have dared for a long, long time.

Dangerously close. For she has my name.

The door to her vehicle cracks open, and she steps into the golden light cast from the house's front windows. Wearing a simple brown sweater and blue pants that hug her legs tightly, she looks around, wrapping her arms around her chest. A pair of glasses are resting on her nose, the thick lenses obscuring her eyes.

Her gaze passes over me without settling.

She's... beautiful. Even from a distance, she is what I have imagined. Summer. *Summer...*

Like the season, hot and blistering and full of light. A season I cannot remember, illuminated by a sun I have not seen in centuries. A sun I may never see again, bound as I am to Hell's servant. Yet here I am, gazing upon it once again.

Her hair is long and gold, pulled back in a high ponytail, messy and slightly lopsided. It careens down her back despite the cinch, as shorter strands spill over her shoulders. It is thick and supple with waves. Golden waves, sunbeams. I understand her namesake.

My fingers twitch to touch her locks, streak through them, and free them to flow across her shoulders.

With the light cast upon her, her hair glows against her skin. Leaning forward, I try to discern her features, but that same light throws her face in shadows, obscuring them, and I only capture a clear image of her silhouette when she picks up her feet and rushes for the house's front door.

She is lithe, her legs long. And thin, too thin. Thin, lithe things are too easily broken. Thin, lithe humans can't afford enough to eat and are poor, yet the house and her vehicle suggest otherwise. The thickest, heartiest attribute she has is her hair. Her chest is shapely, though not as dramatically as her hair.

Yet she also has a job working for Hopkins. She is a woman who works beyond the house.

How much time has passed? I roll my shoulders back and crack my neck. Too long. I do not know the ways of this world. Perhaps human females are now equal to their men.

Something small lands beside me.

A bat. Soon another joins its side.

Summer stops before the door and looks around again. As more bats fill the sky, heading for me, she stiffens, her gaze searching, her body haloed. She *is* light—she is everything I have dreamed about and so much more.

A heaviness grows between my thighs, and it throws me off-guard, forcing my gaze down. Exploring with my hand, I find a large, overly sensitive appendage.

Frowning, I heft it upward.

There, in my hand, is a cock. Cumbersome and as solid as stone, I squeeze it. I try to tug it off, pulling at the tough skin of my groin. Twice the size of my hand and bulging with a steady flow of heat, it grows increasingly sensitive.

Bearing my fangs, I squeeze it hard, testing its attachment to my body. It does not give way. I can't pull it off.

I have never had a cock before. I have dreamed of having one recently. But it was only a dream. Genitalia like this belongs to human men, not gargoyles. Yet here one dangles, growing warmer, heavier by the second. I run my hand up and down its length, palming the thicker tip, then down to cup my engorged testicles.

A groan escapes me, nearly giving my position away. I catch my breath when Summer looks away from the bats and straight at my tree, casting her clever gaze into the shadows. Her lips quiver so slightly, and while I offer a silent apology for frightening her, I become still as stone, tucking in my wings.

Finally, she turns back for the door and lets herself into the house without needing a key.

My frown deepens. The door is unlocked. I do not like that. More bats settle in the branches around me.

I stare at where she vanished, learning my cock with my hand, as hazy memories slip into my mind. My body formed this cock after she bled on my wing. After that dream…

A woman has never learned my name before. No one else has wielded the power to draw my cock from my form before either. They must be connected.

I tug on the appendage, finding it pleasurable—a sensation I'm not accustomed to. A sensation that feels empty now that Summer has vanished.

I need to see her again.

I catch sight of her through the windows and eye another branch with a better view, but before I move, I hear another vehicle down the road. Growling out in frustration, my body goes taut with a new type of tension. The vehicle parks alongside Summer's and two men step out. I sense the older one is bloodkin to her, but my focus is drawn to the man at his side.

Adrial.

My tail wraps around the branch, stopping me from outright attacking.

He looks directly at me, a pleased grin spreading across his face, before turning back to the older man to tell him something. I bristle, enraged. He knows I won't do anything with witnesses around.

And unlike him, I don't have the luxury of hopping into bodies, the freedom of constant movement.

It takes excessive willpower to keep hidden knowing he's now closer to Summer than I am. The older man lets Adrial into the house, and then they're gone. My mind quakes as I drop from my hiding place and search for them through the windows. I'm lucky that in their isolation, this family finds no need for privacy, keeping the panes clear of shades.

They are not afraid of the outside world when they should be terrified.

There are far worse things than me watching from the dark. The colony of bats surrounding me whispers of many wretched beings.

Adrial looks out from the main bay window, and his toothy, triumphant grin expands unnaturally. Despite his human appearance, I would know his evil anywhere. The sneer falls from his face, morphing into a warm smile as an older woman greets him. They shake hands and laugh. They step out of view, and soon after I hear the faint sound of pleasant chatter.

Moving forward, I stop at the edge of the light.

Summer leans against a doorframe at the back of the room, her arms crossed over her stomach. She's pale, nervous, glancing behind her and then out the windows, forcing a strained smile on her face that doesn't reach her eyes. Those eyes widen as Adrial approaches her like they've... met before. Their greeting is awkward, which brings me some comfort.

If she is the demon's pawn, she hides it well.

For some reason, I want her gaze on me. I want to shove my wings between them and rip Adrial's new body to pieces before he can move any closer. They look too good together.

Her expression remains wary, and she takes a step back, fleeing the room and bounding up the grand staircase. She appears on the second floor and then vanishes deeper into the house. The older couple—who I assume are her parents—call after her, the woman following for a few steps before stopping, her features worried. She turns back and addresses Adrial apologetically.

I lift away from the ground, perch in a tree, and search for Summer above.

She reappears on the small third floor, holding a device against her ears and lips. She closes the curtains and vanishes from my sight.

That evening, I watch over them all, learning what I can. A cat prowls the lower floors, hissing occasionally and giving Adrial a large berth. Summer does not return to the main level, which pleases me greatly. I sense when she falls asleep, her emotions settling into placid slumber, her unease replaced with dreams.

Bats come and go as I wait for Adrial to come to me.

He steps out of the house while Summer's father puts on his boots and jacket.

He stops at the edge of the porch. "You're awake, my friend. Fancy that. I did not expect to see you so soon."

"Adrial," I snarl. "Stop your incessant games. They amount to nothing."

"Which one knows your name? Save me the effort." His laugh coils around me, airy with excitement. "I do hope it's the young female, the shop's clerk. That would be fascinating. A *woman*." He draws out the word like it's delicious. "Or have you come out here for me?"

I don't respond. I refuse to give him anything further. I only take—I only *ever* take from him. His power, his freedom, his perverse goals. Everything he wants, that he desires, is trapped inside of me.

He smacks his hands together, driving the bats to screech and worms to wiggle from the earth. "Either way, how fun this will be. I've been waiting."

Despite the centuries since our last confrontation, nothing has truly changed. He needs my name, and I do not know how to destroy him. We will never be free of each other.

Chapter Six

A Plea for Normalcy

Summer

It's dark. I should be sleeping. I turn over onto my back and watch the water hit my skylight in breezy waves, trickling down the glass panes in endless rivulets.

Trying to collect my thoughts.

I don't know how long I stare at the water running down my window, watching as the rain ebbs and the sky clears. I should be dressing and preparing to open the museum. Hopkins has been gone a week, and this is the longest I've ever run the shop on my own. The work is beginning to take its toll because I've started imagining things.

Hopkins would be so proud.

With a groan, I reach for my phone on my nightstand, only to remember I left it at the shop. Thank god I know Ella's number by heart, but I still hate being without my phone—I'm already so isolated out here as it is. My next groan is rife with agitation as I throw off my blankets, grab fresh clothes, and head to the bathroom downstairs.

"You're running late, sweetheart." Dad yawns when he sees me, a coffee in one hand and a Kindle in the other. He's seated in his cushioned reading chair at the end of the hall, his right leg crossed over his knee. It's his favorite reading place. Behind him lies a circular window overlooking the front yard and our driveway.

"I know." I duck in and close the door to the bathroom. Less than five minutes later, I'm showered and dressed, and soon I stand before him, having already recited the plea on my lips a dozen times. "Dad…"

It's his day off. Tuesdays are historically his worst day for doing business, and so he traded it with his Saturday. Such is the sacrifice of a small business owner.

He peers up at me. "What is it?"

I hang my head. "Can you come with me to the museum?"

He gives me that look, that squinty, I'm-trying-to-understand-why look that always ends in a sigh. "You were pale as a ghost last night. What happened? Your mom's upset with how you behaved, and she even made your favorite food."

"I had a rough day at work." It isn't a complete lie.

"Did it have to do with our guest? He seemed rather apologetic. He told us you two met earlier, under bad circumstances."

Bad circumstances?

Hah.

The man my dad brought home had been the same one who'd been upset about the gargoyle. He is new to town, here for business. He must have given Dad a much better first impression since he invited him over for dinner.

I was shocked when he came through the door, already perturbed by my delusion that the gargoyle came to life. He apologized for being rude, claiming he had just finished a long drive and had been excited to see the statue, but it was the sort of apology that didn't meet the eyes.

It was the last straw. Even Mom's homemade macaroni and cheese, the type with breadcrumbs and bites of sausage, couldn't keep me from running upstairs and calling Ella on the landline.

Dad sets down his Kindle and leans forward. "I know your mom's pushing you. I keep telling her to back off and let you find your way. She's worried about you. You haven't been happy since you returned, and she doesn't know how she can help."

"It's not that." I shift on my feet, feeling guilty. "I mean, I was startled to see him. It's just… It's been a crazy couple of days. You don't need to worry—I'm figuring it all out."

Am I?

I'd laugh if I weren't trying to convince my dad I'm fine.

Dad stands and downs his coffee, squinting at me again like he knows I'm bullshitting. "All right, I'll do it, but why do you need me to come with you? You can tell me that at least."

"I forgot to lock up and left my phone—"

"Summer. Really?"

"Yeah, yeah. As I said, it's been rough. Will you come with me? I need to call Hopkins and ask for some time off."

Dad shakes his head, turning for the stairs. "He shouldn't have left you to manage the museum—and you should have told him that before he left. Let's hope no one broke in overnight. Next time, tell me earlier. We could've taken care of this last night. Now I'm stressed *for* you."

My guilt compounds as I follow after him. Someone breaking into the museum would be bad, although that's not what's bothering me. I can't tell my dad the truth. He doesn't need to worry that I'm imagining things too. He hurries down the stairs, grabs his wallet and keys, and heads straight for his truck without putting on a jacket.

Town hall's clock tower looms over us as Dad parks. The museum's historical, red-brick facade is one of many along Elmstich's Main Street. According to the town records, Hopkins purchased it in the seventies, and to this day, he claims the standalone building was the perfect home for his collection.

The sidewalks are mostly empty, but Bread & Bean, the coffee shop bakery in the building next to the museum, maintains its usual clientele. Antique shops, local restaurants, and a few bars occupy the next couple of blocks. Dad's shop, where he sells custom dining sets, end tables, and chairs, is located at the opposite end of the street.

He heads straight for the museum door. I clutch his arm and stop him. "Wait. Let me go first."

If there's a monster inside, I don't want him caught in the crossfire. He pauses and steps aside, furrowing his brows. Standing up to the glass, I peek inside.

"Summer, what's going on?" he asks under his breath.

My gaze lands on the statue behind the counter. He's in the exact position he's always in, looking like he'd never moved at all. Staring at his stoney form, cast in the gray light of a blustery morning, I swallow and shake my head. "No. Nope, everything is fine. Looks clear."

I tug on the door, but it doesn't give. I tug harder.

It's locked.

Dad watches me, his expression concerned as I dig my keys out of my purse. *I could've sworn...*

"Good to see you!"

Dad jumps and I startle, the keys falling back to the bottom of my bag, but it's only Mr. Beck, one of my dad's friends and the owner of Bread & Bean. He and my father exchange awkward good mornings while I find my keys again.

Unlocking the door, I casually step into the museum. Dad rushes past me, stomping through the space, calling out and turning on the lights while I meander toward the gargoyle, staring hard. His cock is there, only flaccid this time, like a Greek statue. Even flaccid, it's still big.

He was erect yesterday. I'm sure of it. Glancing at the replica figurines, I confirm none of them have cocks.

My stomach shrivels. And the only thing I can think of is why? *Why does he have to be hung? What did I do to deserve this?* I take off my glasses and rub my eyes.

Replacing them, I examine him closer, noticing small clues, details that only someone who has spent the last year next to him would know. One wing is arched slightly higher than the other. His left hand is straight where it was once curled.

He did move. He *has* moved.

I'm not going batshit insane. The world is, and it's taking me down with it. My gaze strays back to his groin... *Why does he have such an entrancingly large cock?* I want to shake my fist at the heavens.

Dad returns to the front room, and I step in front of the statue, blocking his view.

"All clear," he says.

"Oh, good."

He gives me that squinty, suspicious look again. "Are you sure you're okay?"

I nod and reach for my phone lying on the counter. "Yep."

"Summer, call Hopkins right now. You're taking some time off."

I'm fighting the urge to remind him I'm an adult when we're interrupted by a loud bang from Main Street. The building shakes, and the floorboards creak. We rush toward the windows.

"Fire!" someone shouts, running by.

Dad heads for the door, and I follow. Outside, smoke billows into the air, right above the coffee shop. People are running out of it.

"Wait here," Dad orders, bolting next door.

I switch off the museum's light, and after giving the gargoyle a last lingering glance, I lock the front door and race after Dad.

By the time I reach the Bread & Bean, the smoke has turned black as soot. The scent of burning wood is joined by the acrid stench of torched fabrics and plastics. A man stumbles out the front door, dragging another behind him as distant sirens fill the air. It's John Beck, dragging his father behind him. Dad rushes to help, and the two of them carry an unconscious Mr. Beck onto the street.

My eyes water from the smoke as I keep the crowd from my dad, John, and Mr. Beck.

Time passes in a stunned haze. A doctor steps out of the growing crowd and mutters something about smoke inhalation and a concussion after examining Mr. Beck.

He's burned. Badly.

The sirens blast my ears as a fire truck and ambulance arrive. Everyone along Main Street has gathered to watch, and my mind blanks as the professionals take control. Dad steps aside as they load Mr. Beck into the ambulance.

That evening, I'm back home, alone. Dad dropped me off and left straight for the hospital to wait with Mr. Beck's son and meet Mom there. She's a neonatal nurse working a twelve-hour shift, and so far, neither has called me with an update.

The news plays in the background as I pace the living room. The fire department managed to stop the fire from spreading, and there were no other casualties. I've called Hopkins a half-dozen times, and I keep getting sent to his voicemail.

I told him about the fire and left it at that.

I've finally settled into the couch with a bowl of cereal when a banner rushes across the TV screen with the words *Breaking News* flashing across it. Leaning forward, I clutch my phone, ready to dial my parents at a moment's notice.

The screen switches from an interview with one of the people at Bread & Bean to another newscaster standing before a gray building with barbed fences all around it. It's surrounded by state and local police cars.

"We've come to tell you that there's been a breakout at Honey Falls Prison this afternoon. Twelve prisoners have escaped and are currently at large."

My heart plummets into my stomach. I stand as the reporter accounts for the incident and pictures of the escaped men appear on the screen. All of them have been convicted of major offenses, from arson and robbery to kidnapping and homicide.

Honey Falls is the next town over.

My phone rings, vibrating in my hand—I jump and shriek. It's Dad.

"Summer, lock the doors and windows," he says the moment I answer.

"I already have."

"Good. I'm going to wait until your mom gets off. Keep the news on. Maybe take Oyster and go upstairs."

"I will. Stay safe," I murmur, wishing I had more to say.

"You too."

It goes to the dial tone. For a few minutes, I stand there, trying to make sense of everything. When I finally manage to move, I head for the front door, double-checking the lock and bolt. I lift the curtain and peek out the side window.

It's barely eight o'clock, and it's already dark as midnight, making me miss the long days of summer. The front lights are on, and I debate whether or not to turn on the flood lights above the garage.

Honey Falls is only forty miles south of Elmstitch and is twice the size. No one would brave a forest trek to end up here... *Right?* My eyes narrow as I try to calculate the possibility.

There's a thud. I think it came from upstairs, and I jerk away from the window.

Oyster darts down the stairs.

I curse under my breath.

He sees me and purrs, asking for attention only because Mom isn't home. He's a stray she took in while I was away at college, and she's the human he really wants. After a few pets, he scurries off before I can pick him up, never one to linger if Mom isn't nearby.

Another thud sounds upstairs. I frown, heading back to the hallway. At the railing, I peer up, listening for any strange noises. There's another distinct *thud, thud, thud.*

My hand tightens on the banister as Oyster returns with a hiss.

"Hello?" I can't help calling out.

Gooseflesh rises on my arms.

Something hit the roof, that's all...

Except there's no storm, no wind—there's little more than a breeze. There shouldn't be any branches falling from the oaks. I wait a minute longer, ears straining, but the thudding doesn't sound again.

Snatching my late grandpa's cane, I creep up the stairs. Trying not to make a sound, the floorboards still creak under my deliberate steps. My breath catches and my legs cramp as I check each room, finding nothing untoward. I double-check the window locks.

All that's left is my attic bedroom.

Shoulders tightening, I trudge to the thin, narrow stairs at the end of the hallway. My bedroom door is open, and a cold draft drifts from my room. Darkness yawns before me. Staring into it, I wait for something to jump out, throttle me to the floor, and eat me alive. Frowning, I head up the steps and freeze at the threshold.

The doors to my balcony are wide open, the white curtains billowing on either side. Soft moonlight flutters in. The corners of my room bleed with darkness.

Heart pitching, I flick on the lights. My room is exactly the way I left it earlier this evening. Everything, that is, except the doors.

"Hello?" I whisper. My eyes burn, unable to blink for fear something will crawl out of the shadows or from under my bed.

I hear a strange whooshing outside, like a bird's wings.

I purse my lips, suddenly so *done* with this spooky shit. Done with fires, fugitives, and moving statues. Stomping to the doors, I step out onto the balcony, my teeth gritted like vices. As I try to look beyond, I realize I've made a big mistake.

The gargoyle crouches on the railing, cast in the moonlight. He straightens, becoming a towering, gothic sight, his webbed wings spanning out from his body, surrounded by a cloud of bats.

My traitorous gaze drops below his waist, fixating on the smooth stone.

His cock. *It's gone.*

"Summer," he rumbles, shocking me from my trance.

I dive back into my room, a shriek tearing out of my throat.

Chapter Seven
PEACHES AND HALF-TRUTHS

Zuriel

Her expression shifts from annoyance to terror within the second our eyes meet. Fear emanates stronger as I say her name.

She stumbles back, her mouth stretched open in a scream as she flees into her room. I reach out to stop her, but her clothes slip from my grip.

I rush into the sanctity of her room—bats trailing after me, her peach scent consuming me—as she stumbles toward the door at the other end.

"Wait," I demand, my voice a deep rasp.

Her shriek turns shrill as her foot catches on a rug, snagging her mad-dash across the room. I snatch her, pinning her fragile human form against my chest. "Stop!"

"No! No, no, no!" She kicks her feet and swings her arms, trying to free her limbs. I close my wings around her. "Let me go!" she cries harder.

"I said stop!" I repeat. "Calm, human!"

She continues to flail, though I scarcely notice her jabs. Her straining makes it difficult to hold her without harm. It's a relief when her cries morph into desperate pants, her limbs easing with exhaustion. She is slight and easy to break and bend.

"Please don't hurt me," she whimpers.

"Calm, female. Calm," I say. "We just need to speak. Nothing else."

I would give her words of comfort if I knew how. Unfortunately, I'm woefully inept in human emotion outside their greed, fear, and sometimes their need for protection. They are weak creatures. I have lived among them for centuries and have learned many things in that time, although my understanding of them is limited—I am an outsider and will remain that way.

Her body wiggles against mine, her breaths labored. The sensation of having her so close excites the new appendage deep within me. I grit my teeth against the pleasure.

Since the last time I've seen her, I've learned to hide my cock, returning it to the stone of my body, even though I remain bewildered by it.

I have a theory, one that may explain its appearance.

Except gargoyles do not mate—they are *made*.

When she sags in my arms, I loosen my grip, disturbed by the terror she's displaying and frustrated by my abrupt arousal.

"I am not here to hurt you. I am here to protect you. All I want is to protect you," I growl. "You do not understand the danger you are in!"

She jerks in my embrace, the only indication she hears me at all. "Please. *Please*, just let me go."

My lips twist. "Not until we speak. I am awake because of you, and because of that, you are no longer safe!"

She is tense despite her terror dispersing. She hitches, trembling as she wraps her hands on my banded arms and grips my tough flesh, shoving me away from her. I don't give, waiting for her to flail again, except she doesn't. She settles. Slowly, surely, she surrenders.

"If I release you, will you listen to what I have to say?" I ask, my voice thickening. Her body is warm and supple compared to mine. She is all soft whereas I'm jagged and cold. I have very few edges that could not be used as a weapon.

I could easily hurt her. So very easily. One thrash of my wings would send her flying across the room. I need to be careful.

"If you release me—" she breathes around the words "—I'll... I'll listen. Yes, I'll listen."

Satisfied, I let her go. She stumbles away, unbalanced as she backs into the corner of her room, and then she pivots, picking up a solid wooden stick. She brandishes it.

I miss her softness, her warmth immediately. My fingers curl as I lower my arms and clench them at my sides.

"That stick will do nothing against me," I say with amusement.

She grips it tighter. Her hair has fallen wildly around her. Its beauty catches my eye.

"You're... You are..." She's shaking so much she can't form the words. Her gaze wanders over my form.

"The one who can protect you—"

"The gargoyle from the museum."

"That too," I agree, tucking my wings inward.

"How?" Her gaze snaps to them and returns to my face. She has blue eyes. Blue like the summer sky. She blinks them wildly, straightening those thick glasses she wears. I want nothing more than to pull them off of her face and crush them in my hand. "How is this possible? How are you speaking? Are you *alive*?"

I cock my head to the side. "You invoked me. You bled on me and then woke me with my name. Don't you know this?"

She seems surprised. No one has ever attempted to invoke me without understanding the risk. Now it seems she did it by accident.

When she swallows, her throat bobs, attracting my eyes to the column of her throat. It flutters like butterfly wings, stealing my attention. It's delicate, like the rest of her. My hand could easily wrap around it.

Bats eat butterflies. And if I am like any creature in this realm, it is a bat. They surround me even now.

She points her stick, glancing at her hand where there's a small cut that is healing. "I did no such thing."

"You did, otherwise I would not be here."

It is easy to falsely blame her for this meeting, and I enjoy the surprise and the curiosity in her gaze. I need to learn how she reacts—is she truly as wonderful as she seemed from the depths of my dark slumber or is she Adrial's pawn?

I suspect she is not.

Perhaps someday I will admit my role in our bonding. A truth I'm still ashamed of.

After the monastery was destroyed, I made a promise: no more humans would be involved.

It was a promise I could not keep. Not with her blood on my wing, an opportunity to bond with her. I *wanted* her to awaken me. It was rash, selfish... I did not resist a connection with her. Curiosity, another new emotion, overcame me.

I am not supposed to feel this way—it is dangerous to have affection for a human—but after all these centuries, I have developed beyond the intentions of my angelic makers.

She shivers. "I'm just a clerk. I run the museum when Hopkins is out. You're mistaken. You have got to be mistaken."

My brow furrows, and she tenses, clutching her stick closer to her chest. Her pulse trembles. "You said my name."

"You're *mistaken*. I don't know you. You're supposed to be behind the counter," she states as if more to herself, her gaze dropping. "Please let me go. I won't tell anyone about this, I promise. Y-you can go back to what you were doing, and I'll forget this ever happened."

"I am not mistaken, woman. We are bonded now, whether you want it or not. There is no turning back. Can't you feel it? Our connection?" Because I can, deeply.

Deliciously. Wickedly... I scan her shapely form, possession clogging my throat. Possession?

A rumble tears from my throat. Possession is a demon's thing.

I stiffen, dwelling on it, stunned by the emotion. I have never felt possessive over anything except my name. To feel this way toward her?

She shakes her head. "No. I feel nothing."

Nothing! When I risk *everything*.

I take a step closer, and she cowers in the corner. "You deny me? Then what was it that you called me earlier?" I ask, taking several more steps, closing in on her. "Whisper it. Repeat it, just this once." *Make me quiver, little female.* It is hard keeping my distance. I want to study her, wrap her in my wings, and breathe her in. I have fantasized endlessly about meeting her. I need to understand why I have formed a cock, this mating genitalia of her species. "Say my name."

"Please... I don't know it," she begs. She makes her body as small as possible, her lips parting and closing. Her face has gone ashen, her eyes wide as moons, staring at my face.

"You do."

She shakes her head, sending blonde waves over her shoulders.

"Say it," I order.

She swallows. Her eyes close.

"Say it!"

"*Zuriel!*"

My name breezes outward, filled with legacy and otherworldly magic. It blooms, unseen, solidifying the threads between us.

I take a deep breath, inhaling peaches, and my body relaxes.

There has been no mistake.

The peace can't last. Just as quickly, tension ignites, erupting through me furiously as a terrible knowledge heats me from the inside, inflaming my tough skin: I should end her now and ensure the continued safety of this world.

Except I can't.

Closing my eyes, I grit my teeth.

I can keep her safe. There are ways.

I can empower her, fill her.

"Listen to me carefully, Summer..." Though I do not sense my demon nearby, I know he is not far. "Never speak my name aloud again. Never whisper it into the darkness, don't taste it on your tongue. It is sacred. My name is beyond a moniker—it's all of me. Many sought it, and who seek it still, if only to grasp at the power they are not allowed to have.

"There is one who needs my name to be free. One who will do anything to obtain it. He will hurt you to reach me. He must never find out," I warn. "You must never tell anyone about me. It is for your safety."

She does not lay down her stick, although I can tell that she is listening, taking in every word I say.

Her brow furrows. "I don't understand."

"Promise me you will not share what you have learned with another."

"I—"

"Promise me!"

She jerks. "I promise. I promise!"

I take a single step back, giving her some space. "Good."

She watches me curiously, easing away from the wall. "Am I... Am I in danger?"

"Yes."

"Then take your name back! I didn't ask for this. Erase it from my mind!"

"What's done is done," I growl, hurt that she wants to forget me so soon.

A ringing bursts through the room, startling us both. I twist, spreading out my wings into a protective arch, baring my fangs.

The sound rises from Summer. I straighten when she pulls the noisy thing—a communication device, a cellular telephone—from her pocket.

Chapter Eight
An Unshakable Gargoyle

Summer

My hand shakes as I check my phone. It's Dad. Glancing at the gargoyle, our eyes connect. He doesn't stop me as I answer the call, my heart pounding in my chest.

"Summer, how's everything at home?" he asks.

I'm terrified. I'm transfixed by awe. There's a literal gargoyle in my room, the same gargoyle that should be in an aggressive crouch behind the counter at the museum. The same gargoyle that I've seen a thousand times throughout my life.

Now he's in my room and he's... *alive.*

"Everything is fine."

Everything is not fine. Not fine at all!

"Good, because Mom and I need you to pick us up. Some asshole slashed a bunch of car tires at the hospital, and they hit both of ours. This town is going to hell."

I struggle to comprehend what he's saying. The fire, the escaped criminals, and now slashed tires? Elmstitch is a quiet, sleepy town, and this turn of events doesn't fit.

Not to mention there's also a gargoyle in my room.

And I'm talking to it, him—*Zuriel*. A name I didn't dream up. A name that's dangerous to know. I try to force his name out of my head. How do you unthink things?

So yes, going to hell seems accurate.

"Summer?" Dad prompts.

The gargoyle peers down at me, watching my every move, no doubt listening to every word. I suspect he would rather I tell Dad *no*. He doesn't know that telling my dad anything he doesn't want to hear will make him suspicious. And oddly enough, I don't want my dad involved. A shotgun isn't going to solve my problems.

My eyes shift to the exit and see my chance. A way out of this corner and beyond my room.

Zuriel let me pick up the phone, and he hasn't attacked me—not really at least—if he has plans to hurt me, he is going about it all wrong. "I'll be there soon," I reply before Dad feels the need to prompt me again. "See you then." I hang up.

The gargoyle growls, baring his teeth, crowding me back into the corner. "Stay with me. We have more to talk about. It is our first night together."

Our first night? There's going to be more? My chest expands and tightens furiously.

He's so close to me, filling my lungs with his fire. He emanates so much heat it's like an invisible sauna has been erected in this corner. Flustered and sweaty, it makes me pant. My cheeks flame with heat, and I swallow, suddenly thirsty. I'm not comfortable this close to him, or any man—male—I don't know.

Part of me still thinks this is a hoax, and any minute now he'll start laughing as he pulls off a mask and reveals himself.

I don't know how I know his name. It just appeared.

I clutch the cane closer. My phone dings, startling me again, and I look at the screen, my hand clenching around the case in a death grip. Dad sent me a text.

Zuriel's wings expand, and it's clear he doesn't want me to leave. He can keep me here if he wants; it would be so easy. He's huge. He wouldn't even have to lift a hand—his wings alone could trap me.

We stare at each other. Like we did in the dream.

He drops his dark eyes first. They trail curiously down my body. My skin prickles, and my brow beads with sweat, as I glance at his thickly arched horns, wide pointed ears, and long dark blue hair that ends at his muscled pecs. With each breath, his corded abs shift.

I hear a click, and my gaze drops to his feet. They're the same as the museum's statue, wide and clawed. It's those claws making the clicking sound, tapping the wood floor as his slender tail stiffens nearby.

When I glance back up, he's staring at me.

Once again, I fixate on his smooth groin. Where the fuck did his cock go?

Oyster clambers up the steps, snagging our attention. He sees Zuriel and *purrs*. Purrs! The cat betrays me, wringing around Zuriel's legs. The gargoyle doesn't respond, returning the intensity of his gaze to me.

I shift against the wall. "So you can protect me..." God, why do I sound so hopeful? Maybe because there might be a way to make it out of this room alive. The idea of protection is much better than murder.

"I can, to a degree." His voice is deep and gruff and not unpleasant. Firm, like a foundation. I hadn't listened to it before, too terrified to take it in.

I lick my lips. "What does that mean?"

"I can only move at night."

My gaze shifts past him and to the skylight. It'll be hours until morning.

Morning. I just need to make it to morning. I can play along until then. Maybe in the daylight, this will make sense.

"Protect me while I drive," I say, appeasing him. We might be able to strike a compromise, anything to escape this corner. "Can you do that from a distance? If I don't go to my parents, they'll ask questions, they'll be suspicious."

He doesn't answer. Instead, he does something else, shocking me.

He steps away, leaving me cold, and strides out onto the deck. I follow after, stopping shy of the threshold. His wings expand, and he takes off into the night sky. He heads to the oak out front and settles on a branch, facing me. The bats follow after, settling on the branches on either side. My heart sinks into my stomach. The moment stretches out before I'm able to look away, to react. Reaching for the doors, our eyes remained locked as I slowly close them and set the bolt.

He can fly.

I take a few minutes to collect my nerves checking out the window several more times. His large, hunched form remains where he landed. I take my time heading out front, closing all the window drapes and rechecking every lock.

He's there when I step outside, waiting for me, crouched within the trees and hidden within the shadows. His eyes glint in the darkness.

There are monsters in this world.

I take a couple of steps toward my car and look back to confirm he's not going to stop me. He hasn't moved.

He's going to let me leave.

He's menacing in his shadowed perch, his clawed feet hanging over the branch. Menacing even when he's immobile like the statue I've spent countless hours looking at—one I've seen all my life. I know every bit of him.

Even his missing cock.

My eyes widen and I dash to my car, cheeks flushing.

I watch through the rearview mirror as he flies upward and into the sky. Clouds drift across the moon. The radio plays as I try to keep my gaze on the road ahead.

Regardless, my eyes flicker up to the clouds. My muscles spasm, remembering how close we were minutes ago, and no matter how I try to make the sensations go away, the ghost of his touch remains.

He said we were bonded. Connected. I don't want to believe him.

I thought appeasement was my best bet to live through the experience. And it worked. I escaped.

Only he's trailing me, and I'm troubled in strange ways.

I reach Bloomsdark County Hospital, the front facade covered with red bricks. It's not large enough for serious procedures, but it's better than nothing. My mom gave birth here, my grandmother did too.

My parents are waiting outside the main entrance, and I park in the pick-up zone to wait for them, stepping out of the vehicle. I cast my gaze on the clouds, scanning them. I can't find Zuriel, and some of my panic dissipates.

A police car is parked nearby, and two officers work from the front seat. People wander around while what looks like every car mechanic in town is in the parking garage. They have a pickup bed full of tires.

My parents approach me, and they are not alone. The beautiful, rude man from the shop walks with them. He meets my gaze and nods sheepishly.

"We were hoping you could do Adrien a favor and drive him home too," my mother says.

Adrien. I'd missed his name before. His smile turns soft, hopeful even, quick to forgive and forget how cold I was to him the night before. "I'd appreciate the favor. Your parents say my boarding house is along the way. I'm too nervous to hitchhike in the dark."

I don't answer, my eyes flicking to the sky when a bat flits by. I glance back to find Adrien has followed my gaze, and when we make eye contact again, he smiles like it was nothing.

He's handsome. *Too* handsome. Why the hell is he in Elmstitch and not in New York City modeling for *Vogue*? He'd be better off there.

I glance down. A worm wiggles across the pavement, and I wrap my arms around my chest.

"Do you want me to drive?" Dad asks, realizing I'm distracted.

I shake my head. "No, I'm fine. Just spooked."

Dad squeezes my shoulder. "We all are. Beck is stable. We'll visit him tomorrow when we return for our cars. Sorry to make you come out here. There aren't enough tires to go around, though they're sending people to Honey Falls to pick up more tonight. I overheard that the state police are on their way. They'll take care of things."

"Right."

Dad squints at me as I scan the clouds once more before getting behind the wheel.

He takes the passenger seat while Mom sits with Adrien in the back. I'm quiet the entire drive, but that doesn't stop mom from filling the car with conversation, peppering him with question after question while prattling on about today.

Adrien is a prospector for a dairy company that plans to expand, and Elmstitch is the first of several rural towns they are considering. They're building a new plant, and I can understand why Dad likes him—he's a businessman who sees more jobs coming to town.

"Do you have someone special?" my mom asks Adrien pointedly, causing me to flinch.

"Unfortunately, I don't. My job keeps me on the road, though I'm hoping that will soon change."

Mom kicks the back of my seat. As if she weren't already making herself clear.

"Summer is wonderful at her work too," she says when I remain quiet. "Hopkins' is the top-rated museum in Bloomsdark county."

It's the *only* museum in Bloomsdark county.

"I'd love to spend more time there. Sadly, my first visit was rushed. I regret how I left."

"It's fine," I mumble, forced to participate.

"I'm sure Summer could give you a personal tour! Won't you, honey?"

"Uh... I think this is our stop, right?" I pull up in front of the converted boarding house with a sign reading *Vacancy*.

"Summer," Adrien says my name slowly like he's feeling it out. "Thanks for the ride. I hope to see you around. I'd love that tour. Maybe we can get back on the right track. I really am sorry for how I behaved the other day. It was unacceptable. The job has been... demanding."

I finally look at him and nod. "Don't worry about it."

He gives me yet another smile as he steps out of the car. It spreads a little too thin.

Leaves fall from a nearby tree, grabbing my attention. Adrien looks that way too, and for the second time that night, I think he's searching for the giant gargoyle too.

"Must be a bat," he decides.

I frown as he walks away.

Chapter Nine

Adrial

Zuriel

When we were younger this game between Adrial and I was new and interesting, and I would have attacked him outright. *Destroyed* his host body with my light. Truly it would accomplish little, for he would only be delayed while he sought out a new host. Yet for a time, I would have freedom. Of course, such a thing was easier before my solidification—back when I was young and naive with no affection for humans or the bodies he claimed as a host.

In my arrogance, I never imagined he could trick me. I had divinity on my side.

But trick me he did, using the image of an angel to nearly claim my name. Thus I was punished with the first failsafe of stone.

It seems impossibly long ago, the memories hazy.

We are older now, wiser—craftier. He sensed my awakening, surmising that someone knows my name, the single most thing he wants besides total malfeasance and pain.

Humans have bled on me before, begging me to bond with them. However, it is not what Summer has done. She is unlike any human I have known. She has given me gifts. Her laughter, her companionship. Her desires. And because of that, I do not assume Adrial will play things out as we have in the past.

Waiting and watching will give me the upper hand... *in time.*

It must.

I can't risk him hurting her. Not before I understand what is happening.

I first learned grief when Adrial destroyed the monastery. And only now am I feeling more. Summer garnered my affection.

Neither emotion should be possible.

Yet she's the first ray of light after losing my mind to an endless void, an internal place I created to safeguard my sanity, where I resided within the sanctuary of a fantastical cathedral cast in moonlight. A place that is at once familiar and foreign. My birthplace obscured and expanded upon to fit my needs. Muddled memories reached me in the depth of this void, and in time, I may have surrendered to the imaginary depths of my head.

Then Summer arrived. She guided me back to the living with a laugh.

Unlike the disjointed memories from the centuries before, I remember every interaction Summer has had with me, the details clearer with every hour I spend awake. I recall her company—her stories. Her voice drew me from my shell, her cadence fun and airy. She lifted me from my stony void by sharing her jokes, laughter, longings, and disappointments... the depths of her loneliness.

It was intriguing.

So few things intrigue me.

I know her better than any human. I knew when she was near, even if she was quiet. Her presence was unmistakably warm and sweet. I was always there, alert and listening.

I've made small efforts to protect her in the past. Working at Hopkins' has not been easy for her, and she has occasionally been left alone with angry customers. After being in her company for so long, day after day, I learned to sense her emotions and experience them as my own. Her anxiety when she was alone with cretins disturbed me. I have tried to comfort her and quell her unease.

There was little I could do but *try.*

I recall her fingertips brushing my wings, warm and curious, touches that emanated heat over my stone body. Her conversations with others, her little grunts of annoyance, and the sighs of pleasure when she sipped coffee from the shop next door. She likes something called mocha. These remnants piece together as I study her from afar, finally able to see more of her. My blood heats and my chest constricts.

My teeth grit as the demon's eyes feast upon her, and I chafe against my restraint. I believe Summer is sincere in her innocence. However, these emotions, my new vulnerability, are they his doing? Is she his unwitting pawn? If so, it is a trick I am falling for.

Adrial steps out of the car and looks directly at me. He smirks.

My hands clench. He's already wormed his way into Summer's family with his silver tongue and trickster ways.

Protecting her will be difficult if she insists on putting herself in harm's way. Despite all my affection for her, she shows only fear of me, and when she asked me to protect her from afar, I felt... *rejected*. It is not a sensation I enjoy. Especially at the hand of someone I've handed power to.

As the car pulls away, Adrial steps away from the house and faces me, his smirk now a toothy grin. Under his human visage, he is always grinning. He's been grinning from the beginning. Even in defeat, he grins.

Around me the bats screech.

"I'm sure of it now, the one who owns your name. Oh, delectable *Sum-m-mer*," he goads, tasting her name on his lips, licking them three times. "Such a pretty one, isn't she? Not my type, but her innocence will be delicious to corrupt. You are too easy, gargoyle. If I had known you liked women, I would have paraded thousands in front of you."

I stare at him, refusing to react.

"Who can resist me in this body?" he flexes the chest of his current form while the house lights cast him in bright light and long shadows. Even his eyes bulge from their sockets, popping out repellently. "I'm enchanting. The poor sap was all too easy to convince, polluting it with drugs and willing to do anything for more. Humans are so susceptible these days, so much fun."

I swallow the urge to bite back, letting him preen.

"My silent friend," he continues. "I believe I have the upper hand. I'll have control over you yet. We could have so much fun together, you and I."

Smug, he chuckles, his appearance returning to normal, and slips inside the house. From it, I smell sulfur and moist dirt. He will probably crawl into the basement and let his worms crawl out. My lips twist in disgust.

Havoc will follow him. It always does.

I retreat to the sky and find Summer's vehicle as she drives down the main road.

The scents of humans gathering, of cooked food and alcohol, reach me, overcoming the lingering smoke and sulfur in my nose. Music plays from some of the structures. A few inhabitants gawk at the burnt building while nobody lingers. It's unusually quiet for the center of a village, already caught in the shadow of a demon's menace.

Summer drives past the edge of town, following the route I've learned. Soon the family reaches their farmhouse, and they make quick work of unloading the car and locking themselves inside for the night. I settle in a tree with my newfound bat companions.

Thirty minutes later, the lights in Summer's bedroom turn on. She peeks at the balcony through the windows although she doesn't open the doors. Her emotions are agitated—she's scared again. Attempting to settle herself, her hands wrap around a ceramic cup. *Good girl.*

She'll need her wits about her.

Adrial's worms won't be able to reach her so far above the ground.

Only the calm does not last long. She turns away from the window and paces the long, skinny room. Agitation blooms out from her and into me.

I fly from the tree, shifting through murky moonlight to perch on the roof of the house. I settle above her skylight as several bats join me.

She looks up, our eyes meet, and she swallows, frightful for a moment, and I become rigid in reply. This time, she does not tell me to leave. Even if she wanted me to keep my distance, I would never disappear.

We stare at each other—for hours it seems.

Through long, slow breaths, I exploit our bond, sending her the energy of safety, waves of my protection. Her eyes hood and finally settle as she succumbs. The empty cup tumbles from her grasp as she surrenders to sleep.

The night passes and the clouds dissipate. There will be clear skies tomorrow.

When dawn approaches, I feel the stiffness starting, spreading from the center of my body. Soon I'll be forced to stillness, and I return to the shop, the hope she comes to find me burning in my chest.

Chapter Ten

Dazzled by Daylight

Summer

    The alarm goes off, and I wake with a start, curling my arms over my chest and sucking in a sharp breath. My eyes go directly to my skylight, squinting as they adjust. The soft gray and gold of morning greet me, not an angular face with fangs and horns or wings with stiff ridges. Squinting harder at the clear skies, I drop my hand over my clock and turn off my alarm.

    He's gone. The bats too. Thank goodness it's daytime.

    Where did he go? Is he outside posing in the trees overlooking my parents' house, or did he head back to the museum? I glance at the balcony—he isn't there either. Untangling my legs from my blankets, I hesitate. I'm wet between my thighs. Glancing across my room to make sure I'm alone, I lift my blanket and run a hand down my pajama pants.

It's not time for my monthly.

Touching the spot between my legs, my cheeks rush with heat. My inner flesh is extremely sensitive like it's been played with. I purse my lips as I streak my fingers over my slippery slit, and they come away wet. Jerking my sheet over my head, I take a peek, shoving my undies away. Dewy, clear arousal coats me, blooming from my pussy and drenching my sheets. Parting my legs further, I test my entrance, discovering feverish heat and swollen skin. A quiet moan escapes me as I fall back onto my pillows, circling my entrance with my finger and then doing the same with my clit.

My thoughts turn lusty as I rub my flesh, abruptly needing completion. *Now.* Caressing harder, grinding with my fingers and my palm, I jerk my hips, biting back a strangled cry. The orgasm evades me, and my need turns desperate.

I feel so empty.

So, so empty.

I want—no, I need something large and forceful driving into me. I want sex. My back arches as I slip my fingers inside, working out my pleasure from within. But they don't fill me. I twist, hoping to find the right spot, and the blanket slips off my face. My gaze lands on the skylight.

Zuriel's large cock.... I imagine him thrusting mindlessly, filling me the way my body craves so poignantly. I pretend his large clawed-tipped fingers clutch at my hips as he drives his massive body against mine. Looking at the corner where he trapped me with his wings, I picture him subduing me, petting me, putting me at ease. He strips me and thrusts his cock between my trembling legs.

"We're bound now, Summer—" Another thrust *"—bound."*

Oh... My mouth yawns open as the fantasy turns frenzied, chaotic, and wrong. If he tried that for real, I'd be screaming.

He covers me with his mass, surrounding me with his wings and—

I erupt, pleasure cascading from my sex to the tips of my fingers and toes. My feet curl, clenching as the orgasm takes me hard, forcing me to buckle and buckle again, each wave crashing into another. I bite back a shriek as I steal my hand away and clutch my bedding, surrendering to the dance, hips shunting. My gaze never wanders from the corner.

It ebbs far too soon, leaving me breathless and stressed and wanting more. I'm not sated. Satisfaction seems impossible.

Then my sweat turns cold, my soaked bedsheets clammy. Embarrassment strikes. Pulling my legs into me, I curse under my breath.

Fuck. I'm so fucked.

Frantic, I replace the bedsheets. My parents watch as I run the old ones to the laundry, reminding me they need me to drive them to the hospital. Blaming my period, I run into the shower to wash off my shame.

An hour later, I'm parking my car and tiptoeing to the museum. I bypass the coffee shop with a sign that reads, *Closed until further notice*, on the front door and give John Beck a little wave through the window. Since our parents are so close, I've known him my whole life, but I've never seen him so dismayed. The sidewalks are quiet. The first of autumn's leaves blow unhindered past my feet.

I see Zuriel through the front windows before reaching the door. A breath escapes me, relieved to have found him returned to his usual posturing. Unlocking the museum, I wonder how he managed to let himself inside. Turning on the lights, I walk up to him, checking him over.

Of course, my eyes go straight to his groin. *Of course.* My embarrassment returns, and I force my attention on his face. Today he's smooth down there. Thank god. I bite back another shameful groan.

Because I'm still wet. I showered thoroughly, scrubbing my skin raw, and yet I'm wet again—fucking *horny* again. I drop my purse behind the counter and palm my face.

He must never know.

Fuck. There doesn't seem to be a better word for what I'm feeling right now.

Curiosity gives me the bravery to face him. "Can you hear me? Do you know I'm here?" I stand on my toes and peer into his eyes. "Can you see me when you're like this?"

I'm no longer scared of him. In fact, upon waking, all I wanted—besides that damn orgasm—was to see him again. He's a gateway to a whole world I never believed existed. He's proof. People spend their entire lives searching for proof like him.

What else here is real? I give an uneasy glance at the entryway to the exhibits.

"I have so many questions," I huff, facing Zuriel and straightening my glasses, empowered by his lack of response. "I guess we'll have to wait until tonight." Today will be excruciatingly long.

I'm extra cautious with the Latin chants and the holy water. By the time I unlock the front door, the skies have brightened. I hope we get a lot of visitors today. I want the time to go by fast.

Nobody shows.

Hours pass and not a single person comes in, leaving me stuck staring at Zuriel, reading his pamphlet a dozen times over, researching all I can about him on the internet. It's research I've already done, but I refresh my mind on the very basic, extremely limited information available.

Digging deeper, I look up the magician who had him last. There's not much about him either. His Wikipedia page has a single paragraph, and Zuriel isn't mentioned at all. I look up the history of gargoyles, how they were once water spouts to protect sensitive architecture from rain, an animalistic protector against demons until the Catholic church adapted them in their cathedrals—and so forth. None of it tells me anything about sacred names, bonds, or mysticism regarding them.

Opening a search engine, I hesitate, about to type his name out, and I decide against it.

I call Hopkins and get his voicemail. I call Ella, but she's in the middle of installing a new exhibition. When I lock up for lunch and go to the bathroom, I return to the counter, finding a missed call on my phone.

From Hopkins.

I've never been so quick to check my voicemail, biting back further frustration that I missed his call. His one call in the past week!

"Hello, Summer. I hope you are doing better, and if you need some time off, take it. I apologize for being hard to reach. Things are taking longer here than I originally expected. I hope you understand. I am certain the museum is in good hands. We will talk soon."

That's it. I replay it, wondering if I missed something. I try calling him back and am directed to voicemail *again*.

Throwing down my phone, I turn to Zuriel and dig my fingers into my temples. "I'm having a bad day. I wish it would just end," I grumble. "I hope you're having a better one."

He gives me a stony, unresponsive reply.

"I can't imagine being stuck in the same position is easy. So I guess you win. Compared to me, I guess you'll always win."

I lean up until my face is directly under his.

"You're a lot less scary when you're like this," I whisper, cupping his cheeks gently. "Will you wake again?"

With his chin resting in my palm, my thumb caressing his cheek, I'm compelled to kiss him, to feel his cold, hard lips against mine.

The museum door thuds, and I jerk back. Flustered, my eyes connect with Adrien's as he calls out through the glass. "Hey! Sorry if this is a bad time. I can come back later."

"No! No. I'm about to take my lunch break."

He's wearing a Sherpa jacket, faded jeans, heavy boots, and a beige beanie, making him look like he stepped out of a rancher spread in an Abercrombie and Fitch catalog. He pulls off his hat and pockets it as I let him in.

"Yeah, I'm on lunch too. I figured I'd stop in and see you before my next meeting." He scans my face as he smiles, taller than me by a head. "I don't want to upend your plans if you're about to go somewhere."

I lick my lips nervously. I'm not used to attention from men like him. I don't get much attention at all from the male gender. Sex wasn't a strong enough motivator for me to go to them—at least until recently. I'm nerdy and academic, prone to lashing out when I'm disturbed. I like my privacy and spend my free time reading, knitting, or watching true crime. Men don't usually fit into those hobbies, and so they tend to disappear quickly when the rare one tries to get closer.

It's suspicious that he's making an effort. My parents like him. I should at least try to be friendly and figure out what's up. Despite his sudden appearance here, the town could use his business, and besides, he won't be here long. The thought eases me, and I smile at him.

"You're not interrupting anything. I'm glad you came. We haven't had any visitors today. It's been rather dull. I guess yesterday's fire is keeping everyone away."

"Is that so?"

"Yeah. Half the block is closed because of it."

"People are too easily scared."

"Yeah..." I retreat toward the counter as he follows. I eye Zuriel, my throat tightening, and pivot back to Adrien. "What brings you in?"

His smile widens though his gaze flashes to the gargoyle before returning to my face. "Well, you, of course. Isn't that obvious?"

"I figured you were here for that tour."

He steps closer, his elbow brushing me as he examines the statue. "It's uncovered today. I assume the repairs are done?"

"Yes. There was a leak..."

"He's a beautiful specimen. A rare breed, there are few like him in existence."

My curiosity is piqued. "He is... There's very little about him on record." My eyes shift to Zuriel. "Do you know a lot about gargoyles?"

"You could say that, although it's purely academic. I move around too much to own any, but..." His head cants as his gaze roams the statue's figure.

"But?" I prompt.

"I wouldn't mind owning this one."

My chest constricts and my heart beats faster. "The museum doesn't sell its exhibits."

Adrien's face hardens. "That's too bad. Don't worry, I had no plans to outright purchase him. I couldn't lift him anyway." He gives me a tight smile like he's tried. "At least now I know where to go when I want to admire him."

"So..." I say, changing the subject. "Do you want that tour?"

"Nothing would make me happier."

I step away from the counter—away from Zuriel—relieved to lead Adrien away from him. He's mine. My mystery, my curiosity. The thought of losing him now, to anyone, makes me defensive.

It's tempting to pretend I'm possessive out of interest alone, but it's deeper than that. Zuriel said I am in danger. Being in danger does not suit me. The fact that I know so little makes me nervous, like I'm a sitting duck as hunters close in, completely oblivious.

I'm a woman—I know all about fear and danger. What not to do and what to do to keep myself as safe as possible in a patriarchal world. Right now, all I have is Zuriel's promise of protection. It's a promise I've latched onto because I'm way out of my depth. I hope, even pray, that I've made the right choice by trusting him. Tonight will tell. If I can make it until then.

"Great," I say, sprinkling sweetness into my voice as I lead him to the entryway. "Follow me into the weird and strange." He crowds close behind me, and his heat envelops me like a flame. It's not a nice warmth—it's the kind that scorches and stabs.

"I love the weird and strange. Are those... peaches I smell?"

Peaches? My lips purse. He's talking about my body wash. I stray deeper into the museum, putting space between us, feeling like I'm leading him into *his* trap. When I turn to face him, he's grinning down at me, blocking my retreat. A shiver courses up my spine. When I meet his brown eyes, I struggle to look away.

"Peaches?" I ask, breathing out the word.

Adrien places a loose strand of my hair behind my ear. I freeze. "Apples are my favorite. Peaches are a close second."

The door to the museum opens with a ding. I look past Adrien's scowl, focused on my escape, and push past him to the storefront. Dad walks through and on his heels is Dr. Taylor, another family friend.

I've never been happier to see them.

"Summer, glad to see you're safe." Dad's face is flushed. "Just stopping in to check on you. I tried calling your phone and couldn't connect to the damn provider." His gaze shifts from me to Adrien, and his worry fades. "Adrien, good to see you."

"You too."

"Hey, Dr. Taylor," I greet him, stepping into the protective space of my dad, where Adrien won't be able to crowd. "I'm glad you stopped in. I was about to give Adrien here a tour."

"It can wait. I don't like you being here all alone, especially with all that's been happening over the last couple of days. Taylor was just telling me the Starbucks off the interstate was robbed this morning."

"They think it was one of those escaped criminals who did it," Taylor interjects. "Though no suspects have been named. Either way, your dad's worried about you being here alone and I am too. When is Hopkins coming back?" He peers into the museum.

"I don't know. I missed a call from him earlier, " I say. "As you can see, I'm fine."

Dad glances around with a suspicious sigh. "But I'm not fine, and neither is your mom. No one in this town is fine right now. It's been one thing after the other. The police are already stretched thin."

"You're a good dad," Adrien says, stepping forward. "Checking in on your daughter."

"It's what any dad would do." Dad huffs. "I got the tires on your mom's car and my truck replaced. Only cost a small fortune. Had Taylor here drive your mom's car back to the house—and that's when we learned about the robbery. I figured we would stop in and check on you before I drop him back off at the hospital. I'll be dropping off and picking up your mom until the police can find the asshat who slashed all our tires."

"They didn't get him on the security cameras?" I ask.

Taylor and Dad both launch into a tirade at the same time, going on about blurry footage and the security guard being on break.

"We need to start a town watch," Taylor argues.

"You'd think we wouldn't need to with the state police in town now! They haven't caught a single criminal yet from the jailbreak."

Adrien pulls his beanie out of his pocket and glances at me apologetically. "I should go."

I feign disappointment as Dad and Taylor rant. "Sorry. Maybe next time?"

"Next time," he agrees. "See you soon, Summer. Watch out for the worms on the pavement."

His words chill me. I head to the window and watch him leave, striding down the sidewalk until he's out of sight. The knot in my chest loosens. Looking down, there are worms up and down the street, wiggling out of the soil.

"He's a nice guy. I think he likes you," Dad says.

I cross my arms. "I don't think so."

"I'll invite him over for dinner again."

"Please don't." I sigh and head behind the counter. "He makes me nervous."

"Nervous? That's a good thing." Taylor laughs, and I frown. "He's a good-looking fella, and he'd give any girl butterflies."

They clearly don't understand, and I don't have it in me to explain—especially when they saved me. I'm glad they're here. I'm glad they sent Adrien away.

I pepper them with more questions, enflaming their usual arguments to keep them here as long as I'm able. After thirty minutes, it's clear Taylor has to return to work—he's inching toward the exit. "I've got appointments."

"Summer, you should close the shop early," Dad suggests.

"Mmhmm, maybe." I don't dare tell him I'm considering staying late.

Despite not wanting to be alone, I do feel better when they depart, taking their arguments with them.

In their absence, the museum hushes into chilly silence, draping me in a veil of apprehension. I lock the door and switch the sign to *Closed*. Turning around, I face Zuriel.

I slowly switch off the lights and head to the counter, keeping my gaze on him all the while, wondering how much he hears when he's completely stone.

I sit on the floor by his claw-tipped toes and wide-spread legs.

I curl my arms around my knees and wait.

Chapter Eleven
JEALOUSY AND DESIRE

Zuriel

I strain against my stone enclosure.

I am useless when the sun is out, and it is maddening.

Even trapped in this cursed form, my consciousness sharpens, and nothing penetrates my unyielding skin like Summer. I seek her voice, listening while her questions grow increasingly frustrated throughout the day.

She should not have touched me, for I am all too aware of my newest appendage, my thoughts drifting, wondering what her body can do to it.

She has given me a new curse. A cock. It does not feel like an appendage that can be sated. It feels everlasting, like the bond we now share, a bond I am becoming desperate to complete.

It is dangerous, this thing between us. It makes me vulnerable.

I ought to destroy it.

Because all these wanting sensations erupted when her caress was followed by a new heat—she blazed with hunger, compulsion, and *need*. The secret of my name binds our reactions together.

My want feeds her want.

Then Adrial neared.

Summer's emotions turned stormy, fueling my own.

Jealousy supplanted reason with raw revenge. I wanted to rip Adrial apart, to gore him with my horns as I wrap my tail around his throat and squeeze the life out of him. I wanted his hellfire to consume us both as I crush his host's body.

Summer is mine. He should not have access to her during the day when I do not!

Thoughts of the demon possessing her body, touching her skin, and stealing her kisses twisted inside me. If he did not leave her alone, I vowed to bestow him with pain.

But along came another human, someone who calmed her and sent Adrial away.

Now Summer is quiet and thoughtful. She hums a sweet song, soothing my thoughts, reminding me that there is good in this world. Once again, we keep each other company in silence.

I crave the taste of peaches—fresh, ripe, and juicy.

Summer, oh, Summer... I replace every note in her hummed song with her name.

As dusk descends, a different type of life rips through me, liberating my limbs. *Excitement.*

The emotion floods me, and I take a deep breath, eager to smell her.

Instead of peaches, I get rot.

"He's been here." The words rip out of my throat. They come out angry. *Betrayed.* I squint at her. "Did he touch you?"

I cower over her, my wings arching. My gaze flicks across her body, and despite my raging jealousy—jealousy and excitement—I'm relieved she's safe and uninjured. It's a symphony of conflicting emotions.

"W-what? You changed—you changed so fast," she squeaks, taking a shuddering breath, sliding away. "I didn't expect... Who has been here?" she asks, straightening against the counter, letting her phone drop into her lap.

I glance around Hopkins' Museum. We're alone, despite Adrial's permeating stench.

"Who's been here?" She becomes bold, demanding even.

"My demon."

I block her way as she tries to stand and restrain her against the counter. Her eyes widen, taking in my wings haloing above her.

"A d-demon? Your demon?" she chokes out. "The only ones here today were me, Dad, and Dr. Taylor. And a prospector from out of town, Adrien."

"Adrien?" I snarl. "His name is *Adrial.*"

The squeak in her voice rises. "Adrien's a demon?"

"A powerful one, lieutenant to the devil. One of the first to fall from Heaven. He would see this world aflame simply for his entertainment."

Her brow wrinkles as she drops her gaze to the floor. "I knew he was too handsome to be human," she says under her breath.

Handsome?

Handsome!?

The word strikes me with unprecedented rage and shame. A growl rips from my throat as my wings rush against my body, thrusting outward, each wingbone stretched and strained.

I am not handsome—such vanity has always been Adrial's concern, not mine. My body was created to destroy his kind, and aesthetics were not a concern. My unyielding form is a weapon, my stony skin, my shield. I am made to *scare* demons and evil humans, not to entice them.

Being handsome has never mattered, not until I heard the word on her lips. No wonder she was terrified of me the other night. I am... *grotesque.*

Grotesque things do not elicit lust within others. Even that, I know.

My nostrils flare as I sniff my surroundings. There are countless peculiarities in the museum, and there are things living here beyond my vast experiences. Shrouding it all is a reminder, a confirmation. *He. Was. Here.*

I'm shaking.

I've felt Adrial's presence in this room before—I knew he visited today, that he has occasionally visited in the last decades, most recently on the day my cock grew—but that was before Summer.

She's staring at me, clutching her limbs tight to her body.

I lean in, closing the gap between us. "Did he touch you?"

"He didn't touch me," she says, her voice tight, breathy. Then she asks, not quite with fear, with anticipation instead, "Will you?"

My breath catches, my chest freezing. *Yes,* I long to touch her. Only she would never want that—she fears me and finds me grotesque.

I try to relax. I'm scaring her. She's safe.

Except it's impossible to be calm knowing Adrial's rot is everywhere. How can I not scare her when I am scared for her? She should be terrified. A demon has his sights on her. A demon who would tear her apart and grin all the while, never mind his determination to learn my name. He knows she invoked me. He wasn't bluffing.

Summer and I need to strengthen our bond. My failure chokes me, and I resolve to do something about it.

She needs it. She wants it. And so do I.

I will claim her as she has claimed me. I can lend her my strength, my light, maybe even more.

First, we must move. Adrial's mark coats these walls, and the museum's wards have not yet fully dispelled it. I can't stay here with her while his lingering menace pollutes the space. If his demonic remnants can't penetrate these walls they will scatter someplace nearby. Something bad will happen—and soon. Demons always leave a trail.

I have heard the whisperings about bad things happening in the town.

I lift away. "We need to leave."

She drops her arms and shuffles to her feet, watching me warily. Her blue eyes are bright, unlike her ashen face and her slightly fogged glasses. Her hair is in a messy bun that has drooped to her neck, fallen strands framing her face.

"What did you mean last night, when you said you could protect me? Does that include demons?" Her voice wavers, evident of her worry. "Oh, fuck—" she glances deeper into the museum, her hand moving over her heart to clutch her shirt "—I need a cross, go to church—something! Is there something in the exhibits that could help? I need to call Hopkins again. *Fuck...*"

"I can protect you," I grunt. *I hope.*

I'm too agitated to explain what I plan to do. She's become part of this, and only her death can unbind us now.

Taking a deeper breath, finding her sweet scent, untouched amongst the rot, I give her my serenity. I breathe more of her in, seeking my own reassurance. Letting my surroundings fade, I focus solely on her and sway her emotions, relieved her heartbeat levels out.

I discover something else about her... an undercurrent of *arousal*.

There's a subtle scent of sex, sweat, and something intoxicating that I can't place.

I stiffen, nearly stone for a frozen moment before my body quivers and wings ripple. My tail coils against the floor as my cock hardens behind its magical binds, threatening to release.

He has done more to her than just visit!

I bare my fangs, clenching my hands. Summer doesn't notice, now pacing on the other side of the counter, her hands running over her hair. She's muttering, reciting exhibits within the museum.

"It's not safe," I rasp through a constricted throat, digging my claws into my palms. "This place has wards, but they are not done quelling Adrial's menace. We must leave. Now." Now, before I'm compelled by this infuriating mixture of her arousal and demon sulfur. It's doing things to my head, making me forget my purpose.

I step around the counter. Summer looks up at me, so trusting... the next question left unsaid on her parted lips.

Her lips... So sweet, so plump while pursed.

I hunger for their taste. Will they be peach-flavored?

Shaking the traitorous thoughts from my head, I wrap her in my arms and constrain her against my chest. She cannot scramble away.

"What are you doing?" She strains back in surprise and bangs her fists on my chest. "Leave where?" She kicks out as I heft her into my arms. "Let me down."

The serenity I've shared with her fades. I force her legs around my waist, clutching her small form tight.

"What are you doing?" Her heels strike the back of my thighs. "Damn it! Can you give me an answer? Let me go!"

"No."

"Let me down!" she screeches, thrashing in my arms as I swivel away from the museum front.

I carry her to the back door where the ensorcelled lock obeys my command, easing my passage in and out of the warded collection.

"Zuriel, let me down!"

She invokes me, and my name burns my ears, demanding I do her bidding. Only she didn't specify when. I'll set her down later, somewhere else. "Do not speak my name."

I spring into the alleyway.

She stops fighting and clutches me instead.

Expanding my wings, I take to the sky. She looses a tiny shriek, digging her face into my chest when the wind whips her hair. Taking to the air calms me—a peace I try to send her. She succumbs to a quiet mutter, her lips caressing my skin as she chants, "Oh my god, oh my god, oh my god. I'm going to die."

I abandon the town, looking down from a height where the settlement becomes a dense pattern of streets and lights. A wide paved road stretches to both ends of the horizon, lit by vehicles that scurry along like bugs, connecting to the distant lights of other civilizations. I'm searching for a stronghold, a citadel, a fortress. A tower in which to lock her away, to keep her by my side until she understands the magnitude of the world she's now a part of. The castle I keep erected within my deepest thoughts is where I would prefer to sequester her.

Unfortunately, it does not exist, and there will be no such place nearby. I examine the land, ashamed I have no home to take her to.

There is a thick forest, beyond which are flat plains for farming. A large lake is near, and mountains loom on the horizon, forming craggy cliffs that give way to caves.

A cave would be safe—there would only be one entrance to guard—but my attention is drawn elsewhere.

The church's spire glints as the holy space draws me near.

I descend upon the grounds, relaxing my grip on Summer. She loosens her arms from my neck and huddles them at her chest. Her sweater isn't enough to protect her against the dark fall night, and she shivers, cold and shaken from our flight. I huddle my wing close to her, protecting her from the breeze.

I release my grip on her hips, and she scowls up at me, squeezing her thighs tight to support herself. I'm entirely aware that her crux is inches from my pelvis, and pressure builds, priming my cock to spring.

She seems to notice too, and her body shudders with something more than cold. Her cheeks flush, and she shoves me away. "I can stand," she says defensively. I release her, finally obeying her earlier command. Her brow furrows and cheeks flush as she swallows, looking to the ground as she asks one more question, "What's happening to me?"

I gaze down at her mutely, hiding my confusion. *What's happening to me?* It is something I'm asking too. I have not been so close to another since the monk. I swallow it down and give her a warning. "I need to check and make sure we are alone."

Her lips part like she still has more to ask, but she stops short and nods, wrapping her arms tighter against her. Leading her with my draped wing, we approach the church's front steps.

She drags her feet.

Her thundering heart pounds wildly in my ears.

She does not want to follow me. She does not trust me, nor am I certain if I can trust her. She did not share my name with Adrial earlier, though she did not seem to understand his visit. My ears twitch, listening to her every movement, trying to understand what she is about.

She gasps when a gust of wind whips past us as we reach the large wooden doors.

"Demons do not trespass on consecrated ground. Even if that ground is no longer used by humans," I say to end the tense silence growing between us.

The surrounding land is overrun, the grasses tall and weeds aplenty, with rusted tools to suggest that someone once cared for it. The property is surrounded by a broken white picket fence, encompassing the small church and crumbling graveyard. The moon peers between thinning branches of an old oak tree, scattering dusky light on the first of its fallen leaves. An unkempt dirt road leads into open farmland.

The church's white facade has seen better days, and thick chains wrap around the iron handles of the double doors, locking them close. The spire rises above the entryway, an empty bell tower beneath its peak. Surrounding the tower, bats flood the sky.

The smell of decay and earth permeates the place—no one comes here, not anymore.

Summer's shivering subsides as she takes in the deserted, overgrown graveyard. "Are you sure we're safe here? I was taught the night is dangerous and wild."

"While you're with me, I won't let anything hurt you. Otherwise, yes, avoid the night, especially the forest."

Taking the chains in my grip, I tear them apart. The thick metal clinks. As I toss them to the ground, Summer bumps against my flexed arm. She shudders again. "God, you're strong."

She compliments me... She finds me strong.

My cock bursts through the magical binding to drop between my legs.

A wanting desire courses through me, ravenous though I've never been hungry. The golden heat within me shifts, warming my cock, driving more mass into its shape. It grows larger.

Perturbed, I push the doors open and usher her inside before she notices.

She doesn't. Not yet at least, and I try to temper my reaction, forcing my cock away as she steps deeper into the church. Moonlight filters through the stained glass, faintly illuminating the old pews facing a wooden stage with a large cross and a pulpit. There are doors on either side, leading to more rooms.

There's no one here.

There's no one for miles.

She turns to look at me, a fresh question upon her lips, but before I can pivot, she sees my groin, where my erection bulges from my form.

Her lips part, and she takes a step back. Eyes widening, she heaves a great breath. Fear erupts.

A growl tears from my throat. "Don't."

She takes a second step back, hitting the first pew. Her gaze rises to my face before falling back to my cock. Her throat bobs as she swallows.

"Summer," I say sharply. "Don't run."

Her heightened emotions electrify the space between us. Her hands drop, clutching the pew's backrest on either side of her, knuckles white with strain. Confusion and panic join her fear. Our emotions ricochet.

I stiffen further, brows furrowing.

"What... what is happening?" she breathes out the words. "Why did you bring me here?"

"I have a cock because of you. For you. I do not know why because I am not supposed to have one. When I am around you, it is hard to keep it contained. It is like it has a mind of its own."

Her gaze rips back to mine, piercing me, driving my need to protect her, to change her with my power. My outstretched hands turn from stone to fiery gold. It's no longer only my cock, my entire being burns, and I sense a gilded light illuminating my erection.

She shakes her head, her cheeks flushing crimson. "I-I..."

My open palms are emblazoned with light. "We will do what we must to keep you safe."

When I reach out, taking a step closer, she flees, darting low and dodging under my arms. She escapes.

"Don't!"

She runs.

Her emotions skyrocket, and I roar, surging forward after her.

She wants to be caught.

Chapter Twelve
BRANDED

Summer

My mind twists, my chest constricting with myriad emotions and sensations I can't keep straight.

I need air.

I need...

I don't know what I need.

My mind melted the moment I saw his cock, unable to react, except to stare at his massive appendage.

He brought me here to fuck me. With his smooth groin, it was easier to forget he was naked, and now I realize how thin the barrier is between us.

I can sense his wicked, frenetic desires, and with them his shaky restraint. A restraint that is snapping. I don't know how I know this—I just do.

"Don't!" he shouts after me.

Glancing behind me at his face, the flames flickering over his palms and his glowing cock, my heart nearly bursts from my chest.

I want him to catch me. I'm terrified of what I'll do if I'm caught. I run faster, deeper into the church.

His claws catch my sweater, and it snags and rips. I stumble forward and dodge as his hands descend. He lands with a thud, falling and crashing through the wood-beamed floor. As he rights himself, I fumble to my feet again and race ahead.

I bolt down the bench, putting pews between us, and dash for the back doors, praying that they're not locked. His wings whip, cutting through the air, and I bend low, scrambling.

My hips slam against the church's stage, and for a devilish moment, I imagine him catching me, stripping down my pants, and taking me from behind like a wild animal. The air *wooshes* out of me.

"Summer. Stop!"

His dark voice slides into me, heavy and full of gruff, guttural need, lending to my hysteria.

"Don't do this!" he roars as I climb onto the stage.

His clawed hands seize my shoulders, and he yanks me back to his chest. His cock rams against me. And I clench—my fucking core flutters! I curse my damn delirious body and grit my teeth, elbowing him. I'm chaotic with adrenaline, knowing what would happen if I stay with him any longer.

He knows. Oh, he knows.

This isn't who I am. I'm Summer, a meandering recent graduate, searching for my dream job. A woman more curious about sex than stirred by it. Everything is different now his heat presses against my back.

"Zuriel," I shriek, using his name against him again. "Let me go!"

He drops me instantly, and I escape his cage of wings. Like silk and velvet, outlined in hard bone, the webbing gives way as I dive for the door right of the stage. He roars anew, and this time it comes out furious, frustrated. I shove the door open, bolting into the dark room beyond, catching sight of another door, one I suspect—I pray—leads outside.

The gargoyle crashes after me. My fear compounds when I find a chain on the exit door. I twist around, retreating within the building.

His wings descend around me, trapping me.

"No!"

Dipping, his claws catch on my sweater as I scramble under his wings. He rips my sweater further, leaving shreds of fabric to flutter over my back. He catches my hair tie, ripping it, and my hair flows free.

"I don't want to hurt you!" he bellows as I push the door open and stumble into the church, sprinting through the front doors.

Freedom!

I halt. Bats, hundreds of them, perch on the steps and the broken railing. They fly ahead, filling the air like a cloud. I've never seen so many in my life.

Gulping, I dash through them, their wings brushing my arms as I rush into the night. The fresh air envelops me like a hug, cooling some of my fiery, terrifying arousal.

Because I am aroused. I've been aroused since I woke up. Today had been hellishly long for so many reasons, and my inopportune lust was only one of them. I can't get Zuriel out of my head. He's been there for days...

I've wanted him since I cut my finger on his wing.

Without time to examine why, I race into the graveyard.

My torn sweater ripples around me, and the breeze tickles my exposed back. Shivering, I sense Zuriel's presence behind me. I'm midway through the graveyard, dodging between old moss-covered monuments when a realization occurs.

He's no longer trying to catch me. He's just following.

Gasping, exhausted, and inhaling sharply, I reach one of the monument's walls and twist to face him.

The next instant, I'm encaged. His massive body drops from above and captures me within an arc of wings.

I tear into him, thrashing at his neck, his shoulders, and his arms. My hands fly as his scent unfolds, masculine and rich, brimstone and spicy, otherworldly and unplaceable. His fists grind into the monument's walls on either side of my head as he leans forward, a deep groan leaving his lips. It slides into me, erupting my nerves with quickening thrills. His lust is mine.

He caught me.

"Please," I beg, with no idea what I'm begging for anymore. I'm flushed, burning, and the cool night air no longer tempers me. "I need, I need..." I gasp in a breath and grip my chest.

He rests his brow on the wall above my head as I strain my neck to behold his wrenched expression. He's so musculature and strong, so monstrous and unreal, I feel minuscule.

The light from his cock illuminates us and ensconced in his wings it's like we're in a world of our own. Even the bats have given us privacy.

He presses his cock—his light—against my stomach. "Summer," he rasps my name.

His member is hot and hard, and my wild hands drop down to wrap around it as I sway my hips back and forth.

"I need you," I cry.

What is happening?

The moment the question streaks through me again, I know he's thinking it too.

He thrusts away. My grip on him tightens.

"Summer," his voice is bewildered. "We need to—"

Missing the cage of his body, I lean into him, tugging him in my hold, kneading his length with my grasp.

My touch is rewarded with a grunt, and his eyes glint with golden fire. It lights his fierce, predatory features and the lust in his gaze—his shock.

He's fearsome, the stuff made of midnight dreams and vintage horror movies. His blue-black skin, his curved horns, and his long hair give him the appearance of a gargoyle, but underneath, he's all male. His cock throbs within my grip. My gaze drops upon it.

I lick my lips at the sight, my slender hands squeezing his member. It's warm and taut.

Golden light bleeds out between my fingers. Fingers that barely wrap around his girth, digging into deep ridges on his underside that lead directly to two heavy oval-shaped testicles where the light deepens to near crimson. With his shaft slightly tapered, his tip bulges out like a mushroom so firm it only gives when I push the pads of my fingers into it.

Gasping, he rumbles my name, sending delicious chills straight to my core.

His hands drape across my shoulders, first combing my loosened locks before wandering under the torn sweater as I explore him, his claws scratching into my skin.

I run my fingers up and down his length. They're hungry, and my hands feast on him.

"Zuriel," I moan.

He growls and clutches my chin, making me face him. He snarls, revealing fangs. "Do not invoke me with lust, female. You play with me. With forces neither of us knows enough about." He thrusts slightly into my hands.

"Then play with me."

Still holding my chin, he yanks my hands off of him with his other hand and clutches my wrists, restraining them between us. "You are not thinking straight."

I stand on my toes. "Neither are you."

His lips twist. His expression darkens with raging lust. He's close to breaking. I can break him. If I can break him, then he can shatter me, and then maybe...

Maybe some of this will make sense. Maybe all of it will.

"Don't," he rumbles the word again.

I lean closer. "Why not?"

His jaw ticks. "You are a devious girl."

He releases my wrists and clamps his hand around my neck, holding me against the monument's wall. He pins me there, and his gaze leisurely roams up and down my body. Aroused by his attention, I arch my back.

His face nears mine, mouth parting into a fanged snarl to say something more, something about the wrongness of this, but I interrupt him.

"Kiss me," I whisper.

His glinting gaze drops to my lips.

He stares at them. "Kiss... you?"

Denied, my hips writhe. "Yes. Kiss me!"

"I need to brand you."

My brow furrows. "Then brand me with a kiss."

He lifts his eyes to mine, his gaze confused and frustrated. "It does not work like that."

I cup his sharp cheeks and draw him toward me. Letting me lead him, he leans down slowly, loosening his hand from my neck.

Our mouths touch, and our kiss burns with frost. My eyes shudder closed while I clasp my arms around his neck. He yanks me against his chest, pulling my feet off the ground, and presses me harder against the wall. I curl my legs around his hips, trapping his cock between us, and it slips past my ruined sweater, sliding against my skin. His ridges dig into my tummy.

Our kiss starts soft, uncertain—like everything has been thus far—though tender. Brushing over mine, his lips quell my frenzy while fueling my need. I lean into him, loosening my hands so my fingers dance down his arms with a caress. His flesh is stiff, yet he shudders under my simple touch. His mouth is cold, slowly warming up. Rubbing my lips across his, he pauses to rest his cheek on mine and burrow his nose against my ear. He breathes me in, setting my fogged glasses askew.

When I look, moonlight brightens his face and deepens the blue of his long hair. His gray horns shimmer like silver. He swipes his mouth over my cheek, whispering light kisses along my face as he traces his way back to the corner of my lips.

Our gaze locks.

He lowers me to the ground and rights my glasses.

This feels like something new, something more than desire, and far, far more terrifying. It's longing and loneliness, and endless, torturous solitude. There's no end or beginning, only right now. It's a moment that is desperate to go on forever because, once it's over, it can never return.

I inhale a shaky breath, knowing I'll never take in as much air as I need.

His brow lowers to mine, and I tremble.

"Summer," he whispers my name.

He lifts me away from the wall and lays me out on the ground, amongst the leaves and dewy grass. Kneeling over me, he lifts the bottom of my ruined sweater and slides it up my chest as his wings drop to either side, blocking out the moon and the evening breeze.

Hands glowing, he slides my bra up, baring me from my breasts to my pelvis. Shuddering, my nipples peak under his gaze. He stares at them, at me, his expression strained. He licks his lips, licks his fangs. However, he doesn't say a word as he sets one of his hands over my left breast, slipping his fingers under my bunched clothes and settling it there.

He places his other hand above my navel. "By this mark, I strengthen our bond. I grant you the use of my power for your protection."

The light shines from his palms, heating my flesh. Warmth floods me, driving ripples of bliss through my chest. The light brightens, and I close my eyes, arching, and digging my heels into the ground.

I'm warm again. So much warmer than before. I'm being filled.

Reveling, buzzing sensations pools between my legs, and pleasure bursts, hot and hard. I cry out and thrash as his light fills me, driving between my thighs. He keeps me pinned as my body dances, writhing as my whimpers escalate.

"Summer," he invokes my name.

My eyes fly open and I scream.

Pain rips the pleasure away.

I don't know when I wake, or that I passed out at all, only that when the darkness recedes, I'm cradled in his arms and we're flying over the town. My clothes have been placed over me, though my skin feels like it's on fire. We descend as the glow of morning gleams across the horizon. My house rises over us as he lands on my balcony and carries me into my bedroom. The curtains billow as he lies me on my bed.

"Find me," he commands. "When you wake, find me."

I blink as he moves back toward the balcony door. With a final look between us, he's gone.

Turning over in my bed, I drift back to sleep.

Chapter Thirteen
BREAKING BREAD

Summer

    My dreams are endless, one leading into another. A lifetime of days drifts by, murky and vivid all at once.

    Through it all, no matter what changes around me, I'm frozen in place. Desperate, I struggle to lift a hand or twitch a toe, discovering I've become still as a statue. I drift again.

    There's light and darkness—mostly darkness. It encapsulates everything with long bouts of silence. My chest aches, melted and solidified by scars.

    There are voices, lots of them, all different. They drift by, one by one. I don't understand what they say, and when I try to listen, they vanish.

    The voices grow distant, farther away. I'm naked, alone in this place.

    I can't move. I'm a statue.

    I can't move! I panic.

    Something finds me. There's a castle in the distance, and bats fly overhead.

Then Zuriel is there, frozen at my side. In the stillness, he doesn't acknowledge me, though it's enough to know I'm no longer alone. Together we watch, listening, as the centuries pass.

The morning glow streams through the skylight as I slowly stir. Blinking rapidly, the grogginess clears. Without my glasses, I can't read the time on the clock. I suspect my alarm should have gone off hours ago—if I'd been here to set it.

But I wasn't here, I was... I was...

In a dream? One that made me feel like I lived a hundred lifetimes.

Memories from last night flash through my mind, the details frantic and difficult to track. Zuriel spoke of a demon—*Adrial*. There were bats. Zuriel flew me to the Old Church where he broke open the building—and that was when his hands turned to fire.

I grasp my chest. He's inside me now, more than before, manipulating my emotions, but as I think this, I understand this distortion goes both ways. I didn't understand the significance of what he meant—I didn't take it seriously enough. And now, I'm afraid it's too late. He wants me.

He has no idea why.

I leap out of bed, grabbing my glasses as I head for the large mirror above my dresser. I'm still wearing the destroyed sweater, my skin marked with dirt and grass. My hair is tangled and knotted, crimping against my shoulders. I lift away the scraps of my sweater and tug off my bra so I can stare at my half-naked reflection.

There are two large handprints.

One is over my stomach and the other covers my left breast, nipple included. The brand's outlines are dark and thick, a rustic gold, and each is filled in with threads of lighter gold, forming tightly-wound swirls and spirals. The design is reminiscent of a human handprint, although more structured and more ornate.

This is what he meant by branding me.

He... *Bastard!*

And I begged him to do it with a kiss. A kiss now cemented on my body.

I tap my fingers to my lips. They lower to trace my altered skin, finding the mark smooth. It's nothing like a scar, and I'm fully healed.

As I explore the intricate details, more memories return of last night. The heat of our chase—how it felt to be caught. I clutch my gilded breast. My heart pounds and my throat constricts, remembering the rush of it all.

He wants me. Our desire spiraled into delirium. We fueled each other, driving each other insane.

I yank down my pants and thrust a hand under my panties. I'm not sore. I'm wet but not drenched. I clench around my tiny finger, face flushing as a fantasy flits across my mind—him pounding into me, branding me between my legs as well.

I yank my finger away.

I wish he'd fucked me.

I want to feel raw and sore, to be burned by his cock. This perpetual arousal is becoming torturous. Groaning, I glance at the drawer of my bedside table, debating a quick tussle with my vibrator.

Instead, I allow the daylight to diffuse my gaze, blurring the heated details like a dream, and I return my attention to the brands and what they mean. My skin has changed. It's evidence.

It's true then. We're bound. Something began when I bled upon his wing, for it was that next night when he first entered my dreams, and I uttered his name.

A name that's dangerous to know because of…

Adrien—*Adrial.*

My fear returns in a rush—real, dangerous terror. Tensing, thoughts cascade as one unknown tumbles into the next. Demons exist. And one of them is here, in my hometown. The fire, the jailbreak, the slashed tires—chaos follows in his wake. He wants Zuriel's name. He wants me to.

Adrial knows who my parents are.

My breath shortens as my reflection blurs.

What am I going to do?

My gaze catches on the glint of his golden brand. Making his mark was important, his highest priority. Instinctively, my hands wander, settling themselves on my chest and stomach, matching my smaller fingers to the silhouette of his larger ones. One hand over my heart and the other… my womb.

Heart and womb, cores of love and creation.

I don't know what the fuck that means.

I work through my breaths, one after another until my heart stops racing. I remember Zuriel's instruction to find him.

Turning away from the mirror, I dig out my phone, keys, and wallet from my pants pocket and stuff my ruined clothes under the bed. Fresh clothes in hand, I'm sneaking down to the bathroom in my robe, hoping to avoid my parents, when Oyster scurries past me and up into my room, the fur on his back raised. I stare after him, confused, and shake my head, ducking into the bathroom.

Minutes later, I race down the stairs, a practiced lie on the tip of my tongue. My phone was filled with countless ignored messages. Dad invited Adrial over for dinner again, and Mom begged me to come home for supper. Then, later that night, Dad asked if I was okay because he saw my car was still at the museum when he dropped Adrial off.

The demon was here.

Turning the corner into the kitchen—my feet halt at the threshold.

Adrial sits at the table with a plate of pancakes in front of him, and he's drinking coffee. He looks up at me and grins, syrup and pancake mashed between his teeth.

"Summer!" Mom cries when she sees me, embracing me and squeezing me tight. She steps back and crosses her arms over her chest. "What a relief it was to find you in your bed this morning. When did you get in? You had me worried sick!"

"Bad service," I mumble, unable to peel my eyes off Adrial. "I, umm... I stayed late, got distracted cleaning an exhibit, and then when I reached my car, it wouldn't start. Bad battery. I must have left a light on. I ended up taking a taxi home. Dad, can you take me to town and help me jump the car?" I peel my eyes away from Adrial to look between my parents.

Acting as normal as I can, I grab a plate from the cupboard.

Dad's lips tighten as he scans me over. "I'll take you to town and jump your car. I'm taking Adrial back anyhow—if Mom hadn't found you sleeping, we were ready to go by the police station. You should have replied to our messages. Or called us from the shop, at least. This isn't like you."

"I tried." My skin feels too tight, guilt compounding with fear. I hadn't thought of my parents once last night.

"Adrien was so worried about you he hitchhiked over this morning," my mom says, anger etching her voice. "You should've answered the museum's phone. With everything that's been going on around here, really, Summer?"

"I'm sorry. I was... in the basement and didn't hear it." I face the breakfast table, stacked with pancakes. With an empty plate in my hand, I have little choice but to be berated and break bread with a demon. I pour a cup of coffee, praying that caffeine can help.

Adrial studies me as I take the seat across from him. I shiver under his stare.

"I hope our gargoyle friend isn't the exhibit in need of more repair," he says.

Nausea hits my stomach. "No, it's... uh, some antique crosses. Water got on them. There's a leak in the basement pipes."

He's still grinning at me when I glance at him, and I drop my eyes to my plate, scared. What can he do to me? My parents? How powerful are demons?

Flashes of the most brutal true crime shows I've seen leap through my head. Terrible things that were all done by humans... supposedly. My jaw clenches and my teeth begin to ache.

"With everything going on, I wish Hopkins would come back," Dad scoffs. "The jewelry shop was broken into last night. Are you sure you want to work today? We could just jump your engine, and you come back home or join me at the shop."

"I'm not going to open the museum. I need to clean up last night's mess and call someone about the pipes."

"You never know what sort of danger lies behind a safe, stony facade," Adrial warns. "I hear your benefactor has been gone for some time. Where is he? Do you know?"

Shaking my head, I swallow a bite of pancake without chewing, lodging it in my throat. I meet Adrial's gaze, and his nostrils flare, a little too wide for a man's. My lip quivers. My brands grow hot. Curling my fingers into my palm, I stop the instinct to run them up my shirt.

Dad sighs. "Keep the doors locked. And keep that mace I gave you close. I want you to call me on the landline every other hour." He pivots the conversation, and I break Adrial's hypnotic stare, glaring down at my food instead. His smile lingers in my mind.

I nod mutely. "I will."

"Do you want me to take a look at the leak?" Adrial offers.

"No!"

My parents shoot me angry glances, and I cram pancake into my mouth.

Throughout the remainder of the meal, Mom kicks my legs no less than five times, clearly disgruntled by my behavior. Oyster never shows. Adrial's constant attention is the worst of it because, between bites and banter with my parents, he doesn't take his eyes off me. At least not for long.

Even when he looks at my parents, the pressure of his gaze remains. His wicked grin. From the corner of my eye, it seems to grow wider than his face.

I focus on the old floral wallpaper behind him. As a child, I studied its repeating yellow and green patterns and memorized them. Only these patterns, this house, no longer feels safe.

I need to get out of here, need to get Adrial out of my house and away from my parents.

My face flushes furiously, and I scrape my plate clean and jerk to my feet, the food like a weight at the pit of my stomach. "Sorry, I forgot, but I need to go to work. *Now.* There's a chemical clean I started last night, and if I don't stop it soon, I'll damage those crosses."

My lies are such bullshit—I don't even believe them.

Dad takes the hint. He squints at me without asking why I'm putting up such an act. I stare back, pleading.

He agrees, taking his plate to the sink. "All right then. I was done anyway."

Adrial cocks his head, his perfectly groomed hair shifting slightly away from his face. Does he know what I'm thinking? I chew on my lips and stand, pivoting for the front door.

Squeezing the three of us into Dad's truck is an awkward, uncomfortable effort. I claim the passenger seat, forcing Adrial to crowd his body into the back. When I blast the radio, Dad gives me a long, hard look, but he doesn't turn the volume down. Grand Funk Railroad's "Sin's a Good Man's Brother" starts to play.

We head to Adrial's boarding house first. In the daylight, I realize the house doesn't look inhabitable. The shingles are hanging, and the lawn is brown and overrun with weeds. It's in desperate need of a new coat of paint, old graffiti marring the side.

He offers to check the museum's leak one more time—an offer I just as quickly rebuff.

He saunters to the front door and turns around, his smile lodged in place as he gives us a salute.

His mouth forms the words: *See you soon, Summer.*

When Dad drives away, it's easier to breathe.

The remainder of the trip is quiet. When we reach Main Street, Dad parks hood-to-hood with my car, turns off his engine without a word, and steps out to grab the cables from the back. I brace for our inevitable confrontation.

Dad knows me, probably better than anyone. He can spot my bullshit a mile away, and I can spot his as well. Whereas Mom ignores the signs, Dad is attuned to them.

Rustling leaves break the silence as I open the passenger side door. The jewelry shop across the street has yellow no-crossing tape across its broken display windows. Closed signs mark many of the stores, and the places that are still open have scarce clientele. It's mainly people I recognize, those who work here.

It's early.

There will be more visitors later.

I hope.

Taking a nervous breath, I unlock my car and test the engine. The station wagon starts, of course, she does. I let her run, proving my guilt, as I step out of the vehicle and apologize. "I must have been mistaken last night. My car's fine."

He crosses his arms and just looks at me, and I'm convinced he's about to chew me out. Waiting for it is almost worse than experiencing it.

"Adrien gives you the creeps," he says.

At first, I'm not sure if I heard him correctly. When the words register, I'm relieved. "Yes."

The buzz of my engine mutes our words. It's my chance to warn him. Unfortunately, every explanation that flits across my mind makes me sound crazier than the last. Dad isn't a superstitious man, and until recently, neither was I. He'd want to get to the bottom of my sudden change in views. He'd dissect it like a frog in science class, convincing me that the world is one-dimensional. Telling him would only make me feel crazier.

Besides, if I tell the truth and he *believed* me, he'd throw me in his truck and drive me far, far away. It would make matters worse. I don't even know what my brands mean.

"I get a bad vibe from him. I don't think he's a good person. Just stay away from him—for me." I rub my face and adjust my glasses. "I think he's connected to everything happening in town, and I know that sounds ridiculous. Please, *please* don't invite him over again. Even Oyster doesn't like him."

Dad's brows furrow. "He does have one fucking creepy smile."

I wrap my arms around my middle. "It's... just a feeling. Call it a woman's intuition. I'll be safe at the museum, people are always walking by outside. I will call you throughout the day."

"You'll ring me if he shows up?"

"It'll be the first thing I do."

He sighs, suddenly appearing tired. "When did you become so passionate about the museum? It's antiques and junk in there. That's what you've always told us." His gaze skirts toward the building's facade, two buildings away. "Do you want me to check the leak?"

"I can handle it. And I've always been passionate about the museum." It's another lie. "I'm not having any luck with getting any interviews. And so I'm... reevaluating."

His face twitches, his doubt evident. "I trust you, Summer, I do. You're a smart girl. Just don't be an idiot, okay? I raised you better than that. Hopkins' Museum isn't going to be your meal ticket out of this town. It's more likely to keep you here instead."

"I'll think about it."

"And don't go pulling the shit you did last night. I don't know how your mother will handle it. We're worried."

"Okay," I agree, giving him an empty promise.

He gives me one last lingering look before patting my shoulder awkwardly. "If you don't call, I'm calling the police. Consider this a warning." He collects his cables and returns to his truck.

When he's gone, I swallow my guilt and turn for the museum, narrowing my attention on the task at hand—I need to talk to Zuriel.

Reaching up, I rub my itching brands.

Chapter Fourteen
All Cats Recognize Demons

Summer

 My brands are unusually warm. I rub my chest fervently, glancing around. There's nobody; I'm still alone. With my hand over my chest, I suspect this is more than paranoia. I eye the distance to the museum, only two buildings down...

 Leaves shuffle behind me, and I jump. Twisting, I see no one, though something catches my eye. There's a cluster of worms wiggling toward my feet. Farther away where the sidewalk meets a short span of dirt, many more are rising out of it. Within seconds, they overrun the sidewalk.

 Sickened and confused, I dodge through the nearest door and into Carol's Cattitude.

It's noisy with meows and squawks, scented like dusty litter. The aisles are cluttered, and glowing blue fish tanks line the back wall with the amphibians and reptiles not that far away.

Carol smiles, looking up from her laptop behind the cash register. "Hey, you're here early."

I catch my breath, freezing at the door. Unlike Adrial, her smile is soft, genuine, and kind. "Did you see the worms?"

"Worms?"

"On the pavement outside."

She walks to the window and hums like nothing is amiss. "Must be the change in season. Did you want to see the cats?" she asks. "We have a couple of new ones."

Carol has been running this store since before I was born. She's in her late fifties now, always smells like clay, and is generally known as the town's kooky cat lady. Seeing her, so typical in her oversized pink sweater with the store's brand crackled across it with her dyed red hair, is like returning to the safety of my parent's home before a demon joined for breakfast.

If the worms don't bother her…

"Sure." I smile back, falling into the safety of my lunch break routine of stopping by. I'm about to walk to the cats when a new idea strikes me. "By any chance, do you have anything that gets rid of them?"

"Worms? Earthworms? No, unfortunately."

"What about bat houses? Do you have those?"

She squints at me. "They're in the back, in the bird aisle. Though why don't you ask your dad? He can probably build a nice one. Summer, is something wrong?"

"No, everything is fine."

Turning from the front window, I approach the rescue cats. There are four today. One of them is a tortoiseshell, and she hisses vehemently as I approach. Leaving her be, I offer the back of my hand to the snowball white kitty who seems much more friendly when the shop's door opens and the bell chimes.

Stiffening, pressure floods my senses like a rubber band around my forehead.

"Good morning," Carol calls out. "Can I help you?"

The cats grow agitated as the door closes and footsteps sound behind me.

Adrial joins my side. "I don't like cats."

My back straightens, and my hands twitch. The cats take turns hissing, spitting, and growling, never taking their narrowed gazes off of him, looming over my shoulder. I don't think they like him either.

I keep my eyes on the cats, pretending, *still* pretending, that he's maybe just a normal human. "How did you get here so fast?" I whisper. "Don't you have work to do?"

The tortoiseshell extends her claws and bites at the bars of her cage. The tag says her name is Genevive.

He leans closer. Too close. Way, way too close. "My work can wait."

My brands burn as his warm breath wafts over my ear. "There was a new finding this morning. Someone tried to claim property I very much desire. It changes everything. My... *work* is on pause until further notice." He straightens up and speaks louder. "How about I take you out for coffee and tell you all about it?"

The hair on the back of my neck rises. "No," I squeeze out. "I should get going."

He never does answer my second question.

His presence looms over me, like a shadow longing to consume. I'm sluggish in his gloom, my head aching and slow. It's difficult to step aside...

Genevive shrieks. A shrill yowl the likes of which I have never heard. Her cry pierces me, and my mind sharpens. Startled, I realize Adrial has stepped even closer, now only a hand's width from me.

I jolt, making up my mind. I leave his hypnotic bubble and walk through the aisles, gathering kibble, a cat bed, and more. He stays near the cats, somehow ignoring their pleading mews and the way Carol occasionally glares at him from the front of the shop.

"Can I help you, sir?" she calls out for a second time.

He lifts his hand dismissively, inciting her nostrils to flare.

Adrial stands there, watching me, beaming with his wide grin. I try not to look at him, try to duck out of his line of sight, but wherever I am, all I can see is his smile. It grows wider, stretching horribly, making my brow bead with sweat and my palms dampen.

Even though my arms are full, I add a bat house to my load. Asking Dad will take time, even if this purchase will invite even more questions.

Finally, I make my way back to Carol—to safety—and drop my supplies. "Hopkins' Museum would like to adopt Ginny, I mean, Genevive," I say, feeling Adrial's bestial grin burning into my back.

Hopkins used to keep a black cat at the shop named Misty—short for Mysterious—he won't mind having another cat around. He never did throw out all of Misty's supplies.

Carol questions me with her gaze, but in the end, she says nothing and presents me with the adoption paperwork, highlighting where she needs me to sign. "Genevieve is a bit ferocious, isn't she?" She observes, peering over my shoulder, her nose wrinkling, her pallor whitening.

I don't know what she's seeing. I don't want to know.

"Exactly," I whisper.

"Weird stuff happening in town. A girl has gotta be careful," she whispers back. "And Ginny's a good girl, I know it. She might need some patience and loving before you break through to her." Her voice dips lower still. "Summer, do you need help? The cats don't like him."

"I'll take good care of Ginny," I assure Carol.

Her gaze narrows, and she slowly nods.

I don't want to involve my dad, let alone her. I've seen enough horror movies to know that involving others gets them hurt, or worse. I feel awful enough for adopting Ginny, wishing I didn't need her help, knowing that through instinct she sees something I still struggle to accept.

Carol rings me up, and I listen to the beeps of her scanner, dinging one by one.

Whatever Adrial is doing, I refuse to turn around and look.

The silence is enough.

I pay, retrieve Ginny, and dash out of the store. Laden with cat supplies and Ginny's backpack cat carrier, I hear the door to the pet shop chime a second time. I pick up the pace. Ginny fusses, putting me further on edge. The bat house bumps the side of my leg.

Get to the museum.

Just reach the museum.

"Do you want help with that?" Adrial asks.

I jump, and Ginny jostles the carrier, going wild.

"Nope, I can manage."

He falls into stride beside me. "What are you doing, Summer? You seem unsettled."

"I think Ginny will be a wonderful companion while I work."

He won't hurt me in broad daylight, right?

"Are you certain? If you crave companionship, I could help you out with that." He says it like poetry, the words twisting upon his tongue and worming their way into my head, while beneath my boots I'm crushing the worms that trail him on the pavement.

My brows furrow. My brands sear with pain.

"That's all right."

I focus my gaze on the museum's door just ahead.

"Summer," Adrial drawls tauntingly.

It's a relief when I catch sight of Zuriel behind the counter.

"You're shaking."

Lowering my purchases, my hands tremble as I retrieve my keys and unlock the door. "No, I'm not. Goodbye," I mutter. Kicking the door open, I can carry everything inside. The door closes behind me, but Adrial slips in.

I spin on him. "I'm keeping the museum closed today. For renovations. You can't come in."

"I'm not just any visitor."

Ginny mews, crying out. I set everything down and open her carrier's door. She springs forth, hair raised and back arched, with a long, low hiss.

"The shop is closed," I repeat, hardening my voice. "Leave."

A bead of sweat gathers on the tip of my nose while my glasses fog. I don't want him taking another step into the store. This is *my* space.

He pouts like he's disappointed in my behavior. I'm compelled to step aside, and only Ginny's agitation keeps me steady. *He's not human.*

I don't like the thought.

I hate it.

Trembling, I take a deep breath. Zuriel mentioned demon rot and markings, that their presence leaves something behind, a *menace*.

"Oh, Sum-m-mer," Adrial says my name slowly. "Don't you want to know the truth?" His face twitches into a hungry, curious expression.

"T-Truth?"

He indicates the statue. "How you became tangled up in all of this?"

I stiffen. Adrial blinks, and his brown irises turn yellow. He blinks again, and they become normal.

"What?" I ask.

"Does he blame all this on you? Say you're responsible for waking him? I'm so sorry. Let me help. I can answer all those questions dripping from the tip of your tongue."

I frown. *Questions.* I have so many of them, and I part my lips, eager to understand. "Why—"

Ginny pounces.

She jumps onto his chest, sinks her claws through his shirt, and digs them into his flesh.

"Stupid cat!" he yells, knocking her away, and shifting his attention. Ginny lands on her feet.

His allure is broken, and I shudder, clearing his poisonous words from my mind. My breath heaves.

Zuriel, I need you.

Lowering my hands, mirroring the position of the two marks, I stop fighting the hot pain, embracing it instead. Zuriel's strength blooms inside my chest. His fire. *It's his fire I feel.*

He penetrated me with it. I understand now. Something did fill me up last night—it just wasn't his cock. Peering down at my hands, I recall how his fingers glowed upon my flesh.

More golden light beckons through the corner of my eyes where Zuriel looms. The heat escalates, snatching my breath, burning me up.

Everything glows as Zuriel's power channels through me.

I'm about to erupt into flames. I want to scream—it hurts so bad!

"Fuck off, Adrial!" I shriek instead, but my voice doesn't sound like mine. There's another, a voice layered behind it. Deep and gravelly, strengthening my command.

Enveloped in flames, light streams from my chest.

There's a thudding sound, and I turn my gaze to the window. A flock of birds has gathered outside. They beat the windows with their wings, again and again, and the thudding continues.

Adrial bellows.

I don't dare look at him directly, but when I take a step closer, his feet shuffle toward the door. His bellow morphs into a high-pitch snarl. I stretch out my hand, my palms now spilling with brilliant light.

Pressure builds in the air, and all at once, it expels.

He's forced outside, and when I hear the door slam upon him, I jump forward and lock it. I catch sight of him then, on the other side of the glass, and it nearly breaks my mind.

His skin is poxed, opening into tiny holes filled with black sludge. His eyes, large and inhuman, bulge like overblown balloons from his sockets. Worms slither around him and through his skin, wet and slimy, leaving viscous brown trails in their wake. His large grin eclipses it all, revealing a mouth flooded with blackened gums, broken teeth, and yellow dripping bile.

His grin dances, turning angry before becoming gleeful and sickening again. On fire, he cackles, a terrible final sound as he disintegrates to ash.

I twist away and cover my face with my hands, slumping to the ground. The birds snap their wings on the windows.

Everything feels like it's melting. Gripping my chest, it feels like I've been torn open.

Curling up into an agonized ball, I sob.

Chapter Fifteen
Waiting for Darkness to Come

Summer

Terrified, I try to relax while shudder after shudder wrenches my muscles. Breathing is still a challenge. I crawl behind the counter, huddling against it and the wall, leaning on Zuriel's legs.

Lifting my shaking palms to my face, I study them. The light has ebbed. The fire in my chest has lulled. Only a metallic taste in my mouth remains. Maybe I bit my tongue.

Ginny approaches me cautiously, rubbing her head against my legs. Stunned and bewildered, I peer up at Zuriel, wiping the crust from my eyes.

I'm safe.

I stare up at him for what seems like hours, my mind drifting in and out of a fugue. Raveling and unraveling, trying to make sense of things that don't make any sense. Sleepily, my gaze trails after Ginny.

When she ducks out of sight, I straighten, jerking all over, and wrench my eyes closed.

Behind my eyelids, Adrial's monstrous form remains, leering at me. It's fading but not fast enough to keep my fear at bay. Try as I might, I can't force him out of my head. My brands throb, tired and spent, reminding me that I'm not alone.

Reaching out, I slide my hand over the hooked claws of Zuriel's large draconic feet and grip them. The stone is cold, and I lean forward, resting my brow on him, letting his coolness ease me. I stay there, just breathing.

I've nearly fallen asleep when the museum's phone rings.

Fuck. I forgot about Dad!

I jump up and answer on the second ring. "Dad, I'm sorry. I was about to call you!"

"Summer," he mumbles, annoyed. "You *promised*."

"I know, I know. The time got away from me. I'm fine though, everything is good. I even saw Carol this morning."

"The cat lady?"

"Yeah." Guilty, I peer at Ginny as she jumps onto the counter. "I, uh, picked up a cat for the museum."

There's a moment of silence that makes my throat tighten.

"Glad you have some company," he finally says. "Does Hopkins know?"

"Yes," I lie to him. I'm getting better at it—I hope. "Of course, he knows."

"I'm guessing you talked to him this morning then? Is he coming back soon?"

My eyes cut to the windows. "Yes," I lie again. "He was very apologetic…"

The birds haven't gone away, and their flock still minds the front door, creating all sorts of ruckus. They feast upon the last of the worms. Behind them, the streets are empty and Adrial is gone. Pulling the landline's cord with me, I close the storefront's curtains, sending dust plumes throughout the room. The drapes haven't been disturbed since spring, and I hold back a cough as I cover my eyes and return to the counter, switching on a small desk lamp.

"When is he getting back? I want to speak with him."

"Soon—and don't you dare. I'm an adult. That's embarrassing."

"He shouldn't have left you alone for so long without a good way to contact him."

"Dad," I warn. "I can use this as a reason for a raise."

He hesitates and finally grumbles, "Do you really want *this* job? Hopkins has a reputation for being a weirdo."

"He's not weird, just eccentric. Making more money here isn't going to hurt me leaving one day," I argue. "Everything is fine." Even when we're disagreeing, speaking to him lightens my mood. He's my rock—he's normalcy. He reminds me not everything has gone to hell and that some things stay the same. "I need to get back to work."

"Call me again in a couple of hours. Don't forget."

"I won't."

Hanging up, I look around. Peering at my hands once more, I confirm they've returned to normal. Tugging up my shirt, my brands appear like they had this morning. They're cool to the touch, and the throbbing has dulled.

I pivot to Zuriel and curl my toes, scanning him from horn to claw.

"Well," I tell him. "I'm here now. With you. Only it'll be hours until you rise and I need something to do." I take in his body, his features. I reach out to touch him but yank my hand back at the last second.

It's different now, touching him, knowing he can feel it.

With a final shudder, I turn to face the museum and start my work by caring for Ginny, setting up her new litter box in the storage closet with a cat door already built into it. I station her new bed next to the front desk.

I clean up the dust in the front room, sweeping, swiping, and vacuuming until the space gleams. The mundane tasks soothe my mind, still reeling at the predicament I'm in. The light that erupted from me doesn't return, which is a relief. If it was a one-time thing, I'm okay with that.

Glancing at Zuriel, my face flushes. My gaze flicks around the museum. Nothing about my life is simple right now.

I complete the rest of the housekeeping chores, focusing heavily on the chants and holy water because I can no longer tell what's pretend and what's necessary, only that some of the tasks warm my brands. Out of perverse hope, I sprinkle some of the holy water over my head and place an antique cross on the front counter.

I'm not superstitious.

I still slip a small vial of holy water into my pocket. Just in case.

I call Hopkins, and as expected it goes straight to voicemail. Annoyed, I leave a message. "I've had to make some decisions while you've been out, and I got us a cat. Her name is Ginny—well, Genevive—and she's great." I pause. "Something, uh, strange has been happening here, and I would appreciate it if you could call me back as soon as you can."

I hang up.

My eyes immediately fall on Zuriel.

Even now, Adrial's demonic form lingers, nagging at the periphery of my every thought. I may never sleep soundly again.

"Thanks for the brands, by the way. They may have saved my life."

I stare at Zuriel, soaking him in. My gaze drops to his smooth groin, wondering where his cock vanished. It was big, that much I remember.

Big. I mouth the word, nostrils flaring as the world turns fuzzy. My body clenches like it's been doing for days now.

There's been no time to cope with what happened last night. We kissed. Zuriel and I almost had sex. I begged him for it.

That's not me. I'm not a sexual person. I've tested the waters and came away underwhelmed. *Books are better than boys.* I have a shirt that says something to that effect in my closet. Sure, on those nights I struggle to fall asleep, I'll whip out my vibrator and reach a quick orgasm. I figured I'd end up with an intellectual, someone with shared interests. I never expected *desire* to become part of the equation.

The world has made me jaded. Men haven't helped. Accidentally clicking on an incel article online has made me even warier of the opposite sex.

On the rare occasion I've had a boyfriend, we never lasted long, deciding we were better off as friends. I never became too attached or said *I love you*, and the breakups were hardly heartbreaking. Once my curiosity was disappointedly satisfied, sex became a relationship responsibility. Part of getting older, I thought.

I'd become fine with it.

Yet last night, I begged for sex from a creature I didn't believe existed until recently.

This desire is going to get me killed. I clear off my glasses again and turn away from Zuriel, wishing I could wipe my thoughts clean as well.

I walk deeper into the museum, down into the basement, stopping at the back corner room with a door that reads *Manuscripts and Old Texts*.

It's one of the few rooms that stays locked—only visitors cleared by Hopkins are allowed to enter. Opening the door, a familiar dusty smell fills my nostrils. More scrolls than books line the expansive shelves. There is a higher shelf that he has explicitly warned me from touching, and I give it a wide berth.

I take a few minutes to review the collection and then gather the books and scrolls that appear most promising, those with titles ranging from *Themistocles' Theories on the Darker Divinities* to *The Modern Take on Ancient Demons*.

I backtrack to the base of the stairs where a cement-floored room opens to several doorways that lead guests through the basement. The green walls are lined with art, while fatigued armchairs and antique tables clutter the edges. What matters is that the lighting is good, and I'll have space to spread out. Settling on the floor, I drop the texts next to me, not knowing where to begin.

I pick up the closest one and flip to the first page.

Chapter Sixteen
OMISSIONS

Zuriel

My limbs loosen, letting me fall from my stiff pose. Waiting until my eyes adjust and moisten, I crack my neck and flex my hands, releasing a growl.

My bond with Summer has strengthened.

Scanning the museum's front room, my nostrils flare, taking in a myriad of scents, including burnt skin and bird droppings, traces of rot, and Summer's lingering fear. None of these resemble blood despite the destruction of Adrial's human form.

She came away unharmed.

She will be spent... My power is not meant for humans. I may have saved her life, though she may be broken in other ways.

Where is she? I take in the drawn curtains. There's a whisper of wings on the other side.

I step out from behind the counter and look down at my feet. A scraggly long-haired cat peers up at me, her bright green eyes piercing. Her tail flicks, once, twice, and after making up her mind, she trots up to stand beside me. When she nuzzles my leg, I reach down and streak my claws behind her ears. Summer's smell is all over her.

I caress my hand down the feline's back. "Good cat. Where is your mistress hiding?"

She runs across my leg once more before darting off into the museum. Some of the lights are on, casting soft gold shadows, giving the space an even older, mustier appearance than usual. Floorboards creak under my foot as I wander from one exhibit to the next. The cat leads me even deeper, where the dangers become real.

I pause at a glass case containing a talon, the claw wrapped in a single translucent hair. It's from an angel of the hierarchy's lowest ring, although the angel's name eludes me. More than glass, it is protected by fresh holy water and enchantments.

The cat mews from the top of the staircase. She looks pointedly down and then scurries away. I head her way.

At the base of the stairs, Summer huddles on the bottom step, facing the antechamber. Stacks of books and unfurled scrolls are sprawled around her.

She's speaking to someone on a phone. Her fingers tap a parchment in her lap, annoyance in their rhythm, too entranced to notice my approach.

"Yes, Dad, I'm still here. Uh, John Beck stopped by earlier and invited me to join him at the Watering Hole, so I'll be out late tonight."

John?

There was no one else here today. I would have sensed them.

Who is John Beck? My jaw ticks.

A wave of infuriating emotions hits me. Alarmed, I'm unsure whether to seek out this John and destroy him or stay by Summer's side. Digging my claws into my palms, I swallow my anger.

Summer is mine!

Not Adrial's, not this John's. It's my handprints on her body.

"Yes, he'll pick me up and we'll walk there together. He's more spooked than I am... Yes, I have a guy scheduled to come in and check the leak."

She sighs, half-responding to her dad, focusing on the text on her lap.

"I'll message you." She hangs up the phone and groans.

"Who is John?" I growl.

She jumps, twisting around as I stride down the steps, my claws clicking on their surface. Her eyes are wide, lips parted. She gasps, her hand thudding against her chest.

"You startled me."

"Who is John?"

She shakes her head, blinking several times as I capture her chin. "He's... It was a lie. I had to tell my dad something so he'd leave me alone for a while longer."

I search her face. "So there is no John?"

She swats my hand off her chin, standing up to peer at me uneasily. "There is a John, but I'm not meeting him. He's just a friend of the family, and his dad's in the hospital from the fire a few days ago." Her lips purse. "Is it night already?"

Unclenching my jaw, I glower over the parchment that has captivated her attention. "The sun set five minutes ago."

"Oh. I lost track of time."

"How?"

The scroll on the floor discusses the nature of demons, archaic in its impression.

She points to a pictograph in the text, illustrating the tail and horns humans identify with demons. Her gaze flicks from the glyph to me. "I was reviewing the library to see what I could find on demons and gargoyles, or something that could help me—us."

Us. I hold her gaze as she crosses her arms. She looks away first, waving her hand over the rest of the texts, disgruntled.

"But there's so much, and most of it hasn't been useful. Only when I read all of this..." She trails off, shaking her head.

"What?"

"If half of what I've read is even partially true, the world is a scarier place than I thought."

She appears so small, her gaze wandering across the countless texts, her demeanor at once stiff with tension and lax with uncertainty.

"I don't want to die," she whispers. "The demon... He's in my head. I-I need him out. What if... what if he gets inside of me, the rest of me? He'll take your name."

She believes me.

Any anger I had at this John slips away, and I crouch at her side, ensconcing her with my wings. "I will never let that happen. He is gone for now. Let the memories fade."

"I'm alone during the day. How can I stay safe when you're not around? When you're far away? I can't always rely on you. I created light with my hands—it came out of my chest. I'm empty and cold when earlier I was feverish and frightened. Now... now I'm just frightened," she trails off and begins to shake. "I had a dream about you earlier—and not a nice one. I was stuck in the darkness for hundreds of years. After a time, I found you, but we never spoke, never interacted."

Her trembling worries me, and I need to know more without alarming her. "It sounds like you were within my mind."

"Your mind?"

"When I am not awake my mind often turns to a dreamlike state. An empty place with infrequent interruption. I am sorry you had to experience that."

Her face falls. "That's awful. It was endless, felt like an eternity."

"It is not so bad after a while. I have also learned to adjust, establishing a home within me, one that reminds me of a place I once knew."

"The castle?" she asks.

I nod, realizing how close we came to one another. I had sensed her, a vague awareness I dismissed as a dream.

She shifts closer. "Will I always dream of this, and you?"

"I do not know. If so, I will seek you out. At the very least, I can provide the comfort of my company."

She nods.

"When you brought forth my light, how did it feel?" I ask carefully, changing the subject.

She hesitates, peering at my wings surrounding us. "At first the brands grew hot like they were burning me from the inside. I saw the glow of—" her eyes streak over the cracks across my chest "—it was the same glow that shines from you. Then I lost control... I said something, though it didn't sound like me, and I aimed that light at Adrial."

"And afterward?"

"He left and... My mind seemed to stop working, my thoughts were fried. It was overwhelming, and I remember crying. I wanted to forget everything, praying my thoughts would remain sluggish so I couldn't remember..." She shivers. "The sluggishness didn't last. Not for long. I crawled to your side. I think it helped, being next to you. And after a while, everything returned to normal, like I was coming down from a really bad panic attack."

I close my eyes. "I haven't broken you then."

"Broken me?"

"You were in danger. I felt it. Tried as I might, I could not run to your aid. And I tried." I growl, straining my wings wide. "However I could drive my strength into you using the brands, and so I did. It was the only thing I could think of."

"I felt you inside me." She clutches her chest again. "I've felt you inside me ever since you placed your hands on me."

"I will always be inside you now."

She meets my eyes. "I couldn't find anything about a bond like ours in these texts. There were rituals for power, for channeling that power, and even capturing otherworldly creatures, making them subservient. I've been reading about blood practices, incantations, sacrifices, knowing I bled on your wing the night before this all began... I've been wondering... Did I start this?"

Her expression is thoughtful, but her uncertainty is evident. Even without her emotions blending into mine, I can tell she needs reassurance.

What kind of reassurance, I don't know.

I stare down at the pages on the floor. "You did not start this, and I am sorry to have suggested it before. I tested you, needing to know you were not a demon's trick, and now I repent for that.

"Before you, there is only one I have been close to. A monk. He died long ago, in a monastery, far from this time and place. He was a good man, taking me in when my punishment first began. Back then, I avoided complete submission to stone, preferring to become a creature of the night, and dared to give him my name. In exchange, he shaped me, sharing wisdom. The angels may have made me, but he was the closest I had to a father.

"By night, I protected him until he died, murdered by Adrial. In his self-sacrifice, he never invoked me or shared my power. From him, I learned loyalty—and grief. His kind face was the last thing I saw before turning to stone and staying that way. His monastery fell soon afterward.

"Ever since, everyone else viewed me as nothing more than a statue, a piece of art, and the few who knew I was something more... they pursued my name relentlessly for greed and power to their detriment. Until you, all those who have bled on me would have immediately given my name to Adrial.

"Until you, Summer. You had no ill intent. At least none that I could discern. You may have seen me as a statue and nothing more, but I remember your presence beside mine for days on end. You came into my life and spoke to me, told me stories and jests, and laughed beside me as if I could laugh with you. None of my previous owners have treated me in such a way. You reawakened my mind, granting me something to look forward to. Affection. The days you were not beside me were—" I clear my throat "—frustrating."

"You heard everything?" she squeaks.

"Yes."

She buries her face into her hands. "God, that's so embarrassing."

"Embarrassing?"

"I told you things that weren't meant to be heard!"

I stroke her cheek with the back of my finger. "And I enjoyed every detail. Your words and company have been the greatest gifts. Gifts I did not deserve, ones I took selfishly."

She lifts her face. "Didn't deserve? What does that mean?"

I drop my hand. "I am being punished."

"Why?"

"I could not destroy my demon. I have one purpose—to keep Adrial in check—and having failed to destroy him, I became stone. I have been in this war with him for centuries, and while I have tried countless ways to end him, he is powerful and it eludes me. However, all is not lost. I became a statue, and through the sheer perseverance of my silent existence, I have limited him. For as long as I am here, anchoring him, he will never be entirely free to do as he pleases. We are connected, he and I."

"What do you mean?"

There is much she would not know. "First, know that demons are incorporeal and need *hosts*, a body with which to interact with the mundane world."

"What I saw..."

"You destroyed his host."

"Wait. So that man..." She blanches. "Was he human? Did I..."

"You cannot kill someone who is already dead," I whisper, though I worry my words offer little comfort. "A human soul cannot coexist with a demon for very long before being driven to insanity. He will claim another form, in time."

"Then he'll always be there?" Panic edges her voice. "Always chasing me, pursuing you?"

Holding her gaze, I nod.

"Why though?"

"All demons have *anchors*. When demons escape Hell, the angels, unable to visit Earth directly without creating an imbalance themselves, create another in their stead. The anchor balances the demon's menace, keeping the realm in line."

"So you were sent here to stop him."

"I was sent here to be his anchor, to limit him, as all true gargoyles are. If I manage to destroy him, then my greatest purpose is complete."

Summer's brow furrows. "I don't understand."

"There cannot be great evil or goodness in this earthly realm without something to balance it out. Destroying him would fulfill my reason for being here, but failing at that, it is simply enough that I exist. I limit his power through my existence, preventing him from wreaking mass havoc."

"Is that why he needs your name?"

"Yes, Summer, that's why he needs my name. If he can invoke me, I will become his servant, and he could use me to do his bidding, amplifying his power and chipping away at the balance. Long ago, he almost learned my name, forcing me into this solid form. It is a punishment as well as a... failsafe. One cannot make a stone talk. Only one with my name can stir me, and even then, merely at night. It is why you will never be safe." I sigh. "And why, as long as you live, I will never, ever let you go."

She eyes me through her dark-rimmed glasses, silent for a time. "Thank you for telling me this."

"You are a good person."

She releases a sad laugh. "It would probably make this all so much simpler if you just killed me now."

Cupping her cheeks, I coerce her gaze, dipping my chin when she lowers her eyes. "I would never do such a thing. I am culpable in this too. Yes, it takes blood to invoke me, except it is easy to combat. Before you, I have never wanted to be invoked," I tell her. "When your blood was absorbed by my stone, I offered you my name from the depths of my fugue, and soon my name reached you. You are entangled in this due to my selfishness. I have never wanted someone so much as you."

Her lips part.

I lean closer, leveling my face with hers. "That is the truth. You are in grave danger because of my decisions. And my demon knows that I willingly gave you my name after the countless tricks he has attempted to take it from me. He knows what you mean to me."

"What do I mean to you?"

"Can't you feel how much I want you?"

Her gaze streaks over my face, and she shudders, leaning into my hands, her eyes hooding. Her arousal returns, the sweet scent drifting to my nose, and I inhale it fervently, stealing whatever I can of hers.

"I want you, little human."

Shifting my hand, I lift her face and lick her cheek from chin to temple. Setting my mouth above her ear, I snag her hair in my teeth, sucking wisps of it into my mouth.

"I want you too. So, so badly." She grabs my wrists. "Please don't leave me."

Her pleading stirs an impulse to roar and preen, to clutch her close and pet her body into submission, to open her up and covet her in every way possible.

"I've been dreaming of you long before last night..." Her voice is lower than a whisper. "I want you so much it hurts. I can barely think of anything else. It makes me angry. It terrifies me. This longing... I could scream and thrash and cry. Do you feel it too?"

As her question lingers, she wiggles out of my hands, leaning back to meet my eyes.

"Yes," I rasp. "I feel everything like you."

"It's our bond, isn't it?" she asks. "Where do your wants end and mine begin?"

"I don't know."

Summer sits taller, shifting onto her knees. Her gaze sweeps over my face, and when she sighs, resistance leaves her.

She presses her lips to mine. "I don't know either."

Chapter Seventeen
The Taste of Desire

Summer

I brush my lips over his. I'm chilled, his mouth cold.

He clasps my face as I rub my mouth back and forth across his. He warms under my touch, teasing my lip with his teeth as I test the tip of his fangs with my tongue. Everything inside me dances and whirls.

I've never felt so alive. My life has never been more at risk.

Knowing he wants me as much as I want him, that our bond muddles my mind and he's offered me the truth of this predicament... I don't know whether I should be furious or relieved.

All I want is to kiss him and pretend that this thing between us is normal.

Clutching his wrists, my nails bite into hard flesh. "If we're going to die, I don't want any regrets."

He leans away. "You are not going to die."

"I will someday. All humans do."

His face wrenches as he climbs over me, constraining my back against the cement floor. "Do not speak of such things. Not when you are so, so ripe…" Like a veil, his hair falls to either side, imitating the spread of his wings. "Do not drive me crazy with more worry, my sweet Summer. There are always ways to continue living, and I am not above using the darkness to accomplish it. Despite my beginnings, darkness is part of me, and I'm nothing more than a monster to a human like you." He shows his sharp fangs, licking them with his meaty tongue as fiery light emblazons the cracks down his chest.

I eye his fangs with intrigue. "I won't bring it up again."

He gives an appeased growl, and his cock jolts from his groin, jutting into my stomach, making me twitch. It's heavy—*big*—resting like a heated plank down my middle. The golden light graces the mushroom tip pointed up at me. It illuminates the bulk of him, casting shadows upon his ridges. My fingers strain, recalling his cock's firmness.

"Stop trying to frighten me," I say. "It won't work."

I'd rather be *with* the monster looming over me than fighting him. The scarier he is, the fewer people will bother me. There's a deep comfort in having him by my side, a primitive comfort I can't deny. My hands clamp at my sides as he raises his hips and lifts his cock off of me.

I moan at its loss, wanting it inside me.

"Is that so?" he rasps deeply, eliciting a shiver through me. "Tell me what to do then, sweet girl."

My toes curl. "What do you want me to say?"

He cups my cheek, his clawed thumb penetrating the corner of my mouth. "Tell me to stop. Tell me this is too much for you."

"No."

"No?" His thumb pushes deeper, pressing my molars. His eyes never move from mine. "If you do not tell me to stop, I will demand more than stories and laughter. Your kisses will only be the beginning."

My heart thumps. Nervously, I slide my tongue over his thumb, flicking it against his claw. I invite the burning cold of his touch.

"Zuriel," I invoke his name, whispering so softly it's barely a breath. "I don't want you to stop."

His gaze brightens, then darkens, his hand gripping my cheek. His thumb drives deeper into my mouth.

I close my lips around it and suck.

His expression morphs, hungry and awed, as his body shudders, his cock tapping my belly. He sinks his thumb further until my lips are against his hand.

I hold his gaze, insisting without words this is exactly what I want, and scrape my teeth over his knuckle. His flesh heats, wet with saliva. Pinned under him, my hips writhe, shimmying my pelvis against his hard body.

It's only his thumb, though I will take what I can get.

Watching his face, I part my legs and tilt my hips. I suck and suck and suck, clutching his wrist to keep his hand in place. My clothes dampen where the head of his cock rests upon me, and I hear the claws of his wings score the floor on either side, bracing his body above mine.

Unable to deny this any longer, he grinds his cock into my abdomen, groaning deeply. His other hand twists into my hair as his brow drops to mine.

"Summer," he groans.

He pushes hard along my stomach.

I close my eyes and moan around him, my whole body clenching.

"Enough!" He yanks his hand out of my grasp, slamming his fist onto the floor, and takes my mouth. It happens so fast. His tongue fills me urgently, tasting everywhere, pushing mine around like a punishment. Like it's a battle. Like he can't help himself.

I shove my hips up, straining for contact. Gasping, I grab his horns.

Shoving me to the floor, trapping his cock between us, he kicks my knees further apart, positioning his body between them. Curling my legs around his waist, I fight him back. All the while, his tongue fucks my mouth.

Consume... He's consuming me.

He rears up, breaking free of my grasp, and staring down at me, he runs the back of his hand over his lips. I reach for him, desperate for his return, but he takes both of my wrists in one hand and pins them over my head.

My brands tingle. They need to be touched. I want him to touch me there.

"Please," I beg, arching my back. "My chest..."

"Summer," he huffs, eyeing me with a predatory expression. Suddenly, he lets go and climbs to his feet. "Wait here," he orders, scanning me, his jaw ticking, before storming up the stairs.

Sitting up, my gaze follows after, losing him as he darts down the upstairs hallway. I rub my balled hands into my eyes, displacing my foggy glasses.

I'm trembling. I'm wet.

He's gone, and the creeping cold returns.

When he returns, I shudder with relief. He's clutching worn blankets and sheets.

He spreads them out on the floor. With mute fascination, too stunned to do anything else, I watch as his glowing cock bobs up and down. The tip drips with precum, making me swallow, wondering what he tastes like.

Layer after layer, he makes a soft place for us, nicer than the cement floor. Finally, I find words. "Why are you doing this?"

I wanted him to take me on the grass in a graveyard, so the cement basement of Hopkins' Museum doesn't bother me at all. Especially since I feel safer here than anywhere else. Even my bedroom or a honeymoon suite strewn with rose petals.

His eyes sharpen on me. "I do not want your back to bruise."

I lick my lips nervously. "Good idea."

He spins, examining the cluttered room, and walks to a shelf. He retrieves a dusty candle, and with a spark from his lighted fingertip, he places the candle on one of the side tables. He turns off the overhead light, casting the room in a myriad of gold, orange, and amber shadows. Light rises only from his skin and that single candle.

"By candlelight, love erupts," he murmurs, approaching me. "I heard that somewhere."

There's no time to question his use of that word, *love*.

Because he's on me, pinning me to the ground as if he never left, his mouth braced against mine. He hauls me into his chest, and I wrap my arms around him.

Except he doesn't lay me on the blankets. His tail sweeps across one of the antique desks, clearing it, as he lowers me to sit at the edge.

"Z," I utter the start of his name. He looks at me, his hands clutching my thighs to spread them out. "Be gentle."

His nostrils flare and his wings ripple. He nods sharply and only slightly loosens his grip.

Then his head is between my legs, pressed against my pants. Clutching his horns, I shudder.

"You smell... I can smell you." He licks the seam of my jeans, abrading the intimate area with his teeth. "I have heard men go wild for such a delicacy, but I never... I never..." He licks and nips. "I need it. I never understood the need before."

I squirm as he soaks my jeans with his saliva, wetting my pussy further. "Oh, god."

Finally!

Chapter Eighteen
CLAIMING A GARGOYLE

Summer

His raspy chuckle fills my ears.

Licking me once more, he hooks his claws into the waistband of my jeans and tugs. When they don't give, I release his horns and unbuckle the clasp, helping him shimmy them down my legs. He yanks off my shoes, leaving me in white socks, my damp panties, and my sweater.

Shoving my knees back apart, he crouches between my legs and stares at my crux, inhaling, compelling me to swallow and curl my toes.

"Sweet, sweet Summer," he coos, leaning forward. "Take your shirt off for me."

Holding prone, afraid I'll shatter, I grip the edge of my sweater and lift it over my head, its soft strands tickling my stomach.

"Your bra," he demands, without looking away from between my spread legs.

He cups my knees as I lean forward and unhook my bra. The straps drop down my arms, and I toss it to the floor with the rest of my clothes. My breasts spill, heavy without support, his brands glinting in the candlelight. My nipples peek, except he doesn't notice, still staring between my legs.

I hold in my stomach, waiting for him to look up at me. I crave his praise. I need him to look at me like I'm the only woman in existence.

His gaze rises, meeting mine. "I've never wanted anything more." His eyes roam lustfully, coveting me. "I would worship your body."

He knows my thoughts?

Sliding his hands up my legs, I relax my toes.

"Do you see my erection?" he asks.

My eyes drop to where it juts from between his legs. "Y-yes."

"It only exists because of you."

He's said something like this before.

"And it wants to nudge between your spread legs, into your delicate human cunt. It craves to wield you until your sweet channel has no recourse but to accept it, *all* of it."

My lips part.

"I have barely come to terms with this, this ferocious desire gnawing inside my gut. This *need* that urges me to claim you from the inside out—to never let you go." His voice is hungry and edged with warning. "I am not a male of your world, Summer. I will not be like any male you know."

I nod.

"I am not human."

My gaze lingers on his horns, his wings. "I know."

He squeezes my thighs. "If I enter you, I will be inside you forever."

I lift a hand to my branded breast. "You're already there."

The corners of his lips lift. "I am."

Lifting a hand from my knee, he hooks a single claw into my panties and shifts them aside. Cool air brushes my sensitive skin.

Spreading my legs further, digging the sides of them into the desk, his smile drops and so do his eyes. Staring at my exposed pussy, he groans, nostrils flaring again. I wrap my hands around his horns and lean back, leveraging, resting my feet on the hard edges of his upper wings.

His breath hits me first, and then his rigid tongue thrusts out to taste me.

He doesn't lick me but jabs at my opening, thrusting directly inside of me. Tiny gasps tear from my throat as his tongue presses and prods, lodging deeper. Clamping around it, his mouth seals against my flesh, his face tight upon my sex. He sucks once and then stills.

To still my squirming, he grabs my butt, holding me firm while he does nothing else, his thick tongue tasting. Pinned upon it, I whimper and shake, trying to grind against him.

And then he jabs.

And jabs.

And jabs again.

I cry out, and his tail slips up my body, teasing my breasts as it approaches my mouth. He fills me there next, twisting his tail between my lips, plunging it in synchronicity with his tongue.

My body convulses. His tongue circles my inner walls, pushing against them. Screaming around his tail, I come hard, fighting my entrapment, kicking out, biting down on him. My hips sway side to side, trying to dislodge him.

When his tongue slips out of me, I sag, heaving, his tail sliding from me too. He wraps it loosely around my neck as he peers at me.

"Again," he demands.

I don't have time to react before his tongue rams back into me.

He keeps my orgasm continuous, his focus honed like he knows exactly what I need. He gives me a moment to rest, only for his tongue to continue fucking me once more. Each time, he stretches at my inner walls, spreading them gently.

At another time, I'm lying across another table, at another angle, but I don't remember when we changed positions.

I lose my panties but don't know when. I'm down to one sock, then they're gone completely.

Eventually, he releases me and stands overhead, his cock bobbing at eye level. He's licking and fondling my breasts, playing with them like he's just discovered them, fascinated by their softness. Languid with pleasure, my eyes hood and I let him do what he wants. Because everywhere he touches, penetrates, kisses, or licks, he leaves bliss in his wake.

His tongue tastes my inner ear, behind my knees, and at one point drifts over my clit, driving me once again to the brink. His fingers fill my mouth, his tail working my pussy as his hands palm my breasts, thumbs rubbing my nipples. He nips at my neck, caresses my brands, and brushes my hair with his claws.

I can feel how much he wants me without ever receiving what I really need.

He doesn't let me touch him back. He doesn't give me his cock.

He reduces me to a begging mess, quieting my objections with gentle, demanding kisses. Kisses that silence the world and make me forget everything—everything except him. When, for the third time, he quiets my pleas in this way, I push him away.

"No more," I beg, gasping. "No more."

Zuriel looks at me, wiping his hand across his mouth—like he does more and more often—smearing my essence across his cheek.

I totter from the desk, my knees giving out as I land on the floor with a sigh. His arms wrap around me, and I try shoving him away. They tighten around me, lifting me back up.

"You're ready," he hums, satisfied.

Ready?

"You act like you've done this before," I accuse as he carries me to the pile of blankets.

"I haven't. And until you, I never even imagined it."

"Then you're skilled for a male who's an amateur." I can't keep the frustration out of my voice, my core still constricting from one of the dozen orgasms.

Zuriel lowers me to the floor and crouches beside me, taking hold of my chin so I'm forced to face him.

"Since being invoked by you, I have had much time to think, to fantasize about what I can do to you. What I want to do to you."

My eyes narrow. "And yet you still don't fuck me."

"You weren't ready." Reaching down, he cups his massive cock and hefts it between us. "You asked me to be gentle."

I lick my lips. "I don't want gentleness anymore."

"Good."

He grabs me and spins me around until I'm on my hands and knees, facing away from him with his tip pressed against me. His fingers spread me open, and despite how I clench around the bulge of his head, he waits, delaying the push inside. His other arm wraps around me, holding my butt up, his legs against mine.

"Easy," he says.

I don't know if the words are for me or him.

Slowly he enters me, releasing his fingers to clutch my hip. With a steady, demanding push, he drives forward little by little, stretching me wide.

My fingers twist into the blankets, and my brow drops. My glasses slip off my glistening face, and I shove them away. I don't need to see, not when my body knows what to do.

Digging my feet against his legs, my whole body constricts around his cock as he stretches me to accommodate him. I fall onto my forearms, ass high in the air, and bunching my hands against my face, I try to relax.

He keeps filling me and filling me, and it's not stopping.

The tight, aching edge of pain never goes over the brink. His tongue and his tail drove me crazy, but his cock makes me submit.

Finally, he lodges as deeply as he can, and a deep, satisfied groan fills my ears. He goes completely still, and in the silence, I realize I'm gnawing on the bunched blanket, my limbs shaking and taut.

He unhooks his arm around me so both his hands can palm and massage my ass. "Are you okay?" he rasps.

"Yes," I whimper.

"You feel amazing, Summer."

My teeth dig into my lower lip. "Thank you."

For a while we stay like that, with me bent over, straining around his girth, adjusting to the edged ridges of his shaft. He continues to pet me, running his hands over my butt, up and down my spine, soothing me into a relaxed state. He tangles his fingers into my hair and kneads my neck, his claws tickling the backs of my arms.

I'm so full, and it takes time for my body to accommodate. Slowly, mercilessly, it does.

The tips of his claws rake my skin, whispering up and down my thighs, sending prickles across my skin. Inhaling, the tension in my limbs dissipates.

"Good girl."

Squeezing my eyes shut, his words embarrass and thrill me. I like his praise.

"Good boy," I murmur back in response, smiling into the cloth wrinkled in my fists.

Zuriel chuckles. His cock jerks, shifting inside me.

I gasp as one of his ridges rubs my inner spot. After the stretching discomfort, the rush of pleasure stuns me—I clutch at the blanket, feeling full. So damn delightfully full. His tail curls under my chest and flicks my nipples. With another shock of pleasure, my backside twitches upward, making his cock slide partially out. Ridge after ridge rubs my g-spot.

Zuriel's deep groan is all I can hear.

He clasps my hips, spreads me wide with his thumbs, and pushes back into me.

"Yes," we both say at once, his a groan and mine a blissful cry. His hands grip me harder, and at long last, he thrusts.

And I can take it. *I like it.*

In and out, his hips heave slowly at first, ensuring I can handle him. In and out, his ribbed erection stretches and works my pussy, one undulation at a time. When I lose him, a terrible emptiness consumes me, turning my whimpers sad, only for him to slide back inside me. Emptiness and fullness repeat until stars dot my vision.

Moving faster with each return, his tail twerks my nipples in unison.

"You feel so good," he growls, grunting with each quickening thrust, his gentleness diminishing.

I brace against him, my hands twisting the blankets beneath me.

"You feel so good!" he snarls again, his hips snapping at the next thrust.

The rush of him, entering me entirely with a single drive, urges me to clench around him. I cry out, orgasming again.

Caught by the frenzy, Zuriel bellows. Hauling me against him, he wraps his arms around me as I writhe, every fiber of my being igniting. Holding me tightly, he thrusts wildly, seating me on his engorged cock. My knees lift off the floor as he holds me upright and upon him. His tail wraps around me and twerks my clit—*fuck*.

He moves my body up and down, faster, harder, his arms encaging me. Gasping with his every frantic thrust, I orgasm again.

"So good, so good, so good," he chants, his voice deep and animalistic.

Reeling on the rhythm of his words, my mind fogs.

With a bellow, he jerks into me. Hard. My eyes snap open and I fall forward. Caught between him and the floor, his arms drop to either side of me as his hips still and his pelvis tightens. His cock tweaks inside me, jutting as he comes.

My spasms continue as his seed fills me up, spilling out, covering everything in slick and wet. With his cheek pressed to the side of my face, he goes quiet, his breaths quick and labored.

Lifting me, he drags his cock out as I whimper from the emptiness. He sets me on the blanket gently and rolls me over.

"Are you okay?" he asks after a time.

I nod.

My eyes open as I face him, his body straddling mine, his wings hooked behind him. He's blurry, and I reach for my glasses and put them on. His gaze searches mine before sweeping over my body, taking me in, narrowing on the crux of my closed legs, my thighs damp and glistening. He seems... *shocked*.

"What is it?" I ask.

"I did not think I would produce seed," he says, reaching down and spreading it over my stomach.

I rise onto my elbows, brow furrowing, still clenching dreamily. "Why not?"

He stares at where his cock lies. "Seed is for breeding. It is something my kind does not do."

It takes a moment for his words to register. My chest constricts as my eyes drop to where he's staring. "We're not... What? We're not going to have..." It didn't even occur to me. He's not even human!

He smiles. "Easy. I did not impregnate you, Summer. It's not possible. Beings between realms can't procreate."

Relieved, I drop back down with a flourish.

Chapter Nineteen
SWEET DELIGHT

Zuriel

My head reels and my thoughts scatter. I cannot look at Summer without wanting to be inside of her, rousing her body to mindlessly dance, her moans filling my ears. A goddess in the throes, there will never be another for me. She is the softness to my hard outlines, my sharp edges. She is a maiden to my monstrous baring. She is the sun whereas I am the moon. If I could, I would hollow her out and climb inside her and relish the embrace of her sweet heat forever.

So delicate, so submissive, she handled my ferocious appetite, a hunger that has mounted since the moment I first heard her laugh.

Standing outside the museum's bathroom, I hear running water on the other side. She wouldn't let me follow her into the small space, so I'm left waiting on the other side of a closed door.

Bracing my arms against the door frames, I rest my brow on the solid wood that's keeping us apart.

I want to see her.

I want to be inside her.

I don't want the night to come to an end.

Yet time passes by—it's well past midnight. We only have a few short hours left until sunrise.

I need her once more before my body submits to stone. I told her as much, and she still insisted on coming up here and cleaning herself. I offered to do it for her, licking her thighs, soothing her dewy folds until she was ready to take me again, but she pushed me away with an embarrassed laugh.

She deserves to be pampered and groomed because she did take me, *all* of me, so completely.

I'm convinced she was made for me. My cock was made for *her*. We fit.

My lips rise into a smile. My sweet Summer has unique needs, if my appendage formed specifically for her.

Our union has warranted my centuries of loneliness. Finally, there's someone who recognizes the isolation of my stony punishment, even sharing it with me through her dream. Someone who is still willing to share their warmth, joining their body with mine.

I am a monstrous creature, a mate no human should want. I am not handsome or soft—I'm hard and unyielding. I was not made for attraction, desire. I am supposed to be fearsome, avoided. My image is used to guard the sanctuaries of humankind, to frighten off the very demons that would corrupt their minds and devour their souls. A being like me was never meant to be invited inside. Never meant to be loved.

Nor was I meant to love in return, to feel any sort of emotion toward humans, toward anyone.

But because she allowed me to brand her, to bare her body and soul in such an intimate way, I needed to prove she would never regret being bound to something like me. I longed to prove my worthiness to her. Worshiping her with my obsession, admiring and petting her, all of it was as much for me as it was for her.

With her every orgasm, I understood her better. I learned her as she already knows me, having caressed my chest, and my wings a hundred times over. I now know how she tastes in every spot, how she reacts with every poke, probe, lick, and touch. My tongue flicks, sliding across my teeth, wishing to graze over her supple skin, to take her tit between them. If she would open the bathroom door, I would entrap it and take the other tit between my fingers, puckering them raw. If only so my tongue could soothe them afterward...

I don't know what I'll do if I lose her. If she breaks because of me or my demon.

My smile drops.

It's time. I must put an end to the demon and send him back to the lake of fire, the abyss beyond this world. It is a task I have failed at, and my ancient hopelessness threatens to overwhelm me—except now I've never been more motivated. I *will* find a way.

The door opens, revealing Summer standing on the other side, clutching a sheet around her frame. When she sees me looming over her, her eyes widen, and her throat bobs.

I cherish her reactions, finding them endearing. Although she should not be shy with me, she owns me.

My smile returns. "Hello."

She eyes me nervously. "I'm done."

"Let's go back down then. Genevive slumbers nearby, and we shouldn't wake her. It would be rude." Except I don't move from the doorframe.

Her head tilts. "How do you know her name?"

"She told me."

"You can speak to cats?"

"I can speak to most creatures, to an extent. Though I would prefer to only speak to you."

"Good to know..." She shifts, looking down and favoring a hip. "Can you move?"

Can I?

When I step away from the door, she scurries past me, darting through the museum and down the basement steps, reminding me of the previous night in the graveyard. Only this time, she's nervous and jumpy, rather than nervous and excited.

I want to taste her excitement again. Her arousal is already fading from my tongue. I stalk after her, debating whether to take her in my arms and recapture her mouth or spin her around, bend her over, and slide my tongue between her legs.

I stop on the last step as Summer scurries about the antechamber, stacking books and scrolls onto a table. Only when she starts to gather her clothes do I descend, catching her before she dons a single item.

I tug the sheet off her body and spin her to face me. "Not yet."

Her lips part, and as the sheet slips away, she hides her breasts and crux with her arms. "Zuriel?"

My cock engorges at the use of my name, so dangerous, leaving her lips.

"Invoke me, tell me to stop," I goad. "I'm not done with you."

Her lips flatten as she holds my gaze. Her cheeks flush prettily, stirring my tongue to strain against the roof of my mouth. I could stuff it into her mouth before she speaks.

"This is our first night together." I seize her arms and clutch her wrists between us, exposing her. "I want more of you before it ends."

"More?" she whispers. "You're not spent?"

"Spent? Is that possible?"

Her eyes widen, and then she smiles, releasing a nervous laugh. "So you're not tired? At all?"

"I never get tired."

"Human men—"

I drop her wrists, grab her thighs, and lift her upon me. "I'm not a human man."

She hitches, her legs spreading to straddle my hips. "No, you're not."

I cup her butt, positioning her back against the nearest wall, and prod my hard cock into her dewy entrance. I growl, driving deeper as she braces, squeaks then squirms, and finally sighs, her eyes hooding as my length buries within.

Tight and sweet, soft and slick, she's still primed from earlier. Her nails bite into my stiff shoulders, clutching as I position our hips, pursuing the angle where she sheaths me entirely.

She sighs again as I settle deep within her, her throat bobbing, swallowing, as she takes me in. When her gaze drifts down, narrowing on the point where we're joined, a wicked smile grows upon her lips. Lodged severely, I have stretched her. There's no room for anything except me. She watches me as I snag her hips and slowly move in and out, conquering her once more.

Her lips part prettily, making me jut. Slipping my tail over the back of her thigh, I prod at her backside.

She gasps, hips hitching as her lust returns voraciously, her emotions ramming into me as her back arches in shock, driving me deeper. I penetrate her with my tail, stuffing her completely as she trembles upon my cock.

Grunting, all other thoughts fade.

She cries out my name, bringing out the beast in me. I pull out and thrust, pinning her hips to the wall.

I fuck her hard, feeling her everywhere, against me, over me, on me. Her hair tangles, her glasses tilt, and her breasts bob. I don't take my eyes off of her even when hers close tight. Pulling out my tail, I wrap it around her waist, squeeze, and shove it back inside her ass.

She buckles and wails, her walls constricting me, deliciously strangling me, gripping and wet. She comes. For *me*.

Triumphant, I spread my wings wide, thrusting my hips upward.

She loses herself to bliss, and I lift her off the wall, wrapping her in my arms. She screams and writhes as I clutch her, thrusting wildly. Her pleasure bleeds into mine, and I come with her, refilling her with my seed, joining her ecstasy with a bellow.

Small thrusts bring us down, and I carry her to the tangled pile of blankets left on the floor. Settling her gently, I spread her legs open and examine where we are joined. She squirms, still sensitive under my inspection.

Her rosy pink opening is wet and warm, stretched tightly around my girth. It is an image I never expected to see, and knowing that I am not one of her kind and she lets me enter her anyway does something terrible to my thoughts. I never want this to end.

She will never be with another. She can never *be* with another. I swipe my tongue across my fangs, ready to fight any suitors who may approach.

I have two goals now. Make Summer mine in all ways, forever, and deal with Adrial, securing our future.

Panting, her breasts shake with the effort. Catching them, she rights her glasses, frowning. "Are you okay?"

"Yes." It comes out as a growl, raspy and possessive.

Her lips purse and I slowly pull out of her. Every time I do this, she moans sadly.

My chest tightens with pride. She likes me inside her.

Holding her legs open, I thrust into her one final time, a delicious goodbye as well as a promise that she has not had the last of me.

Finally, at long last, I shift away, appeased in the knowledge that our first night has been a triumph.

Summer reaches for the edge of the blanket to wipe herself. I knock her hand away and lower my face between her legs.

"You're not—"

Her shocked gasp sticks in her throat as I slide my tongue from her backside to her nub. She sinks into the floor as I lick her clean, soothing her hot flesh. Lapping up my spilled seed, I find it free of flavor, not of this realm. So I swallow her up, returning the taste of her arousal to my tongue. Back and forth, I slide over her, she quivers on my tongue and then softens.

When I'm done, I rise over her. She's breathless and relaxed within the blankets. Her eyes drift open to find mine. She yawns. "It's late. You might not get tired, but I do."

I bunch the blankets and sheets around her, positioning extra under her head to cushion her cheek. "Then it is time for you to rest."

She eyes me sweetly. "Will you do me a favor?"

"Anything," I vow.

"Will you bring me my phone?"

She had last checked the device before using the bathroom. Wondering what she might need it for, I fetch it and hand it over. She grumbles softly as its light floods her face. Tapping her fingers against it, she peers at me.

"Will you take it upstairs and press this button?" She indicates a curved arrow below a series of several sentences. "Service is glitching again. It won't send from down here... and I don't think I can walk right now."

Nodding, I take the phone from her.

"Thank you," she murmurs.

Heading upstairs, I try to read what she's written, but my understanding of modern English is still developing, and besides, I can't parse out her strange abbreviations or tiny pictographs. I press send, wait a moment, and then head back down to the basement.

In a couple of hours, the sun will rise. I'll be stone again soon, and she will leave my side.

My stomach churns at the thought.

She accepts the phone from my hand and sets it aside. "Just making sure my parents don't worry about me. I don't want my dad showing up here unannounced. I don't know how I would explain this." She buries her face into the blankets. "Thank you again... Tonight was... tonight was wonderful."

"You are lucky they care. And you're welcome."

"I am." She gives me a lazy smile. "Will you stay with me?"

"Always." Lowering to her side, I curl my arm under her and pull her against my side, pushing one of my wings beneath her, the other over her. "Sleep, Summer," I breathe, looking up at the cobwebbed ceiling. "I will not let anything happen to you."

My words fall on dormant ears. She's already gone.

Chapter Twenty
When Day Becomes Night

Summer

Sirens wake me, and my eyes drift open. Red and blue lights permeate the museum's curtains, flashing against the ceiling. Glowing like Christmas lights, they're reminiscent of my dreams.

My brow furrows, and I groan, rising on my elbow.

It's morning.

Zuriel's perched above me, solidified anew. I'm lying at his feet, wrapped in sheets with Ginny sleeping nearby. He must've carried me upstairs while I slept. Looking up at my gargoyle, my gaze fixates on his smooth groin, and a smile teases my lips.

Last night was... unsettling, wild, and *amazing*.

Stretching out my aches, I preen. I'm proud to have taken all of him. He worked me, prepared me to accept his burden—he pushed me up against the wall, pounding into me with his massive cock, and filled me with his tail.

I've never had sex like that. I never imagined it could be so wild, so primal. I've never done more than missionary, never realizing I wanted more. No one has ever gone down on me, worshiped me as he has. I felt his frenetic desire and heard his praise.

My cheeks heat, recalling the things he said. Delicious things. My chest tightens with embarrassment while my heart rate skyrockets.

He's more than I ever imagined, ever dreamed, treating me like I'm precious when I'm nobody, a failure. He knows me and still likes me, wants me. He's been listening, eager to know me even better. He's risked everything so we could be together, and despite my fears, I finally feel like there is someone in this world who understands me, body and mind. He saw me as I am, just another human being, and didn't shy away to search for a better one. He came closer.

So close.

I glide my hand under the blanket, testing my opening—I'm sore and swollen, but it's not as bad as I expected. I can accommodate him. When my finger grazes a sensitive spot, I squirm under the sheets. Gazing up at his long, stone tail, I rub my backside, aching there as well.

The distance between us, night and day, doesn't stop me from throwing off the sheets, baring my naked body, and streaking my fingers through my folds. When they're wet, I stand and smear my arousal across his snarling lips.

"Thank you," I whisper, pressing my naked body against him. He's cold as I slide my hands down his chest, over his groin, along his wings. "You can't stop me from touching you now." I laugh, emboldened though still nervous at this new side of my ego. "If you allow me, tonight I want to return the favor." Licking my lips, I lean back and search his fixed expression. "I hope you let me."

If his cock were out, I'd give him a taste of what I mean.

The siren stops wailing, but the flashing lights continue. They're not moving on.

Turning around, I locate my phone and confirm Dad was placated by my final text, at least until five minutes ago. There's a new message waiting. I quickly scan it, realizing what the lights outside mean.

Carol.

Sending a rushed reply, I search for my clothes, dress, and gather Ginny's things. She gives me a wary stare as she steps into the cat carrier—one that reads along the lines of *this better not be bullshit*. "I hope not," I reply.

Approaching Zuriel again, I place a hand in his and caress his cheek.

"I hate leaving you. I know it's dark and lonely in there. I'm sorry it's awful, and I promise to find you tonight. Too bad you're too heavy to carry." I chuckle—he said he likes my jokes—and then sigh sadly. "I guess I wanted to remind you that you're not alone anymore. Neither of us are. I'll find you this evening if you don't find me first. I'll stay safe and won't do anything stupid. I hope you like my gift." I eye the glossy slick across his lips.

Taking Ginny's carrier and the bat house with me, I open the front door.

The acrid stench of bird droppings assaults me as I brace for the sight that assails me next. Several police cars and two ambulances are parked nearby, clustered outside Carol's Cattitude. A news anchor from the local station is reporting across the street. Several groups of onlookers shuffle about with their shoulders hunched.

Menace. Chaos follows a demon's wake.

Stifling my panic, I lock the museum's doors and hurry down the block. When yellow tape cordons off the sidewalk, I take to the street. The pet shop's windows are broken, and two men are being loaded into the back of police cars.

I stop when I see Carol.

Paramedics carry her out of the shop on a stretcher. There's an oxygen mask pinned to her mouth. Her eyes are hooded as she takes deep, shuddering breaths.

I race toward them, sidestepping the taped barrier as useless words spew from my lips. "Is she okay?"

First Mr. Beck and now Carol. Last night, I could forget the cost of a demon visiting my town, but in the daylight... This shouldn't have happened. Carol is innocent.

Sniffling, I calm a little when she glances at me as she's loaded into the ambulance. A bruise forms on her neck. I lose sight of my friend when the ambulance doors shut.

A paramedic approaches me, pointing to the yellow tape. "Are you family?"

"N-no. I work nearby, but I visit Carol during lunch. I just saw her yesterday. Is she all right? Will she be all right?"

"Time will tell. Seems the attackers were more after the money in her register than anything else."

"I have her daughter's number. Do you need it?" I offer.

In a daze, I share Katie's information as they secure Carol in the ambulance. They're done, but I don't budge, can't budge.

By the time the ambulance is gone, I still haven't moved, and the remaining policeman approaches me. "Miss, are you going to be okay?" he asks, pressing a water bottle into my hand. "Drink some water."

"Where are they taking her?"

He eyes my cat carrier. "To the local hospital. Pets aren't allowed."

Then he's gone as well, leaving me with the other onlookers. My chest constricts, holding in the sudden urge to sob.

I'm tangled in this chaos, well over my head, but I have Zuriel. No one else has protection like me, and they're forced into this too. They're up against otherworldly powers without knowing it, with no one to protect them, no one to guard them.

Adrial might be gone for now, but he'll be back. Whether it's today, tomorrow, or next month, he'll be back.

My gaze wanders to the last of the wary onlookers. Some suspiciously glance back at me. Any one of them could be him. Taking a long swig from the water bottle, I walk to my car.

Mom and Dad are waiting for me when I get home.

Mom hugs me tight, as I shake in her arms. It's easy to blame the trembling on everything my parents know, hiding the role I've played. And when I tell Mom it'll be all right, I speak with a confidence I can't justify, reassuring her I spent the night at an old friend's house.

Knowing Adrial had been inside my parents' house on more than one occasion, I hold my mom tighter.

Dad frowns, eyeing the bat house. He doesn't object, hugging me instead, and I squeeze him back.

"Adrien's gone," I whisper to him.

He holds me at arm's length, appraising me. "Good riddance. Our town doesn't need his business, not if he is followed by criminal bullshit."

Swallowing, I nod several times, unbidden tears rising in the corner of my eyes, and I let them fall, unable to hide my relief that they're here and they're okay.

I shower and dress. I call Katie, letting her know I'm thinking of Carol. She was several years ahead of me in school and we're not really friends. There are no updates on Carol's condition, and my stomach twists, hearing her children in the background.

Settling on the couch, I watch Hallmark movies with Mom until the adrenaline wears off. Ginny and Oyster are standoffish with each other at first but reach a truce by midday. If Ginny sits in my lap *and* stays there, Oyster is pacified.

Every once in a while, we check the news. Besides the break-in at Carol's store, nothing else happens in the town. The police have confirmed the attack was by two of the escaped criminals, both of whom are now in their holding. It says that the owner was assaulted though nothing more.

Mom orders delivery pizza, and I try phoning Hopkins again. I have a missed call from Ella, and I text to say I'll call her back tomorrow.

Scritching Ginny's ears, I wonder what it would be like if Zuriel were here, watching shows with a cat in his lap. It would be nice to just be with him like he was my boyfriend, like he wasn't a massive gargoyle that would frighten everyone.

I wonder what it would be like sitting together, sharing time, going out on dates, and laughing over meals.

If he thinks my tasteless jokes are funny, what would he think of the rest of my life?

It would be nice to do simple little things together, but I don't think it's in the cards. Not for us.

My daydreams slip into real dreams as I fall asleep on the couch. Like before, I become a statue, vaguely aware that Zuriel is nearby. This time he reaches out, finding me, soothing me. We spend another eternity, trapped side by side.

When Dad comes home, he helps me install the bat house. He asks the occasional question, each of which I evade until we're finishing the work in contemplative silence.

Later that evening, I'm lazily watching Ginny from my bed. She's settled near the balcony window, her tail twitching as she stares at the birds on the railing. The clear, cold day becomes brilliant as the golden hour begins—sunset nears, and I'm still wearing my sweats.

I'm anxious and unsettled. I promised I would find him tonight—which means I have to go back into town. I think about what I smeared on his lips and groan.

If I don't go to him, he will come to me. I know he will.

And if we're discovered by my parents... I shake my head, horrified as the thought plays out in my mind.

Heart pounding, nerves brazen, I roll over and reach to the back of my nightstand drawer and retrieve my single set of lingerie. I bought it on a whim on an afternoon shopping trip with Ella, back when she first wanted to impress Rebecca. There was no one to wear it for, but it was so pretty I didn't want to leave without it. I've never owned something so naughty.

Ella convinced me it was a rite of passage—buying my first set of lingerie. After that, it didn't take much to persuade me to fork over the money.

I brush my hair out and, instead of tying it back, I let the blonde locks frame my face, tumbling over my shoulders. I squint, struggling to apply extra eyeshadow without my glasses, and debate if I should give contacts another try. Butterflies tickle my stomach.

It was easy to say sensual things to Zuriel this morning when he couldn't react. Now that he's due to wake and can respond, I'm nervous and excited again. Thinking about him helps take my mind off of this morning's events.

He's bigger than me, stronger than me, and knows more about this world's secrets than me.

I have no idea what I'm in for tonight. Putting on the lingerie, I'm relieved it fits me just as it did several years ago. Thank god. I'm desperate for Zuriel to deliver *everything* this is begging for. I want him to look at me like I'm the best in the world because someday, he might realize I'm not.

The lacy red bra is translucent, letting the glimmer of my brand shine through. As the air shift over my crux, the matching crotchless panties suddenly seem like too much, but before I can shy away, I pull my jeans over them. My sweater goes on just as fast.

The panties rub me strangely, making my throat constrict and my cheeks burn. I want to be with him. *Now.*

I want him to be crazy for me. I want to drive my monster mad.

I want to pretend everything will be okay.

Just for a little while longer.

Chapter Twenty-One
Blood Red Lace

Zuriel

The sinking sun releases me, and desperate, I lick my lips, satisfying the desire that has slowly been driving me mad. She tastes delicious.

When my eyes open, Summer is there, waiting for me, looking up, seated upon the counter. Peaches and the sweet scent of her arousal flood my next breath.

She's aroused. *Already.* The knowledge does terrible things to me. I can't believe she's here and she wants me.

Even after last night, she *still* wants me.

Her arousal is on my lips, ambrosia that has kept my thoughts heated and hungry all day long, connecting me to her when she dreamed.

I had made promises, setting intentions that we would... *talk,* figuring out these new feelings between us, but now as I cast my gaze upon her, I'm speechless, starving for another taste. My cock swells, springing from my body, ready for her to make good on her promises.

She smiles, and before she can shuffle away I close in on her, catching her up on the counter with my wings. Genevive slips under my webbing, but Summer cannot escape. Leaning down, I cup her face and lift it to mine.

I lick my teeth. "Summer."

It's all I can say, pushing between her legs, pressing my cock against her. With a single tear from my claw, I could have her bared to me.

"Good evening," she whispers, her voice breathy, her lips moist and pouted.

"You're not still sore?" I nip her lower lip—she gives a soft sigh.

"I was sore this morning, not anymore. I can't stop thinking about you."

"Good. I will make you sore tonight."

We stare at each other, and as time seems to still, I bask in the moment, marveling that she's here, that she's mine. That I am about to be inside her body all over again.

Sky blue, I decide. That's the shade of her eyes, blue like I imagine the sky on a sunny day. Blue as Summer should be, clear of clouds. I memorize the color, so even when I'm trapped in the darkness, I can summon the hue at will.

Summer... My delectable little human who has awakened me in more ways than one.

She looks different today. Her hair is down, and she wears more paint on her face. Breathing her in, her emotions tug at me, scattered. She's aroused in a way that makes her uncomfortable and apprehensive. There's a reason for it, one I can't quite detect.

It's not fear, like the evenings before. And when I inhale, nothing demonic comes to me. Her apprehension eludes me.

There will be no secrets between us.

"What is it?" I demand, searching her face. "What is distressing you?"

Her gaze darts away and she remains silent. I wait patiently.

"I... um... I'm wearing lingerie." She wiggles. I blink, not sure what this word means, and she gulps for air, looking away. "It was a stupid idea. I'm so uncomfortable."

I don't like seeing her so afflicted over something I do not know. "What is *lingerie*?"

Her eyes drift back to mine. Her cheeks turn red.

Is she ill? Sniffing her neck, I sense no sickness.

"Oh." Her mouth stops there, her pretty lips parted in surprise. "It's, umm... Oh, god, you're sniffing me. This is not a conversation I expected to have." She laughs nervously. "It may be easier if I show you."

"Show me?" I lean back and scan her clothes, seeing nothing unusual about them.

She slides her butt to the back of the counter. "You make me nervous when you look at me like that."

"I want to see this lingerie," I growl. "I want to know what it is."

She's even more apprehensive than before. I do not like it.

"Maybe we should talk first?"

I snarl the word "*No*" scanning her body again. Shapely and petite, there is nothing different about her.

"Okay." She huffs. "Stand back so I can undress."

My gaze narrows, but I do as she says, my wings still caging her.

Does this have something to do with her brands?

Did she... adorn them?

Slowly, she slides off the counter. Genevive scurries away, disappearing into the rooms beyond when Summer's feet hit the floor.

Hands shaking, she tugs on the hem of her blue sweater, and turning her face partially away, she lifts it over her head.

Her nerves fire like an electric shock, striking my system too.

My eyes drop to her breasts where an intricately patterned blood-red bra cups them, raising them and pressing them together. Almost spilling out, the edges of her pink nipples appear, my branded handprint rising above, plumped outward. She grabs the counter with both hands, leaning away from me.

My cock jerks, engorging as its light grows to illuminate her. My hands clench, wanting more than anything to cup her breasts and squeeze, to make them even plumper, to tug down the fabric covering her tits so my thumbs can stroke them, squeeze them.

My mouth waters with the urge to suckle her.

"Lingerie," I rasp, licking my lips.

"There's more."

My gaze descends to her stomach, landing on the crux of her thighs. "Show me."

She trembles, lifting her white-knuckled hands off the counter to unbuckle her pants. She slides them down her legs, pulling off her shoes and socks at the same time, giving me a glimpse of her butt. Clenching my hands at my sides, my claws bite into my palms.

When she straightens, her face is flushed, her arms flexed like she has to battle the instinct to cover her body.

"Don't," I plead. "Never cover your body when it is just us."

Her throat bobs as I stare at the tiny red triangle hiding her feminine sweetness. It matches the bra, with a golden ribbon pinning it to her hips. Her arousal thickens the air, barely contained by the delicate red fabric.

"I'll try." Her voice comes out like a squeak.

Dropping to my knees, my nostrils flare as I lean closer and sniff. Her scent makes me shudder.

"Z..." she squeaks again when my hands grip the counter on either side of her.

"I like this... lingerie."

"I'm glad."

"I have never been given a gift, and this—" I inhale her arousal "—can never be outdone."

She's silent for a moment as I nuzzle her panties with my nose, debating if I should use my tongue to shift them aside and explore what's underneath.

"I can outdo this," she whispers.

I chuckle. "I would like to see you try, my little human. I would like to see you try."

She jumps up, sitting on the counter, forcing me back, and as I look back up at her, she opens her thighs, bracing her feet against my wrists. I release the counter and drop my gaze.

She has outdone herself.

There's a slit down the center of the red lace, revealing her glistening sex.

My control snaps.

I grab her legs, forcing them far apart, and dive between her thighs. She cries out, grabbing my horns as I bury my face into her pussy, sliding my tongue inside her, tasting her everywhere. Her hips jerk, her cries shifting to moans as I move my tongue, rubbing it against the small wrinkles that make her dance, working my tongue against them.

Her moans morph back to cries as I slide my tail along the inside of her thigh and tweak her nub in sync with my swirling tongue.

She comes on my mouth, and I drink her down, her sex spilling against my face, wetting it everywhere. This is new—and I want more. Wiping my palm down my cheek, I lick it and my lips clean.

Delicious. Her taste undoes me.

I fall over her, consuming her lips with mine as I grip my cock, raising it to her warm, quivering opening. I thrust inside.

"No, wait!" She pushes at my chest. "Not yet!"

Halfway within her clenching, straining pussy, I freeze, brows furrowed in pain—in pleasure. "What's... wrong?"

She constricts, wiggles, and slides her butt against the desk as her clenching sheath jostles me to her surface. "I want to return the favor first—" She gasps, shoving harder against my chest, quivering in the aftershock of her orgasm.

Groaning in torment, I relinquish her, preferring to thrust wildly and show her who's in charge. "What favor?" I grimace, grabbing my throbbing cock.

Summer points at the wall. "I need you to sit there."

I frown. "Why?"

"You'll see. I can outdo that last gift as well."

Snarling, I do not believe she can.

Nevertheless, I do as she says. I am her servant, after all, her needy gargoyle. Retreating to the corner I pose before, I settle on the floor, leaning against the wall, watching her every move. Gripping my swollen cock with both hands, I squeeze it, *hard*. I want it inside her. It needs to be inside her.

She ties her hair back, eliciting another annoyed grunt from me. I'd fuck her hair too if I could. She stares down at me. I'm at her mercy. She could ask me for anything right now.

I would do anything and everything for her.

She takes her time approaching, working this fantastical *lingerie*—pressed breasts bouncing, lace framing her sex. Watching me watching her, a coy smile spreads upon her lips, and she settles between my knees, her small hands cupping them.

"Summer," I rasp. "Give me this gift soon, or I might…"

"Might what?"

"Might not be able to hold back any longer."

"You won't be able to resist. I promise." Her words come out as a whisper as she settles her hands over mine, tugging them off my throbbing erection. "I've dreamed of this."

A dream… it is one I cannot quite place.

She places my hands on my knees, meeting my eyes. Pinning me with them, she removes her glasses and places them aside. She blinks at me with bare blue eyes.

Leaning down, she takes hold of my erection with both hands and kisses the tip.

I go still, my wings bracing against the wall, arching with strain. Tension floods my limbs as she kisses my tip, again and again, caressing it with her soft lips. She kisses and kisses and kisses.

Almost, I turn back to stone, fearing that if I don't, this will end and she will lift her mouth away. Pleasure streaks down my cock, tightens my testicles, and twists my stomach. My lips part when her hands slide down my shaft, fingertips exploring my ridges as her palms stroke. I swallow, digging my clawed toes into the wood floor and scratching it.

She's touched me before, many times. I have felt her hands on my wings, my chest, and the hard lines of my face. Over the past year, she has even dusted me, ensuring every part of my large form was clean. I hated it, knowing I would never be able to do the same, all while I anticipated it, treasured it.

Now she worships me with her lips, her mouth.

And I want her to never stop.

When she drifts her lips up and down my length, planting tiny kisses throughout, I'm finally able to unlock my hands and spread my fingers through her hair. She peers up at me and our gazes lock—her jaw wide, holding me wickedly—I shudder. I feel it when she smiles, her tongue licking back and forth.

My cock *feels* her smile.

Leaning my head back, I groan, clutching her harder.

She has outdone herself. Again.

When her hands cup my testicles and her mouth swallows my head, when she presses down, swallowing me until my tip nudges the back of her throat, I lose it.

I growl, raising her off of me. There's a pop, the loss of suction. "If you do not stop…" I stare at her flushed face and her wet lips. She licks them.

"I know," she breathes.

My heart hammers. "You want me to come in your mouth?"

She gives me a shy nod, flicking her gaze down. "Maybe."

My head drops back, my horns thumping the wall. "Then make me come, sweet girl." Now it's me who can't look at her, suddenly eager for her to suck me dry. She will have to consume from me all night if she wants to drink it all.

Her lips return to my cock, sucking again. My wings ripple, and my chest tightens as her hands alternate between massaging my testicles and jerking my shaft. I'm big, too big for her mouth to take me completely, but how she tries and tries, driving me to the brink.

Hips twitching, hands fisting as she swirls her tongue, I streak my claws along her scalp, through her hair.

She suckles and sucks without pausing, massaging, kneading, and moaning. Her hands move faster. Gripping, tugging, squeezing, she works me harder, harder, *harder*.

"Zuriel," she whimpers against me, my name muffled, her mouth stuffed. "Come."

I do as she commands.

Constricting, I bellow and grasp her head. Seed pours into her mouth, and she gags around my head. "Summer!" Releasing everything down her throat, I thrust with each pulse. Her throat bobs as she laps me in.

Yes, there was a dream. I remember it now, the manner in which my name reached her, provoking the creation of my cock.

I yank her off me, pulling her face to mine, pressing a bruising kiss upon her lips. Her hands grip my shoulders as I shift her into my lap, thrusting my tongue inside her mouth. She whimpers, straddling me.

I grab her hips and thrust her upon my twitching length, entering her through the slit in the red lace. She pops off my mouth and leans on my bent legs, supporting herself as I work her hips, thumbing her nub. She cries out, increasing the pace until her knees knock the floor as I force her up and down my length. My tail assumes the stroking of her clit.

I tear away her lacy bra, liberating her breasts. I lick her branded nipple when she screams, straining around my erection.

She comes hard, but I do not let her cease when she comes back down, thrusting harder into her instead. With a single claw, I break her panties too, exposing her naked sex. My cock glows brighter and brighter, my seed quickening anew. When I pick her up without stopping, she squeals, frantic fingers retrieving her glasses as I rush her down to the basement. Now if my light bursts, it won't be seen from outside.

I barely make it to the last step before I release. My wings stretch wide as light explodes from me, illuminating the room in a flash—the strength of angels, a gargoyle's gift.

It is bliss, to be so alive, watching Summer's brands ignite their reply, brighter than before.

I hold her close, and she clutches me in return, shivering. We stay like that, pinned together until her legs slowly drop to the ground. I slip away, immediately missing her clutch, wishing we could stay tangled together forever.

Chapter Twenty-Two
No Way Forward

Zuriel

Settling our bodies upon the blankets, I wrap her in my arms and wings, pressing her against my chest as I bury my face in her hair, my cock twitching against her thigh. She must be kept warm, and I cover her naked body with a sheet.

I breathe her in. "You give my life purpose. A purpose beyond that ascribed to me—a reason that is all mine. You make me want to live, not only at night but all the time, as I once did. I want us to be together, always, to never say goodbye again."

Summer shifts in my embrace, looking up at me. "Earlier, I imagined what it would be like to be out in the world with you, like other couples, going out on dates, having you meet my parents and friends, making a life together. I liked it. I like... *you*."

I search her face, my throat tightening. "I do not think I can give you that, sweet one."

"I know and it doesn't matter. I like you more than this fantasy. As long as I have you at night, I'm happy."

My heart drops at her words, knowing her sacrifice. It is not an easy thing to forever wait for the night. "I wish to give you everything."

"And I wish I could save you from turning to stone. I wish I were more than just a young woman, one who can't even get a proper job and is stuck living with her parents…"

I lift her chin. "I don't have a home. Or a job. And while I might be timeless, do not wish away your youth."

Her stomach shakes, rumbling mine with her sweet laugh. "I suppose you're right."

"We will figure it out. For now, you should rest."

Ignoring me, she sits up, eyes brightening. "I've rested all day. That's what I'll do from now on, sleep during the day, dreaming with you, and at night I'll be with you. I need to be with you. More. Always, if I could. With Adrial out there, wanting me, I even thought about sleeping in the museum, but that might be more than my parents can handle, especially my dad." She breaks into another laugh, her gaze streaking across the antechamber. "I don't know how I'm going to explain any of this to Hopkins, if he ever does show up."

"I do not think Hopkins will return. Not until Adrial is dealt with."

She palms her face, rubbing her brow. "So you think he knows—"

I quickly correct myself. "I know little about him, only that he is unusual, for a human who understands my purpose. However, I am certain he prefers to be neutral and uninvolved. His wards and absence are evidence of that, along with the few, real, exhibits with additional barricades."

"The wards…" Her whole body tightens, fear tensing through her. "How long do we have until *he* finds a new host?"

"It may already be done."

She blanches, lifts, and looks at me.

"More likely, it'll take days or weeks. Perhaps longer. He must find someone to manipulate, and the amount of time he dedicates to this search will depend upon the shape of his next scheme. And in a small town like this? It might take him longer. I do not know the state of things."

She nibbles on her lip. "*When—*" she says the word cautiously, testing it out "—when he does return, what should I expect?"

"If he can, he will choose someone close to you, someone you trust. If that doesn't work, he will pick someone in power, who has money and resources he can tap into. Either way, he will approach you, advancing on you or your family or your friends. He'll do it during the day when I am stone."

"What about you?"

"He won't come for me, not until he has my name."

Her brow furrows. "How do we stop him?"

"Summer, I... I do not know. I had long given up hope of overcoming him. Though I vow this encounter will be different." I sit up, leaning forward, and she shifts back until she's straddling me, wrapping the sheet around her shoulders. "I never should have involved you in this. Never given you my name. Even if it was within a dream."

She squints, her hand shifting closer to her brands. "Don't say that. If you hadn't given me your name, we never would have met."

"I have been so lonely," I whisper, lowering my brow to meet hers. "It's a loneliness that may have swallowed me whole if you had not come along." I pause, recalling how dark my world had become before she entered it. "That does not mean it was right, bonding with you. You could not have understood the risk when I—"

"Stop talking like that." She grabs my hand and lifts it to her lips, pressing a tender kiss on my tough flesh. "You have a right to happiness too. Just because you're a gargoyle, an anchor, that doesn't mean you should have lost yourself to the darkness. And besides, things are different now. You won't face Adrial like before. I'm here too, beside you. Maybe... You could use me, our bond?"

I growl. "It is too dangerous. You are too precious to me. I do not want to hurt you, to break you."

"Break," she echoes the word. Nodding solemnly, glancing at the scrolls, her gaze flicks to the many doorways. "There has to be something here that can help us. I haven't even gone through half the texts. Maybe we just haven't found what we need." She looks back at me. "I'm not going to break. I'm part of this now, and unless we run—which I refuse to do—you'll need me to take down Adrial."

"I would prefer to find a solution that will not involve you. If I must..." I frown, hesitant to tell her.

"Must?"

"Now that I am awake, I can destroy myself, another failsafe."

Her eyes widen and her lips part. "You can't do that. Please, don't even consider it. I *will* break if you do."

"I would remove the brands before performing the deed, weakening our bond—losing me is a type of damage you can repair."

Scrambling off of me, she stands, clutching the sheet protectively over her brands. "No! Don't you dare. You will not destroy yourself."

"You must understand, this is part of my duty. When a gargoyle ends itself, the angels send a new anchor. One who has not been cursed with stone. One who will hold their name close."

Tears bud in her eyes. "That's fucked. Did the angels create you to die?"

I shrug. "They simply created a tool to anchor demons, and I am as I have been made. And now, I will do anything to keep you safe."

"Then I don't want to be safe!"

"Adrial will play the long game. It is better for him to exist, weakened by my existence, confident in the knowledge that his anchor has a newfound vulnerability. If you become too much of a nuisance, he'll kill you and encourage another to invoke me. I will not risk your life. As long as you are safe, I do not care about the rest."

Her eyes widen, her lips part, and her breaths shorten. We stare at each other, her eyes searching mine.

"Do you understand what I am saying, Summer?"

Her lips snap closed.

I lean into her, lowering my voice, inhaling her, everything about her—her trepidation, her indignation, her worry, her fear... her lust. It makes me quiver, everything about her makes me quiver.

"I love you."

Her face lowers, her gaze falling to my chest. I can hear her heart thumping wildly at my words.

"I've loved you ever since you started working in the shop, speaking with me, sharing your light, renewing my purpose. You've changed me, igniting my desire to see daylight again. And when I say I will do anything for you, I mean it."

"Anything?" she whispers, licking her lips, peering up at me again. Her eyes narrow, her lips flattening. Drawing back, my nostrils flare. Dropping the sheet from her shoulders, she angrily wipes the tears from her eyes.

I sense her intentions before she can speak them. "Summer," I warn. "Don't."

"Zuriel," she begins, her voice darkening. "You will not kill yourself. Not even for me."

The words blast through me, a command I can't refuse. It solidifies in my soul as easily as I ossify each morning. Naming me, her command seizes the power of my self-destruction, eradicating a gift from my creators. I growl as she lifts her chin.

Naked and unafraid, she's glorious. "We'll figure out another way," she insists, her voice hard.

Rising, I take a step toward her. She holds her ground with anger and determination etched across her features.

"This is not something you should command. Revoke it—"

"We'll find another way. If he's too powerful to destroy, we'll..." Her gaze flicks across the room. "We will trap him."

My eyes narrow. "He will kill the body he's within, flee, and find another. It is an endless cycle, one all demons are burdened with."

"Then we'll trap his soul."

"*Menace.* He has no soul."

"His menace then." She waves her hand dismissively, her mind made up, refusing to acknowledge my fury. "Hopkins has exhibits and wards throughout this place, keeping things in, keeping things out, keeping things safe, correct?"

Hands clenching, I slowly nod.

"Then we'll add Adrial to them. Make him an exhibit for the crowds to eternally gawk at. We'll make him a spectacle, something that will torment him until the end of time."

She brushes past me, picks up her sheet, and drapes it back over her shoulders. She strides to one of the back rooms. When she reaches the threshold, she looks over her shoulder at me. "Are you coming? We don't have much time."

Frustrated and proud, I stalk after her, her viciousness exciting me.

Chapter Twenty-Three
ELLA, CAROL, AND JOHN

Summer

Ella calls me as I drive back to the museum. Sunset is approaching, and I'm rested, ready for another evening. Several weeks have passed since we last spoke, nearly a month since I learned Zuriel's name and destroyed Adrial's form.

Guiltily, I let the phone ring, knowing I haven't been the most attentive friend. We've texted, but I've avoided speaking—I don't want to lie and I can't speak the truth.

I've told her I've been... *busy.* Guess that's true.

So far, the demon hasn't returned. I almost wish he would, as much as I'd like to imagine he's gone forever. There's a constant weight of waiting for something that hasn't manifested, of danger that remains just out of reach. It's impossible to be comfortable knowing he can show up at any moment, any day.

I'm paranoid, always checking over my shoulder, watching the shadows. Dad has helped me install a couple of bat houses, and they offer me some sense of security at home. Everywhere else, the red and gold autumn leaves cover the ground, startling me when they crunch under my feet. I take Ginny everywhere I can. So far, nothing has happened. The town has mostly returned to normal.

I'm the only one who still jumps when people call out to me.

Because despite Elmstitch settling back into a routine, it is far less normal than I realized. Things are residing here that are not human. I sense them through my brands, making it hard to tell if Adrial has returned.

Zuriel and I spend our nights isolated, filling our waking hours with research and preparations.

With each passing evening, sex has become a little more desperate. I'm pretty sure we've had sex in every room of the museum by now. And on most of the tables. We broke a cabinet—it was not my best moment—and before the sun rises each morning, we just sit there in silence, hoping the night wasn't our last.

During the day, I sleep haphazardly, drifting to the place where Zuriel and I are once again united, trapped in a rigid eternity. We've grown adept at finding each other in the dusky landscape, retreating to his castle with the swarms of bats.

I haven't told him I love him. Not yet. I think it's true, except the words catch in my throat. I've only ever confessed my love to my parents and my friends. And this affection I have for him goes deeper than all of that—if I were to lose him, I might fall to pieces. If I were to say how I feel out loud, it would only be worse.

Love is a word for beautiful spring days, and I don't know how to speak of it surrounded by this much darkness.

Zuriel tells me about the universe, of angels, and the realms. And yet, despite his knowledge, I'm teaching him about modern times, recent and current history. I take my laptop to work, and together we compile what we know. He's a quick learner. He's picking up common acronyms and even modern slang.

When he curses, it's cute. Hearing words like *shit* and *fuck* come out of a scary gargoyle with horns, wings, and a tail, just makes me laugh.

I need the laughter.

Zuriel was right. Hopkins hasn't returned. There was another exchange in voicemails—I told him I was keeping the museum closed, working nights. My paychecks are still direct deposited, and I even noticed a raise. I'm getting used to not having him around.

Some days I'm furious with him, sometimes I'm thankful—his absence has given me and Zuriel privacy. On my darker days, I'm dumbfounded, in disbelief that Hopkins thinks I can handle this because the museum has more mysteries and haunts than I imagined.

Zuriel has been battling Adrial his entire existence. In his darkest moods, he wants to take me far away from here, hide me. He needs my positivity the way I need his strength and protection. During these times, I have to reassure him we're safest right here, where we are. On our own turf. We have a plan—not a great one—but a plan nonetheless.

When Ella calls a second time, I pick up.

"Hey," I answer, scanning the buildings and the road ahead.

"Summer! Thank god you picked up. Elmstitch has been all over the news. You had a jailbreak a couple of weeks ago? Now all the criminals are caught? They were filming on Main Street. I saw your museum in the background! It freaked me out."

"Yeah, it's been an interesting couple of weeks. All of that is over, and things are fine now."

Fine. Right as rain.

Ella doesn't hide the concern in her voice. "No wonder you've been quiet. You okay? Is that why you've avoided calling?"

"I'm fine. And I didn't mean to... I've been distracted. I should've called you back. I'm sorry. I wanted to. There was never the right time for it."

"It's fine. I can imagine."

For a beat, we're silent, searching for words, and knowing she's listening on the other side, wanting the best for me, my heart swells with guilt. She's my best friend. We've been through a lot together. I owe her more than a half-assed apology. "Ella, there's a guy," I offer.

"A guy?" She takes the bait. "Tell me everything."

I give her a version of the truth, the closest one I can come up with. My parents already suspect that there's someone special in my life—Mom's hinted she wants to meet them. Thankfully, Dad hasn't pried. They know Hopkins hasn't returned and that I'm under a lot of pressure to complete a make-believe project that conveniently keeps me at the museum every night.

And it's more than that—their friend's health is declining. Mr. Beck's burns have become infected. Mom and Dad are spending more and more time at the hospital with him. I visit when I can, wishing I could confess, tell them everything.

They wouldn't believe me. It wouldn't make anything better.

John isn't taking it well. On top of his dad's decline, he's responsible for repairing the bakery. He needs the income to pay his father's medical bills.

Last night, when the police announced the last of the criminals were caught, we used the excuse to celebrate. Dad made a batch of his award-winning chili, and we delivered it to John. Sometimes it's the little things that help the most.

"He's amazing," I tell Ella. "He's sweet, thoughtful, and kind. Good-looking too, if you're wondering, but in a broody, stoic way."

"And the sex? You've had sex, right?"

"The sex... it's, uh..." Even in the car, I flush, recalling how last night we fucked in front of a mirror.

Ella squeals, understanding my silence completely.

"Don't tell anyone. I'm not ready. With everything happening right now, not even my parents know. A friend of theirs is in critical condition, and I don't want to add anything more to their lives right now."

"Okay, I won't." She pauses. "Sorry about your parents' friend. All things considered, I'm just glad you're all right. You need to stay safe, okay? I want you at my wedding."

I swallow, freezing up, unable to reply. I don't exactly feel *all right*. This ricochet between paranoia and lust is a rollercoaster. Adrial's true form still haunts me. How his host body morphed, eaten by worms. I can't shake the memory of his disgusting grin. My stomach roils with nausea, my vision blurring as my hands tighten on the wheel.

"I'll be fine. Anyhow, how are you?" I ask.

"Busy too, I suppose. So many decisions for the wedding. I want it to be perfect, you know? Oh, and I should send you an email with a few ideas for bridesmaid dresses. Can you tell me which you like? I'm thinking blue to match your eyes. Or maybe an emerald green."

"When are you dress shopping?"

"I was thinking of scheduling something for late next month. Although you don't need to be there, there's no pressure. The travel... I know you're worried about money. Just tell me your size, and I can order it for you."

"That sounds good. Send the email over, and I'll reply as soon as I can." I owe her. "In the meantime, keep me updated?" I park the car and tap my fingers on the steering wheel. A vacation does sound nice, and for a moment, I fantasize about traveling with Zuriel. "Don't worry about the money. I'll see what I can do. Sorry, again, that I've been quiet. I want to be there for you."

"Okay." I can practically hear her smiling on the other side. "I hope you can make it. And it's okay. Life happens, and with everything, I'm glad you and your parents are safe. I'd love to see you. Oh, your man is invited too, if you'd want to bring him along. I'd love to meet him."

"Umm..." *My gargoyle doesn't get out much.* "I'd love for him to meet you too..."

"Sounds good. Talk later? It's really good to hear your voice—just crazy seeing Elmstitch on the news."

I chuckle. "Crazy, yeah."

"Take care of yourself."

"I'll try."

"If you need me, I'll be there in a heartbeat."

"Thanks," I say, not sure how to add, *stay the hell away from here.* "Talk to you soon."

As I unload Ginny, another car pulls up, parking nearby, a pink one I recognize all too well. Katie's at the wheel, Carol's daughter. The passenger door opens, and I spy her mom.

I stiffen. "Carol!"

Rushing to her, I help her rise from the car. She's slow, deliberate in her actions, her motions certain and steady. The bruising on her arms is mostly gone, though there's a scar on her cheek. I have to fight the urge to hug her—that's not something we do. "It's a relief to see you," I say instead.

Katie waves, retreating into the shop while Carol lingers with me. Her kooky clay and cat scent, the sight of her dyed red hair, the pink of her sweater, every detail is more welcome than ever.

"I wanted to see the shop," she says, casting her gaze over the sunset-colored street. "Katie says she's been working hard."

Her shop, like the jewelry store, looks good as new. The windows were repaired weeks ago. Most of the street has reopened, the nightlife busier than usual, and at this hour, the Watering Hole is just starting to draw a crowd. Elmstitch is always lovely in the golden glow of the evening.

Except for Bread & Bean, the red brick facade is still ash-covered.

Hopkins' Museum is another holdout from the merriment. I haven't dared reopen the curtains, and it's not like I can manage the museum and be up all night. It's just easier this way, staying dark and sleeping during the day.

Zuriel's light, it's more than enough for me.

Though people all around town are starting to question... *Where is Hopkins?* I shake my head, tell them to give him a call and ask him themselves.

Carol notices Ginny in my cat carrier and coos at her. "And how is Miss Genevive?"

"She's doing great. Want to say hi?"

"I'd love to."

I open a compartment of her backpack carrier, and Ginny pokes her head out.

Carol scratches her readily. "Looks like she's doing wonderful under your care. I'm glad."

Ginny purrs. For a moment, the tension eases from my shoulders. The sunset, Carol's smile... Life is okay.

With a squeal of tires and the dying roar of a silenced motor, another car parks, drawing both of our attention. John Beck pops out of his old red Mustang—an heirloom he and his father fixed up together.

He looks at us, his expression blank.

"Hi, John," I call out, waving to him.

"You haven't heard the news, have you?" His face is ashen. "My dad is dead." He storms off.

I give Carol a long look, zip Ginny into her cat carrier, and chase after him.

Chapter Twenty-Four
Murderer

Summer

Guilt twists my stomach as I follow him. My parents haven't said anything, so it must have happened this afternoon.

I feel so useless.

John streaks away, his shoulders hunched, and my guilt compounds. I didn't want his dad to die. I never wanted anyone to get hurt.

It's not my fault. Adrial did this weeks ago, and the fire happened before I even knew he was a demon. I hate how I try to convince myself this isn't my fault.

It might have been an accident, but it was still me who bled on Zuriel. It was me who woke him, invoked him, luring Adrial here. Even if it was an accident—even if Zuriel allowed me his name—it still happened. Those events came to pass, and now John's dad is dead.

John and I played together as kids when our parents hosted dinner parties. He was always more interested in his Hot Wheels while I preferred my books, but without a sibling of my own, in a childlike way, I could pretend he was my brother. As we grew older, we drifted apart, and as teens, we had different friends. Since I returned home, we've become acquaintances, friendly, working in adjacent buildings, separated by our different interests.

Maybe he'll push me away, but at least I can offer my time, the chance to talk.

When he whips down the alley between the museum and the bakery, heading for the back door, he pulls up the hood to his coat. I tear after him before he nears the back of the building.

"John," I call after him. "Wait! Can we talk?"

He stops at the bakery's back door, and I jog, catching up to him.

It's cool here, surrounded by brick walls that block the last of the daylight. Rubbish from the bakery's ongoing repairs fills the alley with the lingering scent of ash. Worms wiggle free from the earth, climbing on the equipment. The shadows are dark, lengthening as the sun sets. I'm clammy—except for my brands. They're warming, growing hotter by the second. Ginny yowls, rioting in her carrier, driving shivers down my spine.

I freeze.

John faces me, and when he grins, I'm greeted by an expression that isn't his.

"Hello, Summer," Adrial groans. His voice even sounds like John, spoken with all the wrong intonations. "The bereaved are so easy to convince that the void will provide better comfort than grief. I just had to bide my time."

Heart racing, I take a step back.

Adrial tsks, and I halt.

I close my eyes and curse.

Adrial chuckles.

God, I'm so stupid.

When I face him again, he's studying me with John's brown eyes—maybe they're rimmed with yellow, maybe it's my imagination. The longer I stare, the hotter my brands burn. I take stock of where I am, what's nearby, and what time it is—Zuriel will soon rise.

Darkness is only minutes away.

The museum's backdoor is a few feet from me, on the opposite side of the alley. It's locked, chained, and closed. I would have to dig my keys out of my purse.

When I take another step back, Adrial launches forward.

Pain smacks across my cheek, and my glasses tumble from my face. The taste of iron floods my mouth as I hit the pavement, my glasses skittering out of reach.

"Now, now, Summer, there's no retreating into your damn wards."

Heart racing, I fan out my hands, searching desperately—

There's a crunch. The sound of broken glass.

"Oh, these? Is this what you were looking for?"

I think he bends down and picks up the broken frames. Without my lenses, he's just a dark blur. In the dusky light, there are only shadows and darker shadows. Shapes that scatter and morph, one shifting into another.

Ginny yowls, and eager to free her, I scramble for the carrier, crouching over it, my fingers spidering along its seams, feeling for the zippers, searching... *there*. Her fur brushes against my hands as she flees.

In her wake, it's quiet—except for the throbbing in my head. Blinking, I search for Adrial, except his dark form is gone.

My brands have cooled slightly.

"Summer? Are you okay? I sense Adrial."

Twisting at the voice, I hear the rush of wings as Zuriel's large form draws near. I sag, relieved. "I-I don't know. I think so, but I can't see. He broke my glasses."

He wraps me in his wings and growls. "I will find him, end him once and for all." He touches my cheek, caressing it with his finger. "He has hurt you."

When he grabs my arms and helps me to my feet, I wince. "Let's get inside the museum. He's near."

"First, invoke me. Help me fight him. Give me the strength of my name."

Invoke him? Wincing harder, my head spins, my brands warming. "Give me a moment." I clutch my forehead.

"Good girl. This will all be over soon."

Running a hand across my face, I check my smarting cheek, finding nothing broken. There's a little blood, but it's the piercing headache, intensifying with each second, that bothers me. Zuriel's hand tightens on my arm as I lean down, fumbling with the empty cat carrier, and picking it up. Hoping I'm mistaken, I brush my hands over my burning brands.

"Sweet Summer," he murmurs, continuing to caress me, his wings shrouding me. "Invoke me, command me to destroy him, and I will not be able to stop until the deed is done. This is how it should have been from the beginning. I have left that cretin alone for too long. I will not wait for him to hurt you again!"

I shake my head. "Not out here. We had a plan, remember?"

"Fuck the plan! Invoke me!"

I jerk, startled by his vehemence. When his shadow covers me, I lower my voice, "Please..."

You're scaring me.

Zuriel told me to never use his name. *Never.* Yes, I've said it, when we're surrounded by brick walls and wards. But out in the open, here? Where anyone could hear? It's too risky, too dangerous. It doesn't make sense.

He would never ask me to invoke him out in the open. Never.

Low electricity hums through me, my nerves firing as a hush of tension hangs between us, my palms glowing. They're burning, though weaker than before.

Squinting, my throat tightens as sweat beads down my brow. The light grows, distorting my surroundings, blinding me.

Zuriel squeezes my arm. "Summer. Put your hands down or you'll attract attention."

"Something's not right," I whisper, stalling.

The way he's pinching my arm. I know his touch and *this isn't it.*

Closing my eyes, and twisting my palms outward, I aim them at Zuriel.

His grip on me drops. He staggers back. "Bitch!"

"Adrial," I name him.

I'm shaking, terrified of what I'm attempting. I can't destroy him, not like this. The last time I was near Zuriel and able to look at him. I can't hold this for long. I need to get inside the museum.

I focus one hand on him as I drop the second into my purse, seeking my keys, relieved to find their textured edge. Testing each step, reaching my arm back, I climb the three steps to the backdoor entrance.

"Summer, don't! I am not your enemy!"

His voice sounds so much like Zuriel I hesitate.

It's a struggle to open the door, yanking the chains off and inserting the key. My vision darkens, tunneling around the edges, struggling to separate up from down. My head pounds wildly, sweat dripping from my pores.

"Why command me like this? With my own light? Invoke me!"

I prop the door open, swaying to keep my balance, trying not to faint. My hand falls as I stagger against the threshold.

Adrial rushes forward. "You're too weak, you fucking bitch."

He grabs my wrists, twisting them sharply. Burning flesh floods my nose as I cry out. He yanks me forward, and I fall into him, the heavy door slamming into us.

I'm screaming. The fire in my chest rises into my throat, demanding release. Screams become shrieks as light streams from my mouth, burning my lips and blasting out of me.

There's a crack, the smack of skull against concrete, and then silence.

Everything goes dark.

When I rouse, I'm lying in a warm pool of sticky blood, the reek of copper encroaching upon the sickening aroma of cooked skin. I wipe away the worms that have crawled onto me. My brands no longer burn. My throat on the other hand... The alleyway lights flicker on, the sky purplish.

Slowly sitting up, I find a smoldering form on the ground beside me. Something wiggles nearby—a worm, I think. Touching the mass, I jerk my fingers back. They come away sticky and warm.

John.

He's dead.

I killed him.

I rise to my knees. "Oh, no, no, no."

Memories flood me, scented with car oil and rubber, as I remember the boy who played with Hot Wheels, the man who was so proud of his Mustang. *I did this, I did this. I didn't mean to do this!*

My stomach churns, tangling with self-hatred. I shake uncontrollably.

Murderer.

I back away.

Murderer.

I killed him! He was innocent.

I'll never be able to forgive myself.

A voice crackles, offering a solemn reply. "Then don't try."

Jerking, I shift back to the mass, shocked. "John?"

My vision sharpens upon him.

He blinks with yellow eyes.

With a toothy grin, his mouth stretches open. He rises over me.

And swallows me whole.

Chapter Twenty-Five
His Name

Zuriel

Straining, my limbs rip from their shell. I storm from behind the counter and cast my gaze upon the quiet room. Summer isn't here.

She's nearby.

A meow screeches from outside the front door, and I hasten to it, unlocking and yanking it open, not caring who might see me. Genevive sprints past my legs, scurrying inside.

Trouble. Trouble. Trouble.

With hisses and yowls, her voice surges into me. Her coat raised, and the sour smell of demon rot wafts from her.

Leaning down to offer her my hand, comforting her with a pet, I ask, "Where's Summer?"

Alley. Alley. Demon. Alley.

"Stay here. It's safer," I order.

As I stride outside, several onlookers stare. I snarl at them, scaring them away as bats swarm around me, and advance down the closest alleyway between the museum and bakery.

The putrid rot of blood and death emanates from there. My heart twists. Rushing forward, I unfurl my wings, claws dragging against the walls. My sense of her is faint but not gone. She's wounded, weak.

Her huddled form is propped against the wall at the end of the alley. Beside her lies a charred mass with worms clustering over it, consuming it. Smoke trails from it, rising into the air. The walls are black with char, and drying blood pools around her. Rubbish from the bakery's repairs, heavy bricks, and a burnt oven is sprawled throughout, blocking the museum's back door. I crouch, pulling Summer into my arms.

"You are okay, little one. I am here now." I side-eye the worm-covered lump, unable to make out any features from the black and red mass. "You have destroyed him again."

I still sense Adrial, which means his menace is lingering.

Summer sags against me, moaning when I pick her up. Her blonde strands are dry and frizzy, crisped and dirty. Blood mars her cheek, her chin. Her clothes are burnt and singed. Her eyes are closed tightly, her glasses gone. They're broken, a few steps away.

"Please," she rasps. "I need..."

"What do you need? Tell me."

"Hospital. Hurt..."

Stiffening, I shake my head and peer over my shoulder where the streetlights brighten the road, the bats giving the illusion that it flickers. If I take her to the hospital, I will have to leave her side. I won't be welcome. If Adrial returns, I won't be able to help. She'll be vulnerable, possibly medicated.

"I will take you to the museum," I say.

Her eyes snap open. "No!"

I hesitate. "What's wrong?"

"Don't take me inside. I-I can't leave him." She whimpers, her gaze drawn to the worms. "This is my fault."

I frown. "It's not your fault."

She reeks of Adrial, his sour stench all over her, her presence weak. Calling upon the stillness I know so well, I do not tremble, refusing to show how deeply her condition worries me. Tenderly, I examine her injuries, and despite only finding countless scrapes and bruises, she's limp, unresponsive to my touch. Nothing is broken. This damage seems concentrated in her mind.

Pressing my hand to her temple, I call upon my light.

She sits up, jerking back. "Don't."

"I can help you heal, give you peace. Let me do this."

She shakes her head and rubs her brow, suddenly alert. "My brands... they're not right, and your light makes everything worse."

I lower my hand. Her words sting. "I never meant to hurt you."

"We need to talk. Reassure me everything will be all right."

"We will talk once I am certain you are recovered. You are weak, tormented. I will have your body comforted first."

"I'm fine," she snaps, her face hardening. She pats her chest and runs her hands down her body. "See?"

My brow furrows, flustered by her sudden shift. "You are not fine," I warn. "You are anything but fine. If we must talk before you'll allow me to heal you, we will. What happened?"

"He's returned. Adrial possessed John, and I... I killed him." There's a whimper in her voice, and she never meets my gaze, keeping it fixed on the charred remains. "I killed him because if I didn't, he was going to hurt me, us. I'm... I'm a murderer." She shudders.

Drawing her closer, I ignore the rotten scent still thick upon her as I hug her head against my chest, dampening her shaking. "You are not a murderer. Adrial is."

"I am! It was horrible. I never wanted anyone to get hurt, never wanted this to happen."

Petting her hair, her back, I would do anything to ease her sorrow. "He is gone now. You prevailed, and he will have learned this lesson. Adrial will not approach you so callously a third time, not after you've destroyed his form twice."

"That's not enough!" She rams her fists into my chest. "I've... I've killed two innocent people now. I can't kill another. Who will he take next? My parents?"

My heart sinks. I hate hearing such pain in her words.

"I don't want this bond anymore. I don't want any of this anymore! If he takes my parents..."

My arms tighten around her.

She continues, "I wish none of this had ever happened. How can I live with this? I'm a *murderer*. This has gone too far." She leans back, looking up at me with newfound horror. "You've made me a murderer!"

Stunned, my wings ripple.

She is right. If I had not been drawn to her, had resisted my desire to know her, she would be safe and the people of this town would still be alive, unburdened. If I wasn't so selfish, she never would have needed my power to defend herself.

What a fool I was, for seeking love.

"I hate you!" She lashes out. "I hate you! I hate you!"

Pain erupts at her words, but so do anger and conviction. Cupping her cheeks, I make her look at me. Fury clouds her features... yet there are no tears. "You *are not* a murderer. Adrial is. You defended yourself, and if you cannot accept that, if you must find a way to repent, then yes, you are right to blame me."

"You admit it then, you... *monster,*" she spits. "It's your fault. You are just as terrible as *he* is." Summer's eyes flare an icy blue, piercing with calm rage.

My hands clench. "I am nothing like that demon."

"You are." She clasps my hands, digging her nails into the backs of them. "You're worse—you're a failure. You claim to be created by angels, but there's nothing holy about you. Your uselessness makes you horrible."

I barely remember the angels who made me, so quickly was I cast into this world. Their commands were direct: destroy the demon. The first punishment is stone. The second means self-destruction. As an anchor, entombed in stillness, my success lay in my commitment to the darkness, my obedience to their commands. It used to be enough, the isolation and loneliness, all of it for the sake of this realm. I had resigned my mind to purgatory until she bled on me...

"Admit it," she presses. "Say your name and confess your sins! You're just another fucking monster in disguise!"

My lips twist, urged to speak whatever she needs. Whatever will help her recover from the pain I've forced upon her. Her happiness—is all I have ever wanted.

Summer is right, I am a monster.

And she is wrong. I did not fail, not quite. I have not done as the angels charged me, destroying their escaped demon, and they have cursed me with their failsafe of solidification in return. Despite these failings, my solidarity has had its success—Adrial has remained weakened under my watch.

Her lips twist. "Confess, invoke your name. Confess to me, who you say you love."

"I have failed you, Summer, done wrong to the one I love beyond all others, and I wish to have loved you from a distance, never waking, never giving you my name. But this, this confession you ask of me? Claiming my worthlessness?" Hardening, I straighten. "It is not true."

"Coward!" She scrambles to her feet, disgust wrenching her features as she points to the bloody mass and neighboring worms. "If you loved me, you would claim this death and take this burden from me! I am not the murderer, you are!"

Her eyes flash yellow.

I go still, stopping the horror from showing.

Pressing a palm to my chest, I realize why our bond is no more than a whisper... *Adrial has possessed her.* Except not all hope is lost. There *is* a whisper, a weak thread. A part of her remains, still guarding my name. How he must be torturing her within her own mind, coercing my name from her weakening spirit.

She's fighting, not entirely lost.

Summer launches at me, her fists railing my chest. "It is the least you could do! I never wanted any of this! Who would want a disgusting creature like you? One who manipulates my thoughts and emotions, tricking me into thinking you are something you're not. I do not want to be bonded to the likes of you—I never wanted that. I was supposed to leave this shitty town and do so much more with my life!"

I grab her wrists and tug her off of me. "Stop."

Her lips purse as she spits in my face. Releasing one of her wrists, I wipe her saliva off as her railing continues. "You deserve that and more, beast."

I face her again. "Will you forgive me if I confess?"

She stills, her head cocking, her eyes slitting. "Yes." She yanks her wrist, trying to slip my grip.

I hold firm.

She stiffens further as I cup her cheek and lean down to her ear. I brush my lips against it, tasting Adrial. "I confess, I am a monster. I am everything you accuse me of."

Summer leans against me. "If you truly mean it, you'll say your name. How else am I able to believe you?" Her fingers thread through my hair as she shoves her breasts into my chest. Shimmying against me, her taut nipples stab me. "Say it," she moans.

"The name is—" My lips caress her ear. "Adrial."

Chapter Twenty-Six
Hard Truths

Zuriel

Adrial pushes off me, launching back. My clutch holds, forcing his body—Summer's body—to mine, pinning his arms against my chest. Struggling, he kicks and punches. When that doesn't work, he draws the shadows closer, trying to free himself.

"Get your hands off of me!" he cries out with Summer's voice.

Hearing her, I hesitate. It's not her though. It's Adrial trapped in my embrace.

I wrench his wrists behind his back, holding both in one hand. Picking him up, I haul him tighter against me.

He squirms, wiggling Summer's body, searching for leverage, and I'm forced to grapple him so hard I risk bruising her.

"It's okay," I coo, needing the real Summer, the one I know is inside, to be reassured. "This will all be over soon."

"Yes," Adrial taunts. "It will."

My face hardens. He wouldn't dare kill her—at least not quickly—not when he's so close to what he wants. He'll use her body as long as he is able, torturing my name from her mind, assured I won't kill her either.

He shrieks, twisting against the band of my arm. "Put me down! It's me! Please! You're hurting me! It's Summer!"

I retreat toward the museum, requiring the wards to weaken him, the preparations for his containment. Maybe then I can reach Summer and help her somehow. Adrial stops fighting, stilling as his begging doesn't affect me.

When I walk out into the street, I hear the shouts of pedestrians. Ignoring them, I stride to the museum. I've only been awake for minutes, but minutes are an eternity for Summer to be subjected to Adrial's torment. I don't have much time. Every second, our bond weakens, and at any moment, she could break, granting him my name and making me Adrial's submissive servant until the end of time.

He tears into me anew as I reach the door, writhing as I shove it open. Genevive hisses, running deeper into the shop as I throw Adrial inside. He smacks against the floor as I lock the door, throwing a nearby bookcase in front of it. For what is about to occur, no one should enter. Neither of us will leave.

Pivoting, I face the demon. Adrial is back on his feet with real tears coursing down his face. "Why are you doing this? Why are you hurting me? I thought you loved me?" He wraps his arms around his middle and shakes, trying to appear small. "What did I ever do to you? It's me, Summer. Summer! I love you!"

"Cut the crap, you fuck." I hate hearing that word *love* from her mouth, spoken by him.

Summer hasn't confessed her love for me. Not yet. Still, I can sense it. Her adoration seeps into me, but there has been no time for romantic words, to speak of such things. Doing so would only make our futures harder if we could not be together. I understood her silence. It hadn't bothered me, except now, listening to him speaking as her, mocking her, I crave her declaration.

"I love you!" Adrial crones again.

Snarling, I charge him, ramming my shoulder into his stomach.

He topples to the floor, laughing hysterically, as I grapple him again. Turning him over, I bind his wrists in my hands.

"You won't hurt me." He chuckles as I twist him back into my arms. "Summer is still here. So fragile, this female of yours. Any pain you cause me, she feels." He continues to laugh. "We're one now, she and I. And I'll keep her, *own her*, in a way you never will! She will fester, trapped in darkness, convinced there is no end."

Snagging hair, I force his face up. "You will release her—"

He wiggles seductively and grins. "Or you'll what? Kill me?"

I cover his face with my hand, using my light to fry him.

He laughs louder, the sound echoing, as his menace pours from Summer's mouth, a sinister rush made of the void, throwing me back. I crash into the wall, still gripping hair. Adrial lands in a tangle on top of me, twisting over, ripping Summer's hair to straddle my hips.

The demon spills like smoke, spreading across the room. I curl my wings, shielding my face from breathing it in.

He sucks in a hissing breath, swigging the void down his throat. "You think it would be that easy? You've already lost. I'm stronger than you. I've always been stronger than you!" He writhes over my groin, running his hands down my chest. "If you're good, if you beg, I'll let you desecrate her one last time."

I grip his hips, stopping his incessant dry humping. Summer's body is heated, her nipples peaked, pressing against her tattered, burnt sweater. She's wet with arousal, and I grit my teeth as it floods my nose, provoking memories from our nights together. I shove Adrial away, hating that I'm stirred, except he clenches his thighs, tightening his hold on me.

"What? You don't want to have a last bit of fun? Don't want to feel her once more? It could be so... *delicious*. She wants you, your little Summer. She's begging for you to save her. She's so wet." Adrial grinds her sex into me hard. "Can't you feel it? She hasn't surrendered your name to me yet, but perhaps giving her your dick will do the deed. So, so wet, I can taste it in the air, drown in her desire." He flicks his tongue, snapping it in and out of his lips. "So delectable when forced."

Infuriated, I thrust Adrial down my legs. "You piece of demon shit."

"Shit?" He licks his lips. "I could make Summer shit if that is what you prefer."

Surging back on top of him, I wrap my hands around his neck. "Shut up."

He rolls his hips, ramming them into mine, grinning. "Make me. Please, oh, please, hurt me."

Blasting him with another wave of light, I prepare for his menace to resurface. At first, he eludes my power, but as I'm forced to endure his unrelenting laughter, my rage compounds, and I find the strength to strike again, stronger, more furious than before. Soon his darkness enshrouds me.

I clasp Summer's neck with both hands and squeeze. I force more of his menace from her throat, refusing to let it reenter.

Adrial coughs and gags, his laughter breaking. He writhes his hips as I choke him, throttling his airflow. Despite my efforts, the darkness recedes and is sucked back into his mouth. He contorts his lips into a sneer.

He throws me off him, but I catch and rebalance with my wings.

Bruises form along his neck as he wipes his mouth and rises.

Summer, forgive me.

We stare at each other. He sneers, yellow eyes flickering. He's not playing any longer.

"How much more damage do you think this body can take? You nearly crushed her trachea. She's almost—"

Pummeling forward, I thrust him back, knocking him into the bookshelf blocking the museum's entrance. He staggers, and I clasp his neck again, throwing him deeper into the museum, through the entryway wards and beyond trails of salt.

His body thuds as I chase after him.

Shrieking, he rips from my grasp, launching at me, his fingernails tearing at my eyes. He grips my head.

Suddenly falling, I'm forced from my body, my mind landing in the trenches of Adrial's menace.

The reek of sulfur and brimstone rushes through my nostrils as the shadows darken. My light barely penetrates the darkness, the demon consuming it faster than I can create it. I swipe my claws outward, but he's not there. Blinking, my eyes refuse to adjust.

The gloom expands, growing heavy, thick, more like a wet blanket than air.

In the distance, there's screaming, a chorus of wailing. I wince, brought to my knees. They're all the souls Adrial has devoured. My gums swell—my ears bleed. The shrieks heighten, piercing my mind, enveloping me with their despair.

They're endless, trapped, tortured. My mouth opens, and I join in with a bellow of my own. The sound drowns the screams until my throat throbs. Unable to hold my breath any longer, I inhale Adrial's menace. It winds around my heart and squeezes.

The screams fade, lowering, becoming crunching.

I'm hunched, my wings wrapped around me. Pain courses through them, like the darkness is shredding their webbing.

Somewhere nearby I hear soft crying, barely rising above the crunching. There's whispering and praying. Soft mutters of, "Stop, stop, make it stop." I strike out again, readying to knock Adrial away.

Clenching my hands, I lift my head and search the shadows, focusing on the voice.

The murmuring rises, growing louder somewhere to my right.

Forcing one foot in front of the other, I follow the voice, wandering through the miasma, and I reach a naked form, curled up, rocking back and forth. I recognize Summer's hair, her pale skin, and the subtle, corrupted scent of peaches. Our bond flares, ever so slightly.

I kneel before her. "Summer. It's me."

Trembling, she prays louder, rocking quicker. "No, no, no! Leave me alone!"

I lift my hands to touch her, but when she whimpers, becoming smaller, I hesitate. "I'm not him. Look at me."

"Go away. Please!"

My chest constricts, wanting to draw her to me—hold her, soothe her bruises—anything to reassure her. However, my touch, kind as it may be, could cause further pain.

"Summer," I whisper, shuffling closer. "Let me help you see." Dropping my hands, I settle their backs against the ground, palms lifted, one on each side of her wilted form, placed so she may see their tenuous glow. Draping her in a cocoon of my wings, I shield her from Adrial's menace. The light ebbs, weak—but even in this abyss, it is not entirely dark.

"It's me," I say again, my voice soft.

A few moments pass before she makes another sound, her body stiffening.

"Z?"

"Yes."

Quivering, her arms loosen as she reaches down, cautiously touching my hand. Her fingers slide across my palm, exploring their stretched wrinkles. She turns and checks my other hand, caressing it gently.

Slowly, she raises her head and meets my eyes. "It's you..." Her voice is barely a whisper.

"I'm here."

"How?" Her eyes scatter around. "Is this a trick?"

"It's not a trick." I cup her cheeks. "I'm here. Tell me how I can help you. Please, let me help you."

She shudders. "I'm scared."

"I know, sweet girl. I promise this will all be over soon. I will make it so."

Somebody cries out, another tormented scream. It's joined by a beating thrum, like a drum. The music of Hell. A macabre that nears.

Summer flinches, covering her ears. I curl around her, wings stiffening, as I hold her tight, blocking out the noise. The droning grows louder, vibrations shaking my bones as the world trembles. The drum beats and beats and beats, coming ever closer. I take the brunt of it, solidifying against its force, shielding her. The ominous vibrations strike me.

When the sounds finally fade, I haul her against my chest.

"It's over," I soothe.

"It'll come back."

"Then you need to leave before then."

She raises her head again and runs her hand up my torso, pressing it over my heart. "How?"

"We'll find the exit."

She sits away. "There's an exit?" Her face falls. "There's no exit from here. Not anymore, not for me."

"What are you saying?"

"He might have brought you here, but he's still inside my head, even now. He'll take control again, forcing you back and... I'm not strong enough. I can't resist forever—he will take your name. You have to kill me. It's... it's the only way."

"Like hell I am." I cradle her in my arms as I straighten, picking a direction and walking. "I will not let Adrial have any more of you. There is always an exit."

"You don't understand, he already has me. I was an idiot. I thought..."

The refrain *murderer* rings through my head, loud and clear. "Hush. You're not a murderer."

She leans her head into my chest. "I know."

I cup her cheeks, relishing the glistening blue of her eyes, hating the redness surrounding them. "If you must, give in. Give him my name."

"I would rather die." She leans her face into my hands, into my soft light, her features softening. "I love you."

I clutch her harder, my chest swelling. My light brightens. "Not here," I whisper.

"I wish I had told you sooner," she says anyway. "I love you so much. I've loved our time together, no matter how short it has been. I wouldn't have traded it for anything. You made me feel more than I ever have. You gave me purpose when I had none. Thank you... thank you for trying."

Pain overcomes my joy, hearing the goodbye in her voice, our bond weakening.

"Stop speaking like that."

"I love you. After I'm gone, remember me?"

"Summer," I growl, angry and fearful. "Don't do this." My light burns, growing as she leans deeper into it.

"He's coming," she whispers. "He's almost here. I feel him."

Fury rips through me. Desperate, detesting Adrial more than ever, power bursts forth, erupting from me. My body heats, my eyes emblazon. "I will not let you give up." My wings snap outwards. "I will not give you up!"

Summer's eyes open, her lips parting, staring at me in awe, and she tenses in my arms. "Your light..."

There's a tug, claws grasping, digging into my back, my chest, *everywhere*. I lose my grip on Summer as I'm thrust away. She shouts for me as I reach for her.

I blink. The miasma has vanished, and I'm back in the museum, my gaze inches from Adrial's twisted face.

Growling, I launch at him. My feet slip, and he dodges away.

The floor has no traction, and I look down—there's blood everywhere, hot with its sickening scent.

Gashes cover my chest; my wings are shredded. Muscles torn and weak, pain radiates through me, and my wings remain limp when I try to lift them. I flex my tail, but the nerves cry out, stinging with unanswered pulses. The appendage is strewn aside, chopped off, and lying on the floor.

Staggering, I stumble, catching on my hand.

"Do you like my work? I hope you enjoyed your goodbye." His voice is hard, no longer edged with sinister glee.

Forcing my head up, he's wincing like he's in pain. His breaths are fast and short.

There's no darkness left in the room, none of his menace. I peer back down at my hands and see my light bursting out of them, sizzling the blood on the floor.

He's weakened.

Nostrils flaring, I brace. "Give her back to me," I roar.

It's time to end this.

Chapter Twenty-Seven
The Last Straw

Summer

Zuriel's hands are ripped from me.

I can't lose him, not again, and as the darkness closes in, I lunge forward, chasing his light.

Everything tunnels, his glow dimming, fading into the distance.

No!

No, no, no!

I need him. Running faster, I stop caring about what might lurk beyond my sight, dismissing the terrible sounds of torn flesh and crunching bones. Breaking through plumes of brimstone, I stay strong.

Zuriel found his way in here, which means there has to be a way out.

My chest burns, melting away the fearful ice. My gargoyle's light ignites me, granting me more hope than I've felt since Adrial swallowed me.

Swallowed.

I shudder, pushing the memory away. Regardless, it slithers up my skin. The way his mouth stretched, his teeth grating my skin, catching on my clothes—the pressure of his slimy, enclosed throat, so tight I couldn't breathe.

I sprint faster. I'll run forever if I must.

I need to reach Zuriel and convince him to unleash everything, even if it topples the museum, even if it obliterates me. If he can ignite his light inside here... I know he can destroy Adrial.

This place, whatever it is—the demon's belly, his mind, Hell, or a dimension of it—it weakened when Zuriel glowed. I sensed it when my hope returned.

I chase the distant spark until it slowly becomes taller and wider, the sight amplifying my adrenaline. Gaining momentum, I run even faster.

Grasping hands reach for me, greedy fingers snagging my clothes. I push through, shaking them off, staying on the path, my eyes forward and wide. I'm afraid if I look away, close them for a single second, I'll lose the light.

Approaching, there's something on the other side, but I'm not sure what it is. Colors? Shapes maybe?

Reaching it, halting abruptly, tendrils of warmth course over my skin. It's a portal of some sort, showing me the museum. Zuriel is on the other side, covered in blood—everything is covered in blood.

Lunging forward, my body strikes an invisible barrier. Zuriel stares at me, his face enraged, and the portal shifts, tracking him as he rises.

I rail, pounding my hands against the invisible wall. I shout, hoping he can hear me.

It's me!

I'm here.

I'm... here...

Except my voice doesn't catch, the sound hollow, echoing away. I shove my body against the barrier, testing every inch with my fingers, praying I'll fall through, and that I'll find a weak spot. It indents, giving way like tough rubber, unyielding.

Dripping in blood, wings slashed, and gashes covering his chest, Zuriel captures my attention on the other side. I furrow my brows, horrified by what's happened to him. He shows no sign of pain, but if he can be pleasured, he can be pained.

Zuriel... My nails scratch at the wall. I bite back at the need to shout his name.

He lunges for me, and I try dodging away—toppling as he tackles. He's on top of me, slamming his fist into my face. He does it again, and I flinch, feeling the aches across my body. My nose breaks, the pain a throbbing ache that slowly builds.

He's thrown off me, slammed into the wall, breaking a glass enclosure. He rises, charging me again, teeth bared, ears flared.

He clutches my chin, forcing me to meet his furious eyes.

My mouth widens in a silent scream, consumed by my need for him.

The portal expands, the barrier thinning. Heaving against it, I fall through, and suddenly, it's me he's looking at.

I cry out. My eyes roll back as I fight to remain conscious in my injured body. My head, nose, and neck explode with pain.

"Make no mistake, demon, I will see you mocked, on your knees before Heaven," he growls. "Release her and I might show mercy."

I whimper.

He snarls, hauling me under his arm. "I've had enough of your trickery!"

I wail, pain sharpening and spreading as my breath is slammed out of me. Slumping into his arms, I'm carried to the basement. My vision fades, blood rushing to my head as he throws me into the circle of salt we laid out weeks ago.

Hitting the cement, I groan, collapsing and curling into a ball. Through labored breaths, I slowly rise onto my hands.

He's pouring holy water on the ground. Some of it trickles toward my leg, and like acid, it burns. I shuffle away, backing against the salt, until I'm stopped, like striking an invisible wall.

"This isn't going to work," I rasp.

"Shut up."

Desperation expands inside me, and crying out, my gaze drops to my belly. Nausea morphs, becoming the sensation of hands, pressing outward, pushing from inside me, climbing up my chest. Frigidness returns, an icy chill claiming my chest, rising toward my brands.

"He's trying to retake control." Terrified, I claw at my flesh, shoving the grasping hands inward, delaying Adrial from stretching me wide and ripping me open. "Help me!" I scream.

Zuriel stops, staring at me. I thrash harder, agonized.

"Summer?"

"Stop him!" I shriek, fighting my sobs.

Zuriel rushes closer and cradles me against him. "Hold still."

I barely hear him, writhing as Adrial's hands reach my throat, stealing my breath. Wrapping my hands around my neck, I stifle myself, desperate to stop him from tearing out of me.

Zuriel pins me to the ground. Straddling me, he braces my seizing chest with his hands over my brands.

His touch burns.

There's no comfort in his contact, and a terrible screech rips from my throat, forcing it open.

"Summer," his voice is low, his fire growing, scorching me. "Forgive me."

There's a blast of light, focused on my chest. The pain sears, boils me, becoming more than I can endure. I fade away...

Blinking, I resurface. Adrial's pressure has disappeared, and all that's left are the physical wounds, the aches from before. I wince and clutch my head.

Zuriel shifts my hands and forces me to look at him, our noses close. Blinking away tears, I slump with a cry.

He draws me to his chest. "I'm so sorry," he whispers, his voice hoarse. With one hand behind my head and the other clutching my lower back, he holds me to him. "Please be okay."

Licking my raw lips, I don't know what to say.

I'm not okay.

I still feel Adrial inside me. The pressure of his darkness is building again. "You need to do more," I croak.

His arms tighten around me. "I can't keep hurting you."

I shake my head. "He's rising." My back arcs as the stabbing starts again, starting with my lower belly. "I can't hold out much longer. You can do this. You have to do this."

Zuriel cups my cheeks. "It will kill you."

"Earlier your light illuminated his Hell. Use that. He's contained within me now. Fill me from the inside." I flinch as Adrial's claws morph into worms. They wiggle, squirm, gnawing as they slither up my chest. "Don't hold back." I shut my eyes against the sickening expansion inside me.

"There's another way."

"There's not another way!"

"It won't work—it will only kill you."

"Trust me! I'm going to die anyway! If you don't try—" I sob, feeling Adrial clawing up my aching throat "—he's going to learn your name."

The torture will end if you give me what I want. Adrial's words ring through my head, like the drums from before.

"Please," I beg, shimmying my hands up Zuriel's chest, his head. "*Please!*"

Grabbing his horns, I use the last of my strength, lifting, pressing my lips to his, and kissing him. It's shallow yet wild, frantic with pain.

He holds still and doesn't kiss me back.

"Please," I whisper against his mouth, pleading. "He's almost here. If we don't do this now..." My arms fail me, and I hang my head.

His lips caress my brow.

I long to say his name, if only to declare my love one final time, to lay bare this evidence that he means everything to me. But I don't. And holding back aches. It hurts. Everything hurts, and no matter how I wish for one moment of peace, I know those moments are already spent. I thought I appreciated them while I had the chance.

I didn't appreciate them enough.

There's some relief when Zuriel lays me on the ground.

I grit my teeth, sealing my lips, holding back Adrial's darkness as long as I'm able. With one last pained look, Zuriel rips away what's left of my sweater and bra, settling his hands directly on my chest. His hands warm—they burn, but I'm beyond feeling pain.

Adrial tears at me, shrieking within, his hands squeezing my heart, my womb, my head.

The room floods with light, blinding me. Worms wiggle up my throat, filling my mouth, making me gag, and forcing my lips to part.

I scream. "You piece of gargoyle shit!"

Zuriel's hands shove me against the floor as I lose control, thrashing viciously. Darkness bleeds in, eclipsing the corners of my vision.

Adrial curses and swears, abusing me.

I swallow him down. My insides crisp, and the smell of burnt hair fills my nose.

"More!" I shout.

I can't see Zuriel, only feel him. One hand clamped against my chest, his claws tearing away my pants.

"More!"

Sensing his destruction, Adrial grapples with my life force as he attempts to leave.

Zuriel's mouth closes in on my lips, forcing them open as his tongue drives into me. His light follows, stunning my body. I tumble within, beyond, somewhere, and everywhere.

My gargoyle enters me, penetrating me in every way. Punitive, his tongue lashes against my mouth. He drives my thighs open, his cock stretching me, and thrusting, he fills me deeply. He pumps his light into me. Everything burns as his power pours in, blasting me.

Purifying me.

Adrial recoils.

Limbs locked, I'm unable to move, as the darkness shrivels. The demon writhes.

I bask in Zuriel's light as the demon suffers. He weakens, withering smaller and smaller until he becomes a remnant, his prevailing presence like the subtle flutter of nausea.

White fire encompasses everything. I can't breathe. Can only feel—*barely*.

Zuriel permeates me, becoming me, my body shuddering from the invasion, the effort... the comfort.

The ground shakes with every powerful thrust of Zuriel's hips.
There's a guttural roar, breaking me, and the pain vanishes.
My body explodes.

Chapter Twenty-Eight
An Unexpected Recovery

Summer

Sobbing, I reach for Zuriel, except my hands hit blankets, then lukewarm air. My fingers strain, empty.

There's beeping, the antiseptic scent of the hospital that follows my mom home. Blinking rapidly, I discover I'm in a bed.

He's not here.

"Summer?"

"Ella?" Ella is here?

She gasps and leans forward, her blurry profile barely recognizable.

"You're awake."

My mouth opens, except I can't speak. Tensing, I tug at the blankets, agitated. Moments ago I was fighting for my life, keeping a demon inside, and Zuriel—

Zuriel...

Ella hands me something. "Here."

I squint, seeing a pair of glasses.

"They're yours. A new pair since we couldn't find the old ones. Your mom and I picked them out—I hope you like them."

My chest heaves as I struggle to understand. With shaking hands, I settle the glasses on my nose. They're strange. *Everything* is strange.

Adrial is gone. *Gone.* I *felt* his destruction. I'm certain of it. Pressing my hands to my chest and stomach, I confirm his absence. There's no pressure, no blazing heat, or icy numbness. No hands clawing their way to freedom, and no worms wiggling up my throat. My body is mine again. So is my mind.

I take in the hospital room, recognizing it as a standard issue for Bloomsdark County Hospital. It's daytime, sunlight pouring through the window to my right, illuminating Ella on my other side. The two of us are alone.

"How are you feeling?" she asks tensely, tapping her phone. "I'm letting your parents know you're conscious. God, I'm so glad you're awake."

Awake?

I blink a few more times. The frames of my glasses are thicker than I'm used to, filling the edge of my vision with purple. Swallowing, unsure if I'm dizzy or nauseated, or hungry, I scrunch my nose—there's tubing running up it. It's itchy, and I rub at it.

Ella grabs my wrist. "It's a feeding tube. I should call a nurse—"

I snatch her hand before she draws it away. "No, wait," I say, my voice hoarse. She frowns.

"Please, we need to talk." I squeeze her hand.

"You've been in a coma for two weeks. The nurses need to see you."

A coma... Somehow I survived. *Zuriel...*

"Don't call them yet, please. Can we talk first? I need to know what happened."

She sits back and nods, her expression softening. "Okay." She blinks several times, and suddenly tears stream down her face as she rests her forehead against my hand. "Summer, I'm so glad you woke up."

Unexpected tears fill my eyes. "Me... me too."

"You scared me. You scared all of us."

"I was scared too. I thought I wouldn't make it."

If I made it, Zuriel did too. Right? He had to.

Ella sniffs. "After the earthquake, your dad found you in the basement of Hopkins'. You'd gone missing. He had to break in."

"The earthquake?"

"The strongest Elmstitch has ever had—the seismologists are baffled. We think you hit your head. You don't have any injuries elsewhere. They've done countless scans, and you're completely healthy, except you wouldn't wake up. Nothing could rouse you."

My brow furrows, and I look down at my body. Two weeks have passed. To me, it feels like moments. I release Ella's hand and touch my legs, peaking under the hospital blanket. They're a little hairy, but there are no bruises, no cuts.

Gingerly, I trace my scalp, my nose—it's not broken. My body aches, uncomfortable with disuse.

I place my palms over my breast and stomach but feel nothing from my brands. They've scanned my body, surely someone would have seen...

"There's more."

More? I tense, peering back at her.

Ella's hesitating.

"What is it?" I press.

"It's the way you were found. Your dad has only told your mom and me, but he found you at the bottom of the stairs, your body tightly wrapped in blankets, and nothing else—you were laid out, restful, like you were napping. We're worried about that guy you were seeing... Did he drug you or something?"

I stare at her.

Her eyes soften. "John Beck went missing too. Still is. Is he your boyfriend?"

I look away, shaking my head. "No, not John."

"And there are weird whispers at the Watering Hole that the museum's old gargoyle statue came to life about an hour before the earthquake."

I flinch at her inadvertent mention of Zuriel.

"So I need to ask, and this question sounds obvious, but are you okay?"

I glance back at her. "What do you mean?"

"Please, Summer, you can tell me. I'm worried. We all are. Is there something you're not saying?"

I rub my eyes. I've always told Ella everything. I trust her more than anyone. But this? It will sound crazy, though I want to try. It would be nice to confide in her. If I told anybody, it would be her. She wouldn't stop being my friend. "There's something."

"If you don't want to talk..."

"I do. I *need* to talk about it—"

There's a knock at the door, and whoever it is doesn't wait for a reply. The door flings wide open.

Mom flies into the room, wearing her scrubs. Dad isn't far behind. She hugs me, sobs into my shoulder, and then coughs, collecting herself as she begins to examine my vitals, wiping tears from her eyes. She kisses my brow. "We were at the nurse's station when we got Ella's text. How do you feel?"

Even Dad is glassy-eyed.

"I'm okay. Or at least, I think I'm okay, all things considered."

Tapping on the machine, she speaks in that no-nonsense voice that I only hear at the hospital. "You've been in a coma for several weeks now. You might feel groggy, disoriented, or confused. It's strange... all of this." She clutches my hand, her eyes flicking critically over my face. "You're unusually alert."

Without waiting for a reply, she scurries about, listening to my heartbeat. She checks my eyes and my throat.

I smile apologetically at Ella, and she mouths, "We'll talk later," as she leaves the room.

Once Mom is convinced I don't need immediate attention, she summons another nurse for assistance, since she's not supposed to be the one updating my charts. The attending doctor follows suit.

Finally, after a myriad of tests and questions, Dad settles beside me. "You gave everyone quite the scare."

"I'm sorry. I don't remember what happened. Maybe I inhaled something?" My vision lands on the tiled hospital ceiling. Exhaling, I feel the emptiness in my chest, and the reassurance from before is gone. What if Adrial was a gas leak, a bump on the head?

"I told you to be smart," he says.

"I was smart." Or I tried to be.

His jaw tightens. "Sometimes I wish you were still a child and I could stop you from taking risks. But you're not, and you do. So whatever... *happened,* I hope it was worth it. You're spending way too much time at that museum. Maybe it's time you quit, support your job search in a new way."

"Maybe," I offer. "I'm starting to like it there."

He sighs. "While you were in a coma, there was a funeral for Beck. His son was noticeably absent. The rumor is that he ran away. But all of his belongings are still at home and no one can seem to get a hold of him."

My lips flatten.

"Do you know anything, Summer?"

I picture John's burnt body, mangled as it was, and I wonder why no one discovered it. Someone would've by now if it had remained in the alleyway. If worms hadn't taken it. I shake my head, uncertain of what to say. "I don't know anything."

Dad nods and allows the nurse closer. Dr. Taylor joins him outside, and quietly the two men discuss me.

I lose track of time as I'm inspected, poked, prodded, and scanned. Plans are made for my recovery. I meet with a dietitian, show I can swallow, and am allowed to consume a few bland bites of food. After I prove I can stand and hobble to the bathroom, my muscles more sore than atrophied, my catheter is removed.

In the bathroom, I use the rare moment of privacy to look under the hospital gown. My brands are gone, leaving no mark they were ever there. The uneasy sight amplifies my uncertainty—what was real, I wonder.

I learn that Ginny is still at the museum. Dad stops by to care for her because she refuses to leave the shop, running off and hiding when he tries to pick her up. He says the place is still a wreck from the earthquake, and lowering his voice, he adds there is dried blood, though he doesn't ask whose it is.

Two cops arrive by midafternoon and question me. I offer them vague answers when I know they're hoping for more. Carol and I are the last people to see John, and they know I followed him down the alleyway. They accept my claim that I entered the back door of the museum and must have fallen unconscious shortly after. It seems a miracle nobody asked for a warrant to the museum, to see the dried blood Dad claims to have seen. Suspecting more from Hopkins than before, I can't be convinced that supernatural powers weren't involved.

The whole process drains my strength, and despite the flurry of activity around me and the constant shift of visitors, I drift off to sleep.

Later, I stir to the sound of the door shutting. At long last, I'm alone, the window showing a dusky sky. It's late evening.

Sitting up, my heart races, expecting Zuriel to appear at the window.

I didn't dream of him.

My hands wander, instinctively covering where my brands used to be, except I sense nothing, and my heart sinks.

Minutes pass, and still, no Zuriel.

I'm growing agitated, alert, questioning everything. The only thing I know for certain is that John is missing and his dad is dead, but was that caused by a demon?

Has everything been my imagination?

I need to find Zuriel.

I detach the feeding tube and rummage around the duffle bag my parents packed, finding sweatpants, a T-shirt, sneakers, and a hoodie. Quickly dressing, I'm as quiet as possible. My purse still has my keys.

Sneaking out of the hospital is easy—it helps that I know it well. I dodge past the nurse's station and down the back staircase, leaving through an unarmed door at floor level. Stepping outside, I suck in a breath of fresh fall air and look to the sky, still hopeful Zuriel might appear. There isn't even a bat. It's cold and getting colder. I don't hesitate, running to the bike racks and finding one that isn't locked up.

It's a couple of miles to the museum, and with my adrenaline surging, it passes in a blur. Turning the pedals, I cycle forward. I need to see him. I need to know.

By the time I reach the front door, my legs are rubbery and are about to give way. I stumble forward, unlock the door and rush inside.

He's here.

The museum is a wreck of toppled bookshelves and scattered souvenirs, but he's behind the front desk like he's always been.

Solid, like nothing has happened, in the same pose as always.

I run to him.

My hands brush his cold, rigid body, his wings, his chest, holding his right cheek above his scowl.

"It's night. You can wake up now."

I caress his frozen lips. I look into his stony eyes.

"Zuriel, I'm here. Come back to me."

He doesn't stir. My heart stills.

Tears beading, I collapse into him.

There's a meow, and Ginny rubs her head against my shins. For a while I just stare at her, unable to let Zuriel go, my tears wetting his chest. She weaves between Zuriel's legs, mewing at him.

Releasing him, I reach for her. "Hi, girl. Are you... missing him too?"

She rubs my hand, needing attention. Scritching her, I sit down with my back against the desk.

I look up at my gargoyle. "Was it real? Any of it?"

My mind is muddled, the last weeks becoming difficult to track. I was so sleep deprived, rattled by anxiety...

"Will you come back?" I whisper.

I told him I loved him. That I'd break if he died. I said that, right?

Or was everything just fumes and head bumps? Dreams and nightmares seeping into reality?

Maybe if—I could—

Jumping to my feet, I rummage in the desk drawers, finding a lighter and knife. I wave the flame over the blade, hoping it'll be enough to sterilize, and after making a small cut on the tip of my middle finger, I'm satisfied when a drop of blood bubbles up.

I brush the blood on his lips. "Zuriel, I command you to wake."

Ginny watches, as I suck in a long breath, anticipating.

Nothing.

There's another moment and another. They add up until a minute goes by, until thirty. Nothing happens.

I kiss him. I smear my blood. I say his name.

"Please, please, wake up."

Chapter Twenty-Nine
The Long, Dark Nights

Summer

"Summer, there you are!"

"Ella?" My eyes are crusted shut with dried tears, and I rub them open.

She crouches over me where I fell asleep between the desk and Zuriel, Ginny curled into my side.

"Thank god we found you." Her gaze lands on the lighter and blade. "What are you doing here? What's the knife for? Are you hurt?"

"I... I had to know."

"Know what?" Her face is red and flushed with worry. Tightening her jaw, she settles, sitting down beside me. "We might have a few minutes before your parents arrive. Earlier, what were you trying to tell me? Does this have to do with John?"

I swallow, put on the spot. "That guy, the one I was seeing?"

"Yes?"

I flick my gaze at the statue. "That's him."

She stares at him. "What? The gargoyle statue?"

"Yes."

"Is it the same statue the townsfolk claim they saw?"

I nod. "Nearly two months ago, I learned his name in a dream, and he came to life, except only at night. But this demon wanted his name too—he called himself Adrien, my parents even *met* him, though his real name was Adrial. We delayed him, for a time, and then all hell broke loose. The night of this earthquake must have been when Zuriel defeated him. I was prepared to die."

I look up at Zuriel, memories streaming through me. The way he crouched on my balcony. Our nights of research, of desperate preparations. The way I laid in the crook of his arms each morning as we waited for the sun to rise.

"I had to see him. I thought if I survived, maybe he did too."

Her mouth gapes. "Summer..."

I can't blame her if she doesn't believe me.

Her gaze flicks over my face and she sighs. "You've been crying."

"I loved him, Ella. And I barely told him that—only at the end."

Ella hugs me to her, rubbing soothing hands against my back. "Shhh, it's okay. But you're not making a lot of sense. We need to get you back to the hospital."

"It doesn't make sense," I blubber into her shoulder. "It's insane. I was afraid to tell you, to tell anyone."

She holds me at arm's length, making me meet her gaze. "Thank you for telling me. And, yes, I'm worried about you, but I also believe you're in shock. I'm not going to abandon you."

My chest loosens. I don't think she's going to tell anyone, and it felt good to confess, even if she doesn't believe me. Strangely, I feel saner saying it aloud. I'll stay sane if I accept it was real. Maybe nobody will believe me, but slowly, I decide to trust my mind. There *is* evidence, fragments I can cling to. My parents met Adrien, and others saw Zuriel that night—there was an earthquake.

Except accepting everything was real also means facing this loss. I stare up at my gargoyle's cold, distant gaze.

Ella settles beside me, looking up too. "Tell me more about him."

"He was wonderful."

She wraps her arm around my shoulder, and for the moment, the pain of losing Zuriel is no longer mine alone. We sit in silence, and when Ginny purrs, we pet her until my parents come through the front door.

They insist on taking me back to the hospital, and I don't resist. When Mom asks how I got here, I shrug, though Ella and Dad eye the bicycle abandoned on the sidewalk. There's no point explaining—I'm one day out of a mysterious coma, and I shouldn't be able to ride a bike.

Chalk it up to adrenaline.

Or otherworldly forces.

Zuriel's gone. It's over. I'm done coming up with bullshit excuses.

The rest of that first night, my parents take shifts watching me. Now that I've been identified as a flight risk, the nurses stop by more often. They're wasting their time. I'm not leaving again. I have no reason to.

The dawn light filters through the window when I finally fall asleep. And less than an hour later, I'm woken up.

Still no dreams of Zuriel. It's just another new day, one I'm expected to face.

I'm moved to the hospital's rehabilitation clinic. The window in my new room is bigger, the room brighter. I throw the thick curtains closed and crawl back into bed.

I don't speak much during my first meetings with my physical and occupational therapists, and with this heavy blanket of loss, it's easy to downplay my strength. The entire hospital staff is already shocked by my quick recovery.

Days pass, and only Ella knows how recovered I truly am. She's working remotely from my parent's house, and she visits for a few hours every day. In her company, I don't have to pretend. We don't speak again about the gargoyle, but at least she acknowledges my grief.

The world has turned gray, and it's more than the late fall weather.

Through the long dark hours of the night, I keep the curtains open, looking at the empty sky, searching for something, anything, I don't know anymore. At times I catch the flapping wings of a bat, and my heart flutters, falters, and fails. *It's not him.* Every morning another dawn comes, and I close the curtains, retreating to my bed.

All my life, I've been chasing a dream. Build the right career and maintain the right relationships. I've strategically stacked 'correct' choices, believing that happiness would follow.

And I had happiness, for a time, in the darkest of places. Everything was illuminated by his light, wrapped in the safety of his wings.

Now that he's gone, now that I'm still here... I can't see what happens next.

"You're still thinking about him, aren't you?" Ella asks, finding me at the window at four in the morning.

My heart sinks as I face her. She's stopping by before her early morning flight. This is goodbye.

"Give my best to Rebecca, won't you?"

"Of course." She settles her bags near the door, her brow furrowing. "And you'd better not ignore my calls."

"I'll try not to."

She joins me at the window. "Is this what you're doing every night instead of sleeping?"

I shrug.

"Sleep might help you process everything."

Sleep? How can I when I no longer dream of him? "I'm not ready."

"Will you ever feel ready?"

I don't answer.

She rubs her brow. "Sorry. That wasn't a fair question. If I ever lost Rebecca, I'm not sure how I'd move forward."

"Then what am I supposed to do?"

"Maybe you stop waiting to feel ready—you do what you can. Maybe some days it'll be easier than others, and with time, if you don't lose hope... maybe one day it won't hurt so bad."

Hope.

Hearing the word, there's a flicker of light. It fades quickly, swallowed by shadows.

But it happened.

I'm still capable of hope.

Chapter Thirty
Hopkins

Summer

I call Ella every day. It helps, even when we're hundreds of miles apart. Some days that single phone call takes all my strength. On others, I can manage more.

I start taking antidepressants. I also start sleeping at night, managing a few hours at a time. Mom finds my Kindle, and I start reading books, slowly, one chapter at a time, until eventually, something draws me in and I binge. My parents are eager to have me home, and apparently I want that too because I'm daydreaming about drinking Dad's coffee over family breakfasts and watching true crime on the couch. It helps to have a clear goal in my rehab sessions.

It's these little things that begin to fill the void inside me.

One day, they take me to visit Mr. Beck's grave, the fresh dirt covered in flowers. Dad tells me the family was slowing their search for John. I cry, hating Adrial more than ever.

I'll never forget how the sun shined bright that day, warming the last nice day of fall. It affirmed my newfound resolve, reminding me I can't hide forever. I'm alive and that is a gift that shouldn't be wasted.

I sob even harder when they take me to John's memorial service, my resolve for life growing even stronger.

Now it's clear, the life I've been living won't take me where I want to go—and it took a damn demon for me to see it. It would be easy to continue, moving forward as I always have, but now the destination seems empty. Lonely.

I can no longer be who I was, but I cannot see who I must become.

On the day of my release, I wait for my dad to pick me up, seated in a wheelchair in my room, once again staring out the window. The curtains are drawn back, letting daylight seep in. I don't mind it anymore.

Although, I've noticed a strange number of crows lately.

Squinting, I gaze at the sun even though it hurts my eyes and try picturing it as Zuriel would, letting the heat of its rays warm my skin. He dreamed of seeing the sun again. Even if he can't experience it with me, I should enjoy its glow. Like most things these days, I refuse to take it for granted.

The sun—the light—can always be taken away.

"Come in," I say, when there's a knock at the door.

Only it isn't a nurse ready to wheel me downstairs.

It's Hopkins.

His long gray hair is tied at the back of his neck, the straight part highlighting his eerily symmetric face and stern jaw. He dresses as eclectic as his museum, mixing the bellbottom jeans of a hippie with the baggy suit jacket of a nineties businessman.

I haven't called him since waking up. I haven't even given much thought to it. Another voicemail arrived a few days after I woke, telling me to focus on recovery and not to worry about the museum. He said he's back in town and putting the museum to rights after the 'incident.' He added that I had done well. Whatever that means.

Dad ran into him while checking on Ginny. That's how he knows I'm awake or had ever been unconscious in the first place. Knowing my dad, I bet the interaction wasn't entirely pleasant, and I'm glad not to have been around.

Seeing Hopkins, after all this time, makes me tense with conflicting emotions. None of them are easy to navigate. Part of me wants to scream, rise from the wheelchair, and slap him, while another part wants to tell him to leave me alone. He doesn't just get to walk back into my life like this.

It's not fair.

Except the dangerously curious part of me wants him to explain everything. I want to know what he knows.

"Oh." I straighten. "I thought you were the nurse."

He takes a single step into my room. "I heard you're being discharged today. May I wheel you downstairs? And by the way, congratulations."

"Umm, sure. Congratulations? For what? Being discharged?" I ask dryly.

"On destroying that pesky demon. He's been a nuisance, stopping by the museum every decade or so, checking on our gargoyle friend."

"Oh."

My lips flatten, my heart stuttering. Hearing him speak so plainly puts me at a loss. Such directness should ease my lingering doubts, except I expected him to deflect.

It's over and... Zuriel and I won.

What exactly did we win? Peace?

Terrible shit is still going on all over the world. It's on the news, on my phone, blasted at me from every front.

What does destroying one demon, in one small town, have to do with any of it? What did it solve? There's always going to be death and destruction. There will always be demons.

Hopkins takes the back of the wheelchair and rolls me out of my room and toward the elevators. The rehab staff wave and say goodbye. They've tried to help me, but I haven't exactly enjoyed my time here and didn't have the energy to fake it. I offer only half-hearted goodbyes, knowing they're as relieved about my departure as I am.

While Hopkins and I wait for the elevator, he taps his foot and I examine my hands. They've become pale and boney, the knuckles protruding from my skin. They no longer look like my hands.

Luckily, Hopkins is the silent type, not prone to chitchat in the after hours when he isn't with a customer—maybe that's why I liked working for him.

He breaks the silence first. "I understand if you have no intention of returning to the museum."

"Honestly, I haven't thought about it," I say flatly.

"Very reasonable, under the circumstances."

The elevator dings its arrival, and he wheels me in.

"However, I do hope you'll consider staying on. As you now know, my museum requires a special sort of personnel. You were already quite talented when I hired you between your qualifications, instincts you weren't even aware of, and of course your history with this town. Now that you're fully trained, it would be a shame to lose you."

"*Fully trained?*" I bite out with anger. "I could have died! I feel like part of me *has*."

"Except you didn't. You survived. You're clever, determined, and quite resourceful. I respect that. It's not every day a person is subjected to Hell and returns intact if they return at all. Even those who survive demonic encounters, never quite come back whole. They might be... *broken*."

Broken... A word Zuriel used so often.

Is that what I am? Intact but not whole.

"You could have told me, warned me," I whisper. "I could've used your help."

"Had I known Adrial would possess you, I never would have left."

The elevator doors open, and once again we're quiet as he wheels me out of the building and toward the empty pick-up zone. He locks the wheelchair in place next to a bench and settles beside me.

"Listen," he says. "You never need to set foot inside the museum again, that's fine. But first, please hear me out."

I cross my arms over my chest, refusing to look at him. "I'm listening."

"Now that you understand what the museum really is about, the job changes. From here on, everything will be different. Yes, we'll remain open to the public, but beyond maintaining the front, there's no more nonsense. I'll tell you directly what is what. I'll start teaching you what I know."

My stomach twists. Life was easier when I knew less. I wonder, not for the first time, if there is a way to forget. Except I can't forget... I'm curious, and my curiosity always wins out.

Hopkins' world is Zuriel's world. I can't leave it behind.

"Why didn't you help me?" I ask.

Hopkins sighs, leaning back. "I wanted to. I did. However, my role is... I'm a librarian of things. My duty is to the museum, and to accomplish that, I've taken a vow to never take sides. My collection is a place to contain, preserve, as well as protect relics. The museum is a sanctuary for artifacts from countless ages, species, and worlds from those who would abuse them. I cannot do this job, amassing such power, if I do not remain neutral. This vow of neutrality empowers the wards, deterring those who wish me and my museum harm. If I helped you, I would be taking a side. But I could hire you and observe which relics would respond to you.

"The world is a frightening place, Summer. You know that better than most. And honestly, it's only getting worse. There are few like me left. I do what I can, but I'm only human. And I'm getting old."

Old. He's gray and timeless, but he's too spry to seem elderly. "Uh, how old are we talking?" I ask.

"Old enough to start training an apprentice who can replace me. The collection must be cared for."

Does he want me to become like him?

I side-eye him. "Why should I trust you?"

"Oh, you shouldn't, not completely."

I purse my lips. "You promised real answers."

"Then how about the truth—you can sometimes trust me because there isn't anyone better doing this work. Others are out there, and you've already met some of them."

I nod, remembering Hopkins' strange acquaintances that come by after the shop is closed. They go directly to his office or down to the library.

"Only I don't know a single other person working as I do. Everyone else has an agenda. There may be others who can teach you more and train you better, but I can promise that my instruction comes without bias. I'm sworn to it. How's that? Does honesty make you feel any better?"

Dad's truck comes around the corner, and I wave. "Not particularly."

Hopkins stands. "For what it's worth, I am sorry. It wasn't something I enjoyed, making you handle this on your own. I could only set the stage... Everything was up to you. I knew the gargoyle liked you—he only roused when you were near. Bleeding on him and bonding with him was entirely your doing. And if it's any consolation..." He hands me a small satchel. "Take this—no obligations about the job. It will help you recover. Just review my written instructions and be sure to follow them to the letter. For best results, I recommend performing the ritual when you're alone. Dusk is auspicious. Saying a few prayers beforehand helps. They like that."

I keep my lips tight, refusing to give him a reaction. I accept the satchel as Dad drives up, watching Hopkins warily. Standing, I give him a nod while Dad parks. Hopkins helps me into the truck and then walks away.

Dad glances at the satchel in my lap as he starts the truck. "What did Hopkins want? What's that you got there?"

"A gift. He wants me to stay on, give me more responsibility."

Dad's quiet for a long stretch. We haven't talked about my circumstances, not plainly. He knows how unusual I acted in the weeks leading up to the "earthquake." He discovered a blood-splattered museum and me, laid out in the basement—and I still don't understand how *that* happened. Mom might be able to turn the other way; Dad has been paying attention.

"So a promotion?" He sighs. "It's risky, isn't it, whatever he's asking of you?"

"Yes. I think he wants me to be his assistant, maybe apprentice..."

"Are you sure that's a good idea?"

"No, I'm not," I reply, turning the satchel over. "I'll have to think about it."

"Do that." He's silent for another long moment. "And if you accept the job, can you do me one favor?"

"Sure, what is it?"

"If shit is going to hit the fan again, can you at least give me a warning?"

"I'll do what I can."

With grunting acceptance, he turns up the radio.

Later that evening, I retreat to my bedroom.

It's strange, returning here, with my skylight above and the balcony where Zuriel once intruded. The stars painted on the ceiling remind me of better days when I believed in magic and happy endings before responsibilities whipped that away.

Sitting on my bed, I open the satchel and review the contents.

It's the angel talon wrapped in translucent hair, one of Hopkins' exhibits. His handwritten instructions are to unwrap the hair, twine the talon with one of mine, and wait. That's it. It doesn't say what will happen.

They like prayers.

A little spooked, I clutch the talon harder. These angels... made Zuriel. They made his punishment—the failsafes, first of stone and then of a death I forbade him from taking. Despite all of this, he never told me exactly what they were. Only that they're structured into a hierarchy and only the lowest could intervene on Earth. Like demons, too much light would require balancing, and so they used gargoyles, an intermediary, to anchor loose demons.

I study the red-dusk sky, spinning the talon in my hand, wanting to believe it is a way to communicate with Zuriel.

My heart drops. *Perhaps this is my way to say goodbye.*

Whatever this is, using it requires trusting Hopkins not to screw me over. Again.

He said I had good instincts. I think he's right.

Deciding to trust myself when I have nothing else to go on, I tease the translucent hair aside, twine mine in its place, and hide the talon under my pillow.

I fall asleep faster than I have in months, forgetting all about the prayers.

I stand in a graveyard, the thick wooden doors of the Old Church wide before me. The building is brilliant white, restored, and shining with a light that draws me closer, a light I recognize all too well.

It's not the same shade as Zuriel's. It's brighter, bluer, lacking the warmth that made his light his.

An angel stands at the dais, their features blurred by the light emanating from them, and I have to cover my face, and look to the floor as I near.

"You summoned me?" the angel asks, sounding irritable.

"S-summoned?"

The light glares brighter. "Such ignorance."

"I've defeated a demon. I don't think I have the luxury of ignorance anymore. I was given your talon as a gift."

"Is that so?"

In a rush of feathers and wings, they descend. They tower over me, their light so bright that I squeeze my eyes shut, palms covering my face. There's pressure, a hand upon my brow, and memories flash before my mind.

They replay every moment I had with Zuriel.

The good, the bad. The beautiful, the painful. I watch the weeks unfold until I'm crying, coming to the end. My body writhes to contain Adrial as Zuriel lights me up from the inside.

Only the vision doesn't stop there.

I'm given the blessing and curse of witnessing what happens next.

My body is still, unconscious, purified, and healed by Zuriel's light, except he cannot wake me. After trying fruitlessly he stumbles, his body stiffening. It starts with his fingers and toes as he struggles against unyielding joints.

"What's happening?" I whimper.

"His work is done. He is retiring, becoming stone."

"What?" I gasp. "That's his reward? After everything? Because he accomplished his purpose?"

"Human, it is not your role to question."

Zuriel wraps me in a blanket, setting me tenderly at the base of the stairs. Every moment seems to cost him pain as his body grows increasingly rigid. Finally, he kisses my brow. Slowly, he trudges upstairs, placing himself as he has always stood, positioned to watch my back as I work the front desk.

Cuts vanishing, tail reforming, he claims his post. He freezes, becoming stone. Forever.

When it's done, there is only silence.

I clench my fists, shaking as a new wave of tears streams down my face.

A hand lifts my chin. "So much bravery, from one little human."

"I loved him."

"I see that."

"And now, because we succeeded, he's gone."

"A gargoyle is never meant to find meaning beyond their appointment—"

"But he did! We did… have meaning. Our success depended on that meaning."

"No gargoyle has successfully defeated a demon before."

"I thought—"

"Nor has any gargoyle loved a human. It is… not in their nature, in any of our natures."

There's the sound of humming as the angel considers. "The inadequacy of his kind was never a concern, since the failsafe of stone was powerful enough to keep the realms and their inhabitants safe. However, since Zuriel has been on this Earth far longer than any of his kind, it's possible he adapted to his environment. You have shown me something truly remarkable, and such discoveries are worthy of reconsideration."

Before I can form a question, they press a hand against my chest, and I'm thrust away, out of the church, past the graveyard, and beyond the light of stars.

Chapter Thirty-One
THE STRANGER AT DAWN

Summer

Weak light ebbs into my room as the first of winter's snowflakes gather on the skylight. At long last, I've slept through an entire night.

Thrusting my hand under my pillow, I search for the talon. It's gone.

My heart sinks. I'm not sure what Hopkins thought I might accomplish, *summoning an angel*. Echoes from the dream slowly return to me. With sweetness, I remember Zuriel's tender goodbye, the way he wrapped me up and kissed my brow, but as I recall the conversation that followed, my stomach churns.

Zuriel's eternal entombment was a *reward* for our success. We weren't expected to succeed. The angel didn't really speak of him like he was more than a tool, surprised my gargoyle could ever love.

I didn't even get the chance to speak to Zuriel, to say goodbye, to tell him that I love him. I wish I hadn't waited. I wish I had told him I loved him long before becoming trapped in the darkness, filled with despair.

Turning over, I grab my phone from the nightstand and start browsing my email. There's one of note about a position I applied for several months back. They want to interview me. It's a position I'm qualified for with responsibilities I wanted, except now, no matter how many times I read the email, I'm not inspired to reply.

It's impossible to imagine returning to the real world. Glancing at my bottle of antidepressants, I hope they'll kick in soon. It's been three weeks.

I shove my phone away, resolving to confront Hopkins about his present.

Lazily, I take my time showering, basking in the hot water, and my return to my own bathroom. My jeans are loose, and my makeup is too dark for my new pallor. Examining my reflection, I wonder if the new glasses seem too bold on my narrowed face, and when my gaze lands on my unblemished torso, I quickly cover it with my sweater.

After giving Oyster a quick scratch, I race downstairs, bypass the kitchen, and beeline for the front door, leaving before Mom notices. She's gone from trying to get me a boyfriend to trying to get me a therapist. She knows several, all of whom are her friends.

I don't know which is worse.

The drive to the museum is rote, and I barely glance at the passing houses and buildings. It's hard to believe I've done this drive nearly every day for over a year. Back when I first took this job, I thought it would only be for a couple of months, no longer than a season.

When I park next to Bread & Bean, I pause, staring through the window. Business is bustling, returned to the life it had before. John's sister is running the place now, and confusingly, I'm happy for her—she always loved the coffee shop most.

Hands deep in my coat pockets, I walk past the alleyway where John died. I don't know what happened to his remains and assume there wasn't anything for the police to find. I can only imagine his corpse was obliterated or eaten by worms, vanishing like Adrial's previous host..

Everyone is moving forward.

Hopkins' Museum of the Strange is as I last saw it, the curtains still drawn. Though there's a new sign posted to the front door, written in Hopkins' scratchy handwriting.

Reopening today.

I hesitate at the threshold, wondering if this was a terrible idea.

Swallowing, I unlock the door and enter.

The museum has been put to rights, the gift shop bookcases repaired, and items returned to their shelves. There's the lingering scent of cleaning products. Hopkins is nowhere to be seen, but the room isn't empty. A strange man stands behind the front counter, wiping it down.

Seeing me, he stops. A new employee?

Instead of introducing myself, I freeze, my eyes fixed on the empty corner behind him.

Zuriel is gone.

Breath-catching, I stare at the empty space.

"Summer?" the man asks, his voice low, familiar.

The way he's studying me, he's waiting for me to say something. "Do we know each other?" Even as I say it, I can't give him my full attention. My heart is in my throat, eyes rapt on the empty corner. "What happened to the gargoyle?"

The new guy steps from behind the counter, drawing my gaze.

He stands far too close for my comfort, and I have to strain my neck to look up at him.

He's tall, large for a man. I expect someone like him to be the lead singer of a metal band, imposing though not hard to approach. He's the kind of guy who would never notice someone normal and unassuming like me. He doesn't look like someone Hopkins would hire unless Hopkins is now on the market for a security guard.

Maybe that explains why this guy is here.

He smiles as my gaze narrows, trying to figure him out.

I stiffen.

For a heartbeat, my eyes meet his and then they flutter, racing across his face. His skin flushes and blue undertones appear across his dark lips. Pitch-black hair cascades down his back, matching the thick, arching brows framing his dark eyes.

His skin is smooth and unblemished like it's never seen the sun. It's almost porcelain.

Chest tightening, my heart beats wildly. My brow scrunches, unable to hide my disbelief. Hope bursts in my chest, hollowing out my stomach. The emotions rushing through me are too intense to bear. Because if I'm wrong...

"Is it really you?" I whisper, barely able to form the words, afraid I might be dreaming.

He tucks his silky hair behind a subtly arched ear, like an elf or a... *bat*. His smile widens. "Hello, Summer."

Impossible.

Jolted, I crash into him, throwing my arms around his neck, crying out. He wraps his muscled arms around me, lifting me into a kiss.

Every sensation is familiar and strange, his lips firm like stone yet yielding like flesh. I test my tongue against his, seeking his taste. He runs his fingers through my hair, leaning closer as I grip him, straddling my legs tightly around his hips. Just before the kiss deepens, desperation floods me. Gripping his head, I kiss him everywhere my lips can reach. Chin, cheeks, nose, brows, forehead.

I dot him with kisses. "It really is you."

He holds me tight, elation consuming me as a new warmth radiates across my chest. My eyes brim, and my lips warm, unable to stop kissing him. I run my fingers through his hair, down his back, and along his shoulders, tracing his shoulders, his collarbones. I want to touch every inch of him.

The warmth builds until a fire flares within me, and I gasp again, leaning away to clutch my chest and stomach. The pain fades quickly, leaving only a trace of fever in its wake. Peaking under my sweater, I catch the glint of gold. "The brands. They're back."

"I know," he says.

No longer broken, we've become whole.

"I met an angel last night, in my dreams," I gasp.

"They returned me as a reward. Offered me a new purpose."

My hands return to him, running over his arms and chest. "They made you human—"

He shakes his head. "Not entirely. I'm somewhere between a human and a gargoyle. During the day, I will have this form, while at night I will return to my previous one. And while I'm no longer anchored to a demon, I must continue to guard this realm and the innocents within. As payment for the gift I've been bestowed, I will be an emissary for the angels. I hope that is all right with you."

I blink, still searching his face. "Of course that's okay. I have you back. That means everything."

"There may be times when I am called away."

I nod. "That's fine. Anything is fine as long as you're here. Will you do me a favor?"

He streaks his hands through my hair. "Anything."

"If you are called away, tell me first. Don't disappear on me. I don't think I could bear it. I missed you so much." I don't care if I sound needy. I *am* needy. I can't lose him again.

I won't lose him again.

He cups my face and leans his brow against mine. "I will share everything with you, my Summer. And you will always be able to feel me." His hand wanders down, then up my sweater, as he brushes the brand on my stomach.

It warms to his touch, and my breath catches.

"Until the end of time, we are bound," he rumbles.

"It almost sounds like marriage."

He nuzzles his face along my cheek and my hair. "It is more than marriage. What we share is forever, will be forever."

His words settle in my soul. I test the idea of eternity, scarcely able to comprehend such a thing, and I've never been more reassured, calm, or pleased. I'll never have to worry about losing him again. He's mine. All mine. *Forever.*

We hold one another, going quiet as thoughts tumble through my head: the things I want to show him, the adventures we'll share, the people I can't wait for him to meet. There is so much of this world he has never experienced. Movies, music, books.

He's never had any of it, and I can offer it all.

Wrapping my arms around him, I squeeze.

He holds me just as securely. "I hope you find this new form appeals to you." There's a subtle, insecure waver to his voice.

"I love everything about you. You always appealed to me and were always handsome. In any form."

He arches a brow. "I was?"

I point to the corner where he stood for years. "Long before you woke, I was talking to you, telling you everything. Frightening creatures can be hot, very much so. You'll understand soon enough. We humans are complex." I laugh.

His jaw tightens, still doubting me.

"I love you." I crush my mouth to his, brushing my lips back and forth. "I should have told you how I felt long ago. I will never let another day pass without telling you that. I love you. I love you, Zuriel."

"I love you too, sweet Summer."

I hesitate, then breathe freely. He didn't react to his name. Adrial is well and truly gone.

"I can't invoke you anymore, can I?" I ask, smiling mischievously.

The corner of his lip turns upward. "Not unless I want you to."

"Zuriel, Zuriel, Zuriel." Again and again, I whisper his name, memorizing the shape of it on my mouth, unburdened by outside forces and fear.

Our emotions tangle until the air is thick with adoration. I lean into his chest, listening to his beating heart as he holds me. We steady ourselves in this new reality of ours.

With the rush of small, feline feet, we're interrupted.

Ginny streaks into the room. She mews, weaving between our legs.

"Greetings to you too, Miss Genevive," Zuriel says as he sets me down, and we lower to her level.

"Sorry for the interruption," Hopkins announces, trailing after her. "I tried to hold her back. She does not like to be told what to do, that one." He carries his emerald studded cane. Though he doesn't need it for support, it's his favored accessory when managing the museum. He claims it helps his image. And his museum is all about image.

I blink, startled by his sudden appearance. My anger vanishes, unable to fester now Zuriel is at my side, *because* Zuriel is at my side. Hopkins' gift was far more than I could have ever hoped for.

He strides over to Zuriel, offering his hand. "It is nice to finally meet you."

Zuriel accepts it. "You as well."

"And what should I call you?"

"Zuriel is fine."

"Very well." Hopkins smirks, stepping back, and setting his hand on the cane. "Well, now that you're both here, we have a museum to open."

I glance at Zuriel.

"In the meantime, Mr. Zuriel, if you require accommodations, you may stay at my place. I have an extra bedroom, and while it's overflowing with junk, I believe we can make it suitable, at least until you establish yourself."

My toes are tapping, taking all this in. It's overwhelming, and I'm still reeling.

"Thank you. I will need time to decide," Zuriel responds.

"Of course, no rush. Now if you will excuse me." He nods to the clock and squares his shoulders, walking to the front doors. "It's time to unlock the door."

There's the shuffle of customers outside awaiting the museum's reopening, and with the curtains closed, I didn't realize anyone was waiting.

Surprised, I open the closest curtains, lifting them aside so light can flood the room. It's been ages since this space was lit by natural light, and I tie the drapes in place as Hopkins greets the day's first tourists.

Cautiously, Zuriel nears the window.

Eyes wide, he rests a hand upon the glass as fat snowflakes drift to the street. They sparkle as the sun pierces through the clouds. Zuriel's lips tease into a smile. It's innocent, filled with wonder, and makes me smile too.

I go to him and lean into his side. "There's so much I can't wait to show you."

"I can't wait to be shown."

He stands taller, wrapping an arm around my shoulder, holding me against him. We welcome the day's first customers.

Together.

Ready for anything that might stand in our way.

EPILOGUE: THE VOW

Zuriel

Sitting in the passenger seat of Summer's car, I study the landscape drifting by. We left Elmstitch four hours ago, at the crack of dawn, to drive to a place called Washington, DC, and more specifically the Smithsonian American Art Museum for Summer's friend's wedding ceremony.

Gritting my teeth, my stomach churns.

"We're almost there. It's only another two hours," Summer whispers, trying to reassure me.

Two hours. Lifting a brown paper bag, I breathe into it.

"We should have flown overnight," I wheeze. "We could have arrived sooner."

"Yeah, when pigs fly," she murmurs. "There is no way you could carry me. And our luggage. And Ella's wedding gift. Take another Dramamine." She points to the plastic bag at my feet.

I shuffle through it and find the medicine. "It says right here on the box I'm not supposed to take another dose today." Closing my eyes, my stomach upends again. I groan weakly. Cars are my weakness. I've never been brought so low. Until today, I have not left Elmstitch by vehicle, and the moment Summer hit a road called an 'interstate' it was all over for me.

"You'll be fine. Clearly, two isn't enough for someone as big as you."

"I would rather be fighting demons."

"You're being a baby." She laughs softly. "Take the medicine and try to nap. I'll keep sending you good vibes."

Vibes. A modern slang word that accurately explains our bond. I pour out a pill and chuck it back, leaning into my seat at the same time. Clutching a fluffy pillow to my chest, I try to relax. Summer sends me these good vibes, though she's also focused on the road, as she should be.

"I appreciate you," I groan.

Keeping my eyes closed, I listen to the music Summer chose for this journey, calling it a road trip playlist. The first song was about a journey lasting five hundred miles and then five hundred more. Now it's something slower, sweeter, the sound of *hallelujah*. An apt word, even under these nauseating circumstances. Summer is by my side, soothing me as the Dramamine's drowsiness takes effect, and I drift.

"We're here."

Startled—waking this way is still new to me—I stiffen, thrashing my arms outward, readying to attack whoever might assault Summer.

"You... okay?" Summer asks beside me.

I look past her and scan the hotel parking lot. There's no threat. I relax my arms and respond. "Yeah, yes. Are you?"

She chuckles, opening her door. "Come on, let's go check in! We don't want to be late!"

The next few hours involve getting situated and greeting friends of Summer that are also here for the wedding. They're all people she went to graduate school with, and they all know one another already. Being as cordial as I can, I try not to embarrass her, but people find me odd. I don't talk like them and know the things they know. Not yet at least.

Summer and I came up with a backstory that I'm a foreigner, though we never tell them from where. If they ask, we make them guess.

Despite this, I make an effort to be nice—thoughtful even.

Because these are Summer's people. Because Summer rightfully thinks it would be nice if I had *friends.* If only the concept of maintaining relationships with *more* humans did not make me more anxious than a car ride. By necessity, I have socialized with her parents, Hopkins' friends, and the folk around town, constantly uncertain if my mannerisms are too aggressive or abrupt. Summer says I should just be myself. However, it's difficult to read the emotions of anybody, to trust anybody—except for Summer.

Only they're important, these humans, and I try asking them about their lives, building a better understanding of modern humans.

If community weren't so important to Summer, I would as soon snarl at everyone until they left us alone. I would much rather be alone with my mate, wooing her, kissing her, and peeling off her clothes.

Once this is over, that is exactly what I will be doing.

Watching her dress for a rehearsal dinner, my mouth salivates as she strips to her undergarments, tiny white ones that make her look far more innocent than she is. She notices me staring in the mirror before her and gives me a sly smile.

"Zuriel, don't," she gasps as I stand and tug her dress out of her hands, pushing her against the reflective glass. "We don't have time."

"Then we best be quick."

If there's one medicine to make me feel right in this world, it is her. Dropping to my knees, I drag down her panties, shoving my face to her crux. She clutches my head, her fingers straining against my scalp.

I lick her wet, probe her with my fingers, and nip her clit, growling like a beast in a rut. When she begins to melt, unable to stand any longer, I lean back until I'm lying on the floor and pull her down to straddle my face. Quirking her clit into my nose, I thrust my tongue inside her until she comes, crying out my name. I drink her dry and spread her pussy with two of my fingers, pressing them inside of her. A reminder that my cock is coming later.

She flops with a moan, and I rise, taking her into my arms.

Kissing her clit one final time, I slide her panties back up her legs as she lies panting. Grabbing her little blue dress, I pull it over her, righting it as she catches her breath.

She peers up at me, flustered. "Damn you."

With a playful growl, I zip up the back.

I'm hard, aroused, unsated. She's going to have to deal with this all evening. Perhaps it is cruel, but it will make the next few hours interesting for me.

We leave the hotel and walk to the museum where the rehearsal will take place. When she leads me to a large, ornate building with steps and giant columns, I am awed. We're ushered to a side room by one of the attendants inside. With everything so grand and overwhelming, Summer has to tug me by the sleeve to keep me moving.

"We can explore later," she promises.

Summer quickly introduces me to Ella's parents before leaving me to join the others. Sitting in one of the chairs at the back, I peer around, taking in the hard but graceful lines of the architecture surrounding me, my gaze drawn to the distant artwork, eager to examine each piece closer as Summer and a group of others gather at the front.

This museum is different from Hopkins' in every way. I had expected something cramped with the lingering aroma of old books.

Summer glances at me and smiles, and I can sense her excitement, her joy. Her love. It rushes through me, lightening my heart, settling me more than the blush of lust painting her cheeks. I shift my cock lower, glad to have her purse to hide my bulge behind.

She points me out to a woman at her side.

Ella, if I had to guess. She waves, and I awkwardly wave back.

I stiffen when Summer and several others, including Ella, leave and soft music plays. They file in again shortly, and I watch with fascination, catching Summer's eye as she walks down with another man. I'm unsure what to think of this, but it is over quickly, and Summer waves for me to join them at the front.

Wrapping my arm around her, I'm easily the tallest one of the group, towering over the others by at least a head, if not more.

"Guys, this is Zuriel," Summer says.

The one I believe is Ella eyes me. "The gargoyle? I can see now where he gets his nickname." She chuckles. "Fuck, you're tall!"

The woman closest to Ella—she must be Rebecca—laughs, offering me her hand. "Do you play basketball? If you don't, you should. You'd make a killing."

Taking her hand, I make sure I'm gentle with it.

I'm still inhumanly strong. As Summer's father discovered when he first shook my hand.

"I do not," I say, having heard of the sport—she is not the first to make this joke—but knowing nothing about it. "Maybe I should start."

"Yes, you definitely should."

We continue with a light banter before the brides are called away. Ella hugs Summer goodbye and leaves with the rest of her party. Summer lingers back with me.

"Do you like her?" she asks, hopeful.

I cock my head. "She is fine."

Her shoulders sag, and her eyes roll to the ceiling. "You don't like anyone."

"I've lived long enough to have high expectations. It will take more than one meeting to garner my favor."

Taking my hand, she squeezes it. "You'll like her in time, I know it. If there's anyone in this world I would bet on you liking, it's Ella. She's a good friend. Rebecca is pretty cool too."

"You're probably right."

As dusk nears, we race back to the hotel, barely making it on time. As we enter our room, I transform out of my man suit and back into the stone skin that I know. Summer shuts the door just as my wings slice through the flesh of my back, ripping out of my fading human body. She tugs on my hand, leading me to the bed, and I grin, eager to see her white lingerie again.

The night passes quickly. Summer showers and passes out the moment her head hits the pillow. I stay up for a while, sitting in a chair by the window. The view is interesting, something I could have never imagined. Silver and gray buildings line the street, their countless windows sparkling, reflecting the headlights of cars. Stores are marked with a mirage of neon colors and an industrialized aesthetic. At the far end of the street, there is a park with a small patch of grass, a few benches, and some trees, but there's no wilderness, no pure darkness.

The bats did not follow us, and I am glad they did not. They are not suited for a place such as this. With the help of her father's experience and tools, Summer and I have constructed several large bat houses in the forest around her family's yard. We have built a few up outside Hopkins' house as well.

Despite the city's dazzlement, I long for Elmstitch and the countryside.

Humans have advanced a long way since I was last amongst them. Gone are the gothic cathedrals and castles, replaced by hotels and city halls. There is not a stone gargoyle in sight.

Closing the drapes of the windows, I turn toward the bed. Summer is on her stomach, her legs tangled within the blankets that have fallen to her waist. A small snore leaves her parted lips.

I do not tire as she does and spend many of our nights just watching her—and watching over her. When sleep took me that first time several months back, my dreams felt like I was back within the shadowy realm of my mind. I did not like it.

But I pretend for her. I will do anything for her.

My life is different now. It is my own. As of yet, there has not been any communication with those from above. I hope they never have a reason to reach out to me. Now that I have a taste of freedom—true freedom, with barbeque ribs and the taste of Summer's lips with syrup on them—I want nothing more.

Climbing gently into the bed, I curl my body around hers, using my wings to shield us both.

I drift.

At five a.m. sharp the alarm blares, and I jump out of bed, brandishing my wings, baring my fangs at our attacker. Summer mumbles, flips over, and turns off the incessant beeping.

"You need to stop doing that," she croaks, a hand searching for her glasses on the side table.

Grumbling, I relax, loosening my wings.

"All I want to do is sleep for another five hours." Her voice sounds so muddled and sad.

I offer a light smile. "What can I do to help?"

"Did you sleep at all?"

"No. I did not need it, and I would not even if I did. This place is too crowded for my liking. There should be more than a door and a lock separating us from other humans."

She pouts. "I'd kill to have the energy you do." She shoves the blankets aside and throws her legs off of the bed, sinking her feet into a plush pair of bat slippers she bought several months back. Looking up at me with pleading eyes, she sucks in her lower lip.

"What?" I ask.

"If you want to help... could you make me a cup of coffee?" She points to a device on the other side of the room. "I would greatly appreciate it."

"Coffee is love."

"Yes. Yes, it is! I'm glad you're finally seeing the light."

I scrunch my face, making her laugh, the sound sending shivers of delight down my spine.

As she turns for the bathroom, I take action, setting about the job she asked of me. I hear the shower run as I lift the coffee packages to read them. By the time the water turns off, I have her bitter drink ready. Steam drifts out from under the door as I knock on it.

With a fluffy white towel clutched around her, she opens it and startles, placing her hand over her chest.

"What's wrong?" I ask.

"I'm not sure I will ever be used to your form shifts." She takes the cup and places it on the bathroom counter.

"It is strange." I look down at my human body and flex my muscles.

"You're naked. I think that's the hard part. When you're a gargoyle I don't notice your nudity as much. Maybe it's because you were that way as a statue. Maybe it's because your gargoyle form has a..."

Her gaze darts downward and she blushes.

"Retractable cock." I finish for her.

"Yes." She chuckles, forcing her eyes to meet mine. "Now, step aside guardian. And put on some clothes! You're too distracting, and I need to get dressed. Today's a big day."

The morning moves fast. Summer spends the next hour fretting over every detail of her dress, make-up, and hair, insisting that she look perfect for her friend's ceremony. There's going to be a lot of people and she wants to make a good impression. And at the same time, she doesn't want to stand out. I don't know what she's worried about. She's beautiful with or without clothes, make-up, or an updo.

But by the time she's done and asks me what I think...

I don't know what to say. My eyes widen, scanning her from head to toe several times over.

"Zuriel?" she prompts, her brow furrowing. "Did I overdo the make-up?"

I shake my head. "No. You look like an angel." My voice comes out breathy and hot.

She's in an emerald dress that shows off her bodice and hugs her curves. Against her pale skin and ringlets of hair that frame her face, she looks like a living gem. Beautiful, eye-catching, mesmerizing. Her lips are a deep ruby red, her eyes lined with black, her cheeks subtly pink... It would make any male crazy. Strands of her hair stray from her bun, slipping across her shoulders. I reach out and swipe them back.

When she smiles up at me, my chest tightens. "I would kill for you," I rumble. "If I were still petrified. I would kill for just a glimpse of you like this."

Her smile widens into a grin, and she pushes at my chest teasingly. "Good thing you're not petrified."

I smirk. "Oh, Summer, but I am."

She glances at my very stiff cock. "I told you to get dressed... We don't have time..."

"We could make time."

"Do not tempt me! I refuse to be late. Not today." She turns toward the bed and throws my suit at me. "Get your dick under control and dress like a good gargoyle."

"And if I don't?"

She scrunches her face. "Then you'll receive no present from me later."

I laugh. "Then I better obey."

Later that morning, I escort Summer back to the museum. We receive countless looks from the pedestrians on the street, those who oggle her and others who squint at me. It is uncomfortable to be beyond Elmstitch where there are now more stares. Fortunately, one growl from me sends onlookers running.

Summer grins, shaking her head.

By the time we reach the museum a small crowd already gathers—friends, family, and attendants—conversing and preparing for the big event. Unlike the evening before, there are red and white roses everywhere, making the severe interior flush and sensual. Vibrant in her emerald dress, Summer looks at home amongst the flowers, tiles, and columns.

It makes me wonder what a wedding between her and I would be like. I picture silk, lace, and black satin offset by dark blue and purple. It would be small gathering lit by candlelight and far from an industrialized city.

The bats and Genevive would want to attend.

This wedding, though rich, is nothing like ours would be.

Summer squeezes my hand. "I have to go. Just find a spot to sit until the ceremony."

I grunt, showing only toughness.

Though she senses my true vibe. "You don't have to make small talk unless you want. Love you."

She dashes from my side before I can stop her, disappearing with another bridesmaid around a corner. With a sigh, I find a seat in the back.

The morning comes and goes, the ceremony with it. Despite my intentions to pay close attention and learn how this marriage rite may progress, the moment Summer once again walks down the aisle with the strange male's arm curled with hers, I forget the rest. My eyes never stray from her.

Through it all, the one thing I hear is the vows. The brides promise many beautiful things to one another—the vow of loyalty, *until death do us part*, stuns me most of all. Summer glances at me then, holding my gaze and blinking back tears.

She's busy all afternoon taking pictures with the wedding party, and while I play the part of a lingering shadow, we have little time together. We share snippets of conversation and brief hugs, but most of our time together is spent small talking with her friends.

With every moment, I battle my need to steal her away, claiming her as mine, ensuring my loyalties are abundantly clear—this is not what she has asked of me. So I'm polite, mostly quiet, helping her make the most of this limited time. I may be overstimulated, but I am not alone.

In time it becomes not so hard to do this. Everywhere I look there are smiles, laughter. Everyone is happy. I have never seen so much happiness. It makes my chest constrict and my heart warm.

There is good in the world. Even if I am not aware of it, there is good.

That evening at the reception Summer is finally freed to me as sunset nears. We sit at a large round table with the wedding party and their partners. They drink champagne and eat food. When they glance at me they avert their eyes and lower their voices.

It has become a very long day, and while my body feels no fatigue, I have grown tired of this event.

Stuffing filet mignon in my mouth, I chew with frustration.

Under the table, Summer squeezes my thigh, and leans into me. "Don't worry, they're just curious about you. They've never seen me with a guy before, and well, I can't imagine they ever saw me with a six-foot-five metalhead."

I swallow my meat. "Is there something wrong with metalheads?"

I apparently dress like one, often wearing the faded large tee-shirts of old groups that I've found at Elmstitch's thrift store. They are the only ones that fit and are usually black. After enough questions about it from others, I took on the persona. It came as a natural way to blend in. I'm not wearing one of my shirts right now. The suit makes me a blank slate amongst all the other males with suits.

"Stop being so nervous," she says. "And there's nothing wrong with metal-heads."

"I'm not nervous."

"Yes you are. It's making everyone else nervous. It's also very cute."

"Just because you can sense my feelings, it does not mean your interpretation of them is correct," I grump.

Summer laughs. "It'll be sunset before you know it. Drink your champagne—" she indicates the bubbly drink in the glass in front of me "—and relax a little and… try and enjoy yourself. You might find you actually will." She releases my thigh after another squeeze. "I'll be right back. I'm going to the restroom."

"Wait—" My nostrils flare with panic.

She's already threading through the guests and walking away.

Turning back to the table and the strangers around me, I sigh and grab the glass.

Sipping my champagne, my eyes widen and I inhale. Lifting the glass to eye level, watching the bubbles, I am surprised by the peachy cream flavor. Summer's flavor. Although it's more direct, sharp, alarming with a quick carbonated pop. I take another tentative sip and close my eyes.

"So how did you and Summer meet?"

I peek to my left and at the lanky male sitting at my side. Noticing he's the same one who was paired with Summer at the ceremony, I force my fist to relax. "We work at the same museum."

"Oh! That occultist artifact place… Hopkins' something…"

"Hopkins' Museum of the Strange."

"Yes. That's the one! Sounds like a cool place."

"We keep the inside temperate, otherwise the older artifacts will degrade." I tilt the rest of the champagne down my throat, focusing on the flavor of peach.

The guy frowns, then laughs. "A sense of humor, I like that. Summer and I were in the same internship. That's how I met her and Ella."

Uncertain about what humor there is within my words, I nod. Someone comes up behind us and fills our wine glasses.

The male lifts his and takes a drink. "I'm Jordan."

Not wanting to be awkward, I do the same. "I'm Zuriel."

"Interesting name."

"Everyone says that."

He eyes me. "It fits."

"Thank you."

Maybe he is not so bad after all.

Our conversation tapers off, and I focus on the wine. There's a depth of flavor here, more than I have the experience to register, though I'm certain it's not as good as the champagne—not enough bubbles. By the time I've finished it, my mood is better.

Much better.

So great, in fact, I'm at the bar ordering another, grinning like a fool. With it in hand, I face the dance floor, scanning the crowd for Summer and her vibrant dress. I sense her nearby, eager to find me, wondering where I am.

Our eyes connect across the room, and she smiles with relief. She excuses herself from the others and steers for me, eyeing the wine in my hand, the smile on my face.

"You're happy," she gasps, placing her hand on her chest. "Really happy."

"You were right. The champagne helped my mood. No wonder humans enjoy alcohol so much."

"Woah." Her face flushes. "I can tell. How many have you had?"

"Just the champagne, a glass of wine, and this one." I raise my cup and take a swallow. It's already nearly gone.

"In fifteen minutes? I wasn't gone that long!"

"Is that bad?"

"Yes!" But she says this laughing. "I'm cutting you off after this one. It'll be dark soon anyway."

"In that case..." I polish off the wine and set the glass down. "Let's dance." I snatch her hand and tug her to the dance floor where other couples are swaying. Following their lead, I wrap Summer in my arms.

She holds me as a new song plays, the tempo slowing. Resting her head on my chest, we drift from side to side. More couples join us on the dancefloor, including Ella and Rebecca. The ballroom grows quiet as the song plays and people circle up to take pictures of the newlyweds.

"I love this song," Summer murmurs.

She is content, comfortable, blooming with love that ebbs into me. I thread my hand into her hair and hold her close. "What's it called?"

"Unforgettable. It's by Nat King Cole."

I store the information in the back of my mind.

We string slowly around the dancefloor while others do the same. No one is paying attention to us anymore, too absorbed in their own romances to care. The song ends and another one starts.

Bleary eyed and tired, Summer looks up at me. "I love you."

I pet her cheek with the back of my hand. "I love you too, my sweet delight." I lean down and give her a soft kiss that makes her hum and fall further into me.

I am not from this world, and I do not belong amongst these people and their celebrations. I was never supposed to intermingle with humans, never intended to dance, to move, to live. Everything that was supposed to happen, didn't.

Everything that I believed was not wholly the truth, not the only possibility. And with Summer, the possibilities become endless. I belong by her side. There is nothing I desire more than to be wherever she is. Love didn't belong to me, and she gave it to me all the same.

Tightening our embrace, she leans into me, infusing me with her adoration and peace.

Peace...

Peace on earth may never happen, but peaceful moments will continue always. I brush my lips across the top of her head.

She looks up at me and smiles... only for it to immediately fade.

"Zuriel! You're changing!"

The music shifts, assailing the room in an upbeat frenzy. Summer wrenches my hand and yanks me off the dancefloor.

"Summer, where are you going?" Ella says when she sees us rushing past her. "Wait!"

"I can't!" she yells.

I feel my body expand, my wings straining my suit. For some reason, I'm not worried.

"Zuriel, move!" Summer yells once we are in the hotel lobby. "Your skin is turning gray." She dashes to the elevator and slams her palm on the button. One of the doors opens.

Chuckling, I flex my fingers as my claws descend, following her into the enclosed space.

When the doors close, she turns on me. "Oh my god! Your suit is ripped down the middle."

I peer down at my displayed chest and shrug.

"How can you be so calm?" she squeaks, grabbing my shirt and trying to tug the torn sides closed.

"Maybe because I just don't care."

"You're never allowed to have alcohol again!"

I press my mouth to hers, thrusting my tongue between her lips and kissing her quiet. My cock stirs as I slide my arm along her back and haul her against me. With a final, piercing rip, my suit splits, liberating my wings.

My cock extrudes, straining my pants.

When I tug up her skirt, indulging impulses I've restrained all day, she sinks into my embrace. She whimpers, flooding me with her desire.

The elevator dings. The door opens, closes, and we miss it entirely.

I tug down her bodice and cup her breast under her bra, teasing her nipple with my thumb. Moaning, she falls against the wall as I haul her leg up my hip. My bulge rips free. I bend and arch, pressing it between her legs.

There's another ding.

"Summer!?"

We tear apart and face Ella, who's standing wide-eyed in the middle of the open elevator door.

"I can explain!" Summer squeals, righting her dress. "Don't scream!"

Ella's gaze streaks from my outstretched wings to my clawed feet and finally settles on my face. Her mouth parts as the elevator doors close. At the last moment, she stops them with her hand.

The doors swish open revealing her narrowed, intense gaze. She shuffles into the elevator, only turning to ensure her voluminous dress passes the threshold. Summer grabs my shredded suit jacket off of the ground and thrusts it in front of my groin. I hold it in place.

"Ella?" Summer asks tentatively as her friend presses the button to the top floor and turns back around to face us. "I'm sorry..."

Ella eyes me up and down suspiciously. "You weren't lying. He *is* a gargoyle."

"I wasn't."

"I kinda liked thinking you were a little crazy."

Summer snorts. "You wish."

Ella and I stare at each other as the floors pass.

"You're not going to tell anyone are you?" Summer asks.

"Can't you just turn yourself back into a human?" Ella answers with a question, directing it at me.

My wings ripple. "I'm only human during the day. I do not have control over my body's shift."

"That's got to suck."

I nod.

"Ella..." Summer prompts. "We need to get him out of sight until morning."

She crosses her arms and sighs. "You're in the hotel across the street?"

"I was thinking if we made it to the roof, we could fly over once it's dark enough and hopefully enter from the top."

Ella's eyes somehow widen further. "You can fly?"

"I can."

"Fuck. Now, that's really crazy."

For discovering the truth of my nature, Ella is far more calm than I expected. Even Summer tried to run, and when she couldn't, she grabbed a weapon.

"You are quite comfortable," I say, "with what is in front of you."

"Somehow, I'm not surprised. Maybe I will be later because it hasn't hit. Honestly, I'm more shocked catching Summer having sex out in the open. Never would've pegged her for an exhibitionist."

The door opens behind her.

"You guys can stay in Rebecca's room." Ella glances at Summer who's hiding her face in her hands. "Oh stop, Rebecca and I have done worse. She has the room for another day, but we'll be in the bridal suite tonight. In the morning, we'll find Zuriel some clothes so you can leave the hotel." She ducks her head out of the elevator and checks both ways. "It's clear. Let's go!"

She dashes out, and we have little choice but to chase after her. Pulling a card out of a hidden pocket in her dress, she unlocks a room halfway down the hall. Ducking in, the room is nicer than ours despite the disheveled state. With a sigh of relief from Summer, Ella shuts the door behind us.

"Thank you. Thank you. Thank you!" Summer launches at Ella and hugs her tightly. "I love you."

Ella embraces her back with a quiet laugh. "I love you too." She leans back and grabs Summer's shoulders. "You're okay? When you ran by downstairs, you looked panicked. Though now, I guess I know why."

"Yeah, I'm good. I hope we didn't ruin your night."

"Hah! I think this makes it better. I'll never forget this. I should get back down there though..." She drops her arms and looks at me. "I'll see you both in the morning. Have fun."

"Say goodnight to the others for me!"

"Will do. Stay out of sight." Ella opens the door, and with a final curious glance at me, she leaves.

Leaning against the door, Summer slumps. "Holy crap that was close!"

"You worry too much." I purr. "Most people will think I'm in costume."

"That's not what I'm worried about," she huffs and points at my crotch. "Your dick is what I wouldn't be able to explain! It glows, Zuriel! Remember? Oh my god, this was a bad idea. There's kids here. What if Ella screamed? Or wouldn't understand? We're never leaving Elmstitch again!"

Dropping the ripped jacket, I saunter closer and peel her off the door. With a flushed, exasperated expression, she looks up at me. She shakes, still worked up.

I need to distract her. "Summer, will you move in with me?"

She blinks, startled from her worries. "Move in together? Is this the alcohol talking?"

"No, I have given this much thought. Managing my transformations is difficult for us, and I've learned of a farmhouse for rent. It is not far from town with plenty of privacy."

Softening, she laughs. "Some privacy does sound nice." Her face twists, her mortification returning. "Oh my god, I can't believe that just happened, that Ella saw—"

"It will be all right. You're safe now."

Proving my point, I hoist her into my arms, carrying her to the bed. Shimmying her dress up her thighs, I run my claw under her panties, finding her clit.

She wiggles, languishing under my touch, squirming. Licking, I push her disheveled bodice aside and suck at her nipple, my finger working her the entire time. She writhes. Crowding over her, I examine her scrunched face, the way she bites her lip. She's about to release, and I press her harder.

"What do you think?" I ask. "Should we live together?"

She whimpers. "This isn't fair! Asking this way!" With a gasp, she comes, hitching her back, her body relaxed and tight all at once.

Dropping closer, I kiss her softly, stroking her gently as she lands.

Eventually she opens her eyes and peeks up at me. "Do you mean the farmhouse near the apple orchard?"

"Yes..."

Grabbing my horns, she steadies herself and smirks. "I was thinking the exact same thing."

For a moment, I'm as still as the stone I once was, her words taking a second to seep into me. All day I had hoped to ask her this, nervous she might not be ready, that she may hold some reservation now we're no longer fighting for our lives.

"Zuriel, I always wanted you," she reminds me. "It's always been you."

Feeling her sincerity and loyalty, I find the words for my new vow.

"Beyond life and death, I will forever be yours."

AUTHORS' NOTE

Thank you for reading *A Gargoyle's Delight*! If you liked the story or have a comment, please leave a review or rating! Continue onto *The Scarecrow's Queen* if you want more monster love within the town of Elmstitch.

Turn the page for a preview of book two, *The Scarecrow's Queen*...

THE SCARECROW'S QUEEN

BOOK TWO OF MONSTER'S DUET

ONCE, I WAS FEARED by all who gazed upon me. For the past century I have served, defending my crops in solitude, baring my scythe as an omen.

But when the crops aren't seeded, I find myself standing over a field of dirt and weeds.

It is her fault.

The female who has inherited the farm. She might be the new queen of these lands, but in her wake, she brings only ruin.

So, I will scare her away. I will claim these fields, and she will learn to fear me!

Until one evening, she is attacked by the crows. She cowers behind me for protection.

Her terror and desperation stir me into action…

Nobody, not even a god, is allowed to frighten what is MINE.

PROLOGUE
A Preview of The Scarecrow's Queen

Hollowstalk

It was like any other winter day on Sylvie's farm. The cornfields were sheared low, jagged gold-brown needles sticking out from the dusting of snow, tight in their linear rows. Acres of dead crops surrounded me. They spanned out, opposing the horizon of a frozen morning sky interspersed with streaky white clouds. Clouds that would vanish by high noon, leaving nothing between the sun and me.

The farmhouse and barns sat undisturbed, the bordering forest still as stone. The road leading to and from this land was packed tight with cold dirt.

It was nearing midmorning, and old lady Sylvie had yet to make an appearance—which was unlike her. She rarely missed her tea and biscuits, let alone her searing perusal of the land from the front porch, always wrapped in her faded flannel robe. Through the dingy windows of her kitchen, nothing stirred. The drapes to her upstairs bedroom were closed, and there was an absence of smoke from the chimney.

Instead, crows gathered.

At first it was one or two at a time, pairs hopping around the dead stalks. They gave me a wide berth, acknowledging our pact. Except as the morning came to an end, their numbers grew to dozens. They gathered on the rickety wooden fence lining the road, the railing of the porch, the roof, and fields on either side, closing in on me. They settled on the branches of the forest. With each passing minute, more arrived.

During the cold months, we had a truce, they and I. There was nothing to destroy, no crops to eat, and so, there was nothing for me to protect. I did not need to scare them away, to ensure the harvest wasn't ravaged.

They weren't here for a meal. They would not disobey the Crow King today.

Their sharp gazes lingered on the house, and as more of them arrived, so did mine.

That evening, nothing changed. The farmhouse remained dark as the crows grew in their number.

And the next day, it was the same.

The same can be said for the next one too.

By the fourth evening, thousands of crows had gathered, so great a number they called forth their god. Large and menacing, his shadow wandered the farmhouse's periphery, silent and predatory. All through that night, he stalked the grounds.

The next morning he and the crows were gone.

A car arrived driven by a man I recognized, one who visited on occasion, both human and timeless. He let himself into the house, and shortly after, more vehicles appeared. They lined the dirt driveway, and their drivers met with the timeless man. They followed him into the house, and when they came back out, it was with a bulky bag on a gurney.

It was then, to my dismay, I realized Sylvie Shorewood, my queen, was dead.

Printed in Great Britain
by Amazon

50934610-9e6d-44f8-921e-7e1d4c3c0223R01